A WAR OF WORDS

The holographic image flickered to life in Dirk Radick's hands. The figure that appeared was clearly his nemesis, Angela Bekker.

"Star Colonel Radick of Clan Wolf, by now you know I have left nothing of value in the fort. All you have won is a building. Its loss means nothing to me or my Clan."

Radick's eyes narrowed with rage.

"No doubt you are looking for a fast battle. This I deny you, as I denied you the contents of the fort. Know this, Dirk Radick, you are where I wanted you to be, when I wanted you to be. I have controlled this situation and will continue to do so. You are on Toffen now, in the territory of the great Ghost Bear. And when we fight, I will remain in control of the situation.

"In other words," she said with a sly smile, "I have already beaten you." The image flickered off.

Radick gritted his teeth. "I will break her ... crush her ... and leave nothing but a bloody smear on whatever rock she is hiding behind! Attack at once!"

Don't miss the first action-packed
book in the *MechWarrior* series—

MechWarrior
Ghost of Winter

By Stephen Kenson

Every warrior faces his baptism of fire.
Surviving it is another story. . . .

ROAR OF
HONOR

Blaine Lee Pardoe

A ROC BOOK

ROC
Published by New American Library, a division of
Penguin Putnam Inc., 375 Hudson Street,
New York, New York 10014, U.S.A.
Penguin Books Ltd, 80 Strand,
London WC2R 0RL, England
Penguin Books Australia Ltd, 250 Camberwell Road,
Camberwell, Victoria 3124, Australia
Penguin Books Canada Ltd, 10 Alcorn Avenue,
Toronto, Ontario, Canada M4V 3B2
Penguin Books (N.Z.) Ltd, 182–190 Wairau Road,
Auckland 10, New Zealand

Penguin Books Ltd, Registered Offices:
Harmondsworth, Middlesex, England

First published by Roc, an imprint of New American Library,
a division of Penguin Putnam Inc.

First Printing, October 1999
10 9 8 7 6 5 4

Series Editor: Donna Ippolito
Cover art: Peter Peebles
Mechanical Drawings: FASA Art Department

 REGISTERED TRADEMARK—MARCA REGISTRADA

This book is dedicated to the people who matter to me most, my wife, Cyndi, and my children, Victoria Rose and Alexander William. Without them I'm just a guy who spends too much time in front of a PC.

It is also dedicated to Central Michigan University, my alma mater. CMU is the place where I learned I could be a writer if I really wanted to.

ACKNOWLEDGMENTS

Many thanks to the real-life John Sprague, who taught me how to play the pipes, read music, and have more rhythm than I thought possible. Yes, folks, I do play the bagpipes in real life. Sprague (Sprange) and other friends, such as the real-life Joe Scarry, Mark Natelson, Paul Ishimaru, Catherine Graham, Angela Herberger, Paul Sorrentino, Phil Breedveldt, Jim Lark, Joe DiGiornio, have all made appearances in the novel, even if in name only. When you have to crank out a novel in record time, sometimes it helps to borrow names from your coworkers and friends. Any relationship between the characters in the book and real people is pure coincidence (wink, wink).

Special thanks to Dan Plunkett, Cullen Tilman, Greg Johnson, Kevin Rivenburg, and Bob O'Connel for, well, the hell of it.

I also gratefully acknowledge Bryan Nystul who, in three E-mails and one phone call, helped me make this simple idea into a book, as well as providing me a wealth of information on the Ghost Bears. Bryan suggested taking on the Wolves in the first place and helped me narrow down a title (from a list of spoofs such as Bears on the Border, Bear En Guard, Bear Pack, and BRT [Bears Right There]).

Also thanks to G. Gordon Liddy (who I had the honor to meet on my last book tour), and Don and Mike, who provided me countless hours of entertainment while I edited and did the re-write on this beast.

Finally, to the BattleTech fans. One thing is for sure, they are a loyal lot, though some take it a mite too seriously. Remember, folks, it's pretty doubtful that three-story, humanoid, robotic war machines are going to be running around in the thirty-first century. The idea is supposed to be fun, and I hope you find that kind of fun in this book. If you don't, no doubt you'll roast me on the Internet. Such is life. . . .

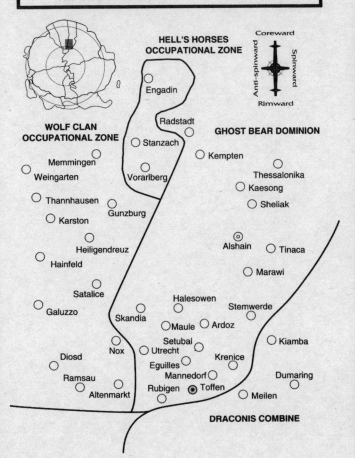

RIMWARD CLAN TERRITORIES
circa 3062

Map Compiled by *COMSTAR*.
From information provided by the *COMSTAR EXPLORER CORPS*
and the *STAR LEAGUE ARCHIVES* on Terra.
© 3062 COMSTAR CARTOGRAPHIC CORPS.

**HELL'S HORSES
OCCUPATIONAL ZONE**

Coreward
Spinward
Anti-spinward
Rimward

Engadin

Radstadt

**WOLF CLAN
OCCUPATIONAL ZONE**

GHOST BEAR DOMINION

Stanzach

Kempten

Memmingen

Weingarten

Thessalonika

Vorarlberg

Kaesong

Thannhausen

Sheliak

Karston

Gunzburg

Heiligendreuz

Alshain

Tinaca

Hainfeld

Marawi

Satalice

Halesowen

Galuzzo

Stemwerde

Skandia

Maule

Ardoz

Setubal

Kiamba

Nox

Utrecht

Diosd

Eguilles

Krenice

Ramsau

Mannedorf

Dumaring

Altenmarkt

Rubigen

Toffen

Meilen

DRACONIS COMBINE

Prologue

Minsk Mountains
Strana Mechty
Kerensky Cluster, Clan Space
14 February 3059

Outside the cave a horizontal wall of snow driven at cutting speed blurred her field of vision. Star Captain Angela Bekker pulled her parka tighter as the icy fingers of the chill wind reached into her. The small fire at the mouth of the cave offered some comfort, but not much. Not after what she had been through.

Farther back into the cave lay Sprange, still moaning from the mauling he had taken in the ghost bear attack of two days ago. He and Angela had been part of a group of forty-eight Ghost Bear warriors braving the dangers of the Minsk Mountains in their Clan's annual Clawing rite. Only the highest-ranking unClawed warriors in each of the Clusters—the rough equal of regiments—were eligible. Once into the mountains the group had broken up into smaller hunting parties of some ten warriors each.

It was solemn rite, Ghost Bear warriors climbing into the frozen regions of Strana Mechty to hunt the mighty creature for which their Clan was named. Armed with nothing more than long spears, only the bravest and strongest could ever hope to defeat a ghost bear in single combat.

Half the hunting parties never returned at all, though at least one warrior usually did succeed in killing a bear.

Angela Bekker's team, however, did not have much luck. Just before the storm, they had split up in hopes of covering a wider area. Though each carried survival gear and even a defensive laser pistol, only the spear could be used in the actual hunt. They also carried rations, but those had been used up several long and grueling days ago. Now the storm had turned this from a ritual hunt into a test of survival.

Angela and Sprange had been blinded by a blizzard almost as fierce as this one when a ghost bear, hidden under a mound of snow, had suddenly risen up and attacked. It had bitten and mauled Sprange before he had a chance to react, his spear lost forever in a powdery white drift. He would have died had Angela not wounded and driven off the huge beast. She had saved Sprange's life and they both knew it.

Angela drew in a long lungful of air through her nose and felt her nostrils freeze with a bitter sting. Glancing over at the crumpled form of Sprange, she thought back on all the years they had known each another. Created from the same batch of genetic material, the two had been together since birth. They had spent the whole of their young lives growing up together in a sibko, enduring the harsh training that would forge them as Clan warriors.

"You should go down the mountain," he moaned. His broken ribs and right shoulder seemed to make even breathing difficult and painful.

"Be quiet," she commanded, but without harshness. "We are Ghost Bears. We are sibkin. I will not waste a perfectly good warrior to save myself."

"You have always been the stronger," Sprange said, shifting position slightly. "You earned your bloodname and rank in just a few short years. I am not your equal and we both know that. You should save yourself." There was respect in his voice. Clan warriors prized a bloodname above all else. The right to bear a surname, each one descended from one of the founders of the Clans, had to be won on a field of combat. Only the finest warriors could compete for a bloodname. Only the best ever won one.

And only the cream of those ever slayed a ghost bear in the Clawing, Angela thought.

She had won her bloodname piloting an old War-hawk OmniMech. BattleMechs and OmniMechs were the pinnacle of military technology and had dominated battlefields for the last three centuries. Standing nearly three stories tall and roughly humanoid in shape, a heavily armored 'Mech could move at incredible speed. It also carried the firepower of a tank platoon—a startling array of missiles, lasers, and other implements of death and destruction.

Another gust of wind buffeted the last flickers of their small fire, which began to smoke as it died. There was little left to burn. Now, with the day starting, they did not have much time if they were ever going to do what they came for. There was no loss of honor in failing to kill a ghost bear during a Clawing, but Angela Bekker was not one given to surrendering an ideal. Trying to flush out one of the mighty creatures seemed impossible. The ghost bear was notorious for the way it hid itself in the massive snow drifts, patiently waiting for its prey to come to it. There had to be another way to end this ordeal. Otherwise she and Sprange would die here in the cold.

Her mind played over everything she knew about the legendary ghost bears as she fought back another wave of shivers. They were hunters, powerful, white-furred creatures that stood over five meters when they rose to strike. The cold did not bother them. They ruled these pitiless mountains, where they managed not only to survive but to thrive. It was said they could smell blood for kilometers and would hunt their prey by smell alone.

Then the idea came to her. It was a dark thought, one that would ask great sacrifice on her part. Honor was at stake, and for Angela Bekker little else mattered. From her earliest days in the Prowling Bear sibko, she had been steeped in the idea. Sacrifice was expected from a warrior for the sake of glory or victory, and she resolved to win the honor of slaying a ghost bear. Silently, with great care, she wedged the shaft of her spear into the earthen floor, then braced it securely against a large rock protruding from the ground. The sharpened tip pointed toward the opening of the cave.

"What are you doing, Angela?" Sprange asked weakly.

She did not look at him, too busy testing the shaft of the spear to be sure it would hold against any weight brought to bear against it. "I am going to kill a ghost bear," she said finally.

"Is one coming?" There was no fear in Sprange's voice. He sounded almost relieved. He would not survive another encounter with one and had resigned himself to death. It was the way of the warrior, and for a warrior to die during the perilous Clawing ritual did not bring shame.

She looked back at him. "One will," she said, drawing her utility knife. The blade shimmered in the dying light of the fire, and she stood silently looking at it for a moment. She then stepped just to edge of the cave opening, her feet crunching on the snow.

With one sweeping move of the blade in her left hand, she severed the fourth and fifth fingers of her right.

Angela screamed, but it was more the fierce howling of an animal than the sound of pain. Blood sprayed in the air and against the cave wall. She felt a warm rush suffuse her body, then she doubled over in agony. The knife slipped from her fingers, and almost instantly was buried in the snow piling up at the cave entrance. Angela drew her small laser pistol and fired at the cut place on her hand. A wisp of smoke brought the smell of burning flesh as she cauterized the wound. She wailed again, less loudly this time, but now it was in pain.

With her good hand, Angela picked up the two severed fingers and tossed them out into the snow. She half-staggered to the back of the cave where she had braced her spear. Her breathing was rapid, and left clouds of steam in the air as she fought back the agony in her hand.

"It is only a matter of time now," she said, standing to her full height as if to tower over her own pain. Her blood would be the bait.

"We will both die here," Sprange said.

She looked at him and smiled. "There is no fate more fitting for two Ghost Bears, quiaff?"

For the first time since he had been mauled, Sprange smiled. "Aff."

The minutes passed slowly, then suddenly the cave

entrance darkened as a shape loomed before it. Angela lowered her stance slightly, breath still ragged, heart pounding through every part of her body.

The great ghost bear lumbered into the cave, its bulk just barely able to fit. It was oddly silent as it came, as ghostly as its name. It was enormous, and its white fur looked silvery by the firelight, especially around its neck, a sign of its age. The bear spotted its prey at the rear of the cave and seemed to explode with a roar that shook the very rock walls around them.

Angela did not flinch. She focused on the eyes of the ghost bear, staring deep into its soul. For the creature to have lived so long, it was indeed one of the greatest of its kind. It stared back at her, not like an animal but like a fellow warrior taking the measure of his foe. It took a step forward, then seemed to coil back slightly. She knew what it was doing, The great ghost bear was preparing to spring.

Angela lowered herself slightly and reached out to where she'd rigged up her spear. The ghost bear did not hesitate. It leapt with a speed and agility that seemed impossible for a creature of its size. It came right for her, its eyes still locked with her own. It was as if this most magnificent of beasts was leaping at her very soul.

In that instant she angled the point of the spear directly at the leaping bear, keeping the base of the shaft still anchored against the rock. The ghost bear, caught in mid-flight, impaled itself on the spear, which drove straight through its body and out its back. Time seemed to move slow, and the cave and Angela's awareness of the moment became a blur. Sounds in the cave were muffled, a dull roar in her mind. She did not remember rolling, but somehow came up beside the great creature as it lay dead between her and Sprange. The ghost bear's huge teeth had ripped her light blue parka as it fell.

The end was so sudden, so stunning, that she hardly knew how to respond. First, she had to make sure the bear was indeed dead, and prodded it with her foot. The beast gurgled slightly, a death rattle that would haunt her dreams for years to come. Dizzy either from her loss of blood or the exertion, she looked over at her comrade. Sprange stared at the beast that had nearly killed them, his mouth agape, his eyes wide. He turned to her slowly.

"I do not believe it," he said.

Angela nodded. "The ghost bear is a hunter that knows the wisdom of waiting for its prey to come to him. I have only done what it teaches."

"What have you done to yourself, though?"

Angela looked at the charred flesh where her two fingers had been. "I did what was necessary. I am, after all, a Ghost Bear warrior."

She got up and retrieved her knife. "Now we do what we must—we survive."

Two days later they were found by a patrol, Angela garbed in the hide of the great ghost bear she had slain, Sprange being pulled behind her on a makeshift skid.

PART ONE

Ristar

There was a soldier, a Scottish soldier
Who wandered far away and soldiered far away
There was none bolder, with good broad shoulder
He's fought in many a fray, and fought and won.
He'd seen the glory and told the story
Of battles glorious and deeds nefarious
But now he's sighing, his heart is crying
To leave these green hills of Tyrol.

Because these green hills are not highland hills
Or the island hills, the're not my land's hills
And fair as these green foreign hills may be
They are not the hills of home.
—"The Green Hills of Tyrol," traditional Scottish song

1

DropShip Featheringham
Descent Approach to Alshain Spaceport
Ghost Bear Dominion
2 January 3062

"I still don't know," the bondsman whined, but Star Captain Constant Tseng did not let him finish. He struck him across the mouth with the back of one hand, sending the man sprawling. Not one of the technician castemen working around them so much as glanced up from their labors to see what was going on.

But Star Captain Angela Bekker saw it all as she crossed the deck of the 'Mech bay, and she knew the blow was meant not so much to hurt the bondsman as to shame him. It was all part of his instruction in the way of the Clan.

"Clan warriors do not speak in contractions, you surat," Tseng was saying. He seemed to tower over the bondsman, but in reality it was more bravado than size.

Angela continued toward them, impressed by Tseng's

air of command. When he reached out a hand to help his bondsman back to his feet, she was even more impressed. Few bondmasters would have done the same.

She and Constant Tseng had become friends during the space journey to Alshain. Both had been ordered to Alshain, where they were to report to the commander of Delta Galaxy to discuss "redeployment strategy." She and Tseng, the only bloodnamed warriors aboard the DropShip *Featheringham,* had bonded quickly during the long days while their JumpShip recharged its batteries between interstellar jumps, and now as the DropShip made its journey to the planet's surface.

During their many talks she had learned that Tseng had taken his bondsman during a raid by an Inner Sphere force against the world where Tseng's unit was garrisoned. He told her that the man had fought well, taking out two Ghost Bear warriors before he fell to one of Tseng's laser barrages. In accordance with Clan tradition, Tseng opted to capture the man and adopt him into the ranks of the Ghost Bears. But first the captive would have to live as a bondsman, something like an indentured servant, until he proved himself worthy to become a member of the warrior caste.

Her boots echoed on the deck of the huge 'Mech bay, where the air stung slightly of chemicals, coolant, and more than a century's worth of sweat. She recognized the smell; it was the scent before battle, before victory. As she approached, the dark-haired Tseng paced in front of his bondsman, who seemed to be trying to figure out just how much trouble he was in with his master.

Tseng caught her eye as she came up, and she returned the look with the slightest of grins. "Are you sure this one is worthy of our Clan, Star Commander?" she joked lightly.

"Aye," Tseng returned. "He will be, if he can master the concept of bidding."

She chuckled. "This one has trouble with bidding? Perhaps we should bring a newborn cub to explain it to him." Cub was the Ghost Bear term for the Clan's young trueborns—genetically engineered warriors bred from the genetic material of only the worthiest Ghost Bear warriors. Trueborns were considered the pinnacle of Clan society, and were the highest caste. Freeborns, on the other hand, were spawned "naturally," and they filled most of the places in the lower castes. A few freebirths did manage to enter the warrior ranks, but they were a rarity. The trues generally despised the frees, finding something disgusting in the nature of their conception and birth, and tensions between trueborn and freeborn were common.

Dressed in the sorry remains of a tattered shirt and a pair of trousers, the bondsman stood to his full height between the two Clan warriors. "I ask to try again," he said.

Tseng turned to his bondsman. "Very well, Barthelow. Explain the concept of bidding for a Trial."

The bondsman drew a deep breath. Surely he knew that Tseng and the others were trying to break him, attempting to mold him to the ways of the Ghost Bear, but some fight in his warrior's soul probably still yearned for escape. He drew another long breath and spoke as if reciting the words Tseng had drilled into him. "The Clans do not fight mere battles. A Clan warrior engages in Trials. The defender will state what forces he will defend. The attacker then must bid to defeat his foe with the minimum amount of force possible."

"And why is that?" his bondmaster prompted.

"I believe it is to minimize the amount of potential loss."

"Partially correct, but what you believe is not important. What is important is what *I* believe," Tseng said. "There is more, bondsman. Why not simply engage as your former commanders in the Inner Sphere do, with every bit of manpower and BattleMech hardware available?" He did not conceal his scorn.

The bondsman shook his head, but did not lower his eyes. "I do not know."

"At least this time you did not use contractions," Tseng said. "Star Captain Bekker, perhaps you would be so kind as to inform this surat-dung as to why we do not attack with everything we have."

Angela regarded the bondsman for a moment. "Honor," she said.

The bondsman looked puzzled, but she went on before he could interrupt. "To use every bit of your strength to achieve a goal shows no honor. The blood in our veins as Ghost Bears is red with honor. If I outnumber you four to one and attack and defeat you, what then? Nothing. There is no honor in such a cheap victory. If I bid down and take you with even odds, there is some honor in that. But if I bid the least possible amount of force and beat you with that, then I have achieved the greatest honor. If you learn nothing else, learn that honor is the lifeblood of this Clan."

"If I may, Star Captain?" the bondsman said. "If you underbid and lose, then there is no honor, quaiff?" He was careful to use the traditional Clan interrogative.

Tseng looked over at Angela. "This one is not a mindless soldier, is he, Star Commander? His questions are apt."

"Aye," Angela said. "But if an officer underbids and stands to lose, he or she can either end the trial or call in the last group of forces he bid away before the final bid.

There is a loss of honor in raising the bid, but in defeat, there is no honor."

Tseng turned back to his bondsman. "You are learning, Barthelow, but that is enough for now. You have tasking to attend to. I wish you to clean the legs of my *Warhawk*." He pointed to the gantry alongside his stout OmniMech. "I want them spotless enough to eat off of. And I want it done in an hour."

"Aye, Star Commander," Barthelow replied, then scuttled off to do as he was bid.

Tseng watched him walk away for a moment, and Angela noted that he held himself with an ease and precision inbred and trained into him from birth. There was something proud about him. But nothing so petty as ego. In her long talks with Constant Tseng aboard the DropShip, she had not seen the slightest hint of the blowhard or the braggart. No, what she saw was a warrior who believed that the spirit of the Ghost Bears breathed in his soul.

"Well, Star Captain, what do you make of him?" he asked.

She looked over his shoulder and saw Barthelow heading toward the massive OmniMech, bucket and rags in hand. "He has potential. Bidding concepts are not difficult to master, but an understanding of nuances cannot be learned simply by rote. He might comprehend the importance of bidding, but he has no firsthand knowledge of the rite. Still, you have done the Clan well by keeping this one."

"We will touch down soon," Tseng said. "Are you not curious about why we have been ordered to Alshain?"

Constant Tseng had been speculating about their orders for most of the trip, as curious as a Fire Mandrill.

Angela did not mind. At least he was not gossip-mongering like some. A number of other Ghost Bear warriors aboard ship had also been ordered to Alshain, the new capital of the Clan. Rumor had run like wildfire among them, but she wanted no part in spreading or feeding those flames. "I have been giving it some thought," she said. "I assume we and the others have been ordered here as part of a general reorganization of the Touman."

The Touman was the formal military organization of the Clan. At the lower end was the Point, a single BattleMech or five Elementals. Then came the Stars, each one consisting of five Points, followed by the Binaries and Trinaries, two- and three-Star combinations, respectively. These were further grouped into Clusters of two to five Binaries or Trinaries, and the Clusters into Galaxies, the largest Clan military unit. Some units had been weakened in the invasion, and rebuilding their military had become a prime objective now that the Ghost Bears had consolidated their holdings in the Inner Sphere.

Memories of the invasion and its aftermath were as fresh in Angela's memory as if they had happened only yesterday and not more than ten years ago. The Ghost Bears were among the handful of Clans that had won the privilege of participating in the great crusade to liberate the Inner Sphere from centuries of self-imposed tyranny, but the Clans were not of one mind in seeking to vanquish the cradle of mankind. The Crusader Clans wished to conquer the Inner Sphere to save it from itself. The Wardens believed their role was to guide and protect it. Though the Ghost Bears had begun the invasion as Crusaders, they had gradually evolved to become Wardens. Crusader or Warden, all of the invading Clans had come with one goal . . . the conquest of Terra.

The Clan that won control of the homeworld of humanity would become the supreme Clan, the ilClan. They would restore the golden age of the Star League, which had fallen three hundred years before and forced the ancestors of the Clans to leave the Inner Sphere forever.

The Inner Sphere forces had initially crumbled before the technological and fighting supremacy of the Clan onslaught. But eventually ComStar, which controlled both Terra and all interstellar communications, had challenged the Clans to a proxy battle to forestall the invasion. That battle had been fought on the cursed world of Tukayyid, where, in a stunning turn of events, the Clans were defeated. The Truce of Tukayyid ordained that the Clans could not resume the invasion for a period of fifteen years.

And while the other Clans fought among themselves and sought ways to circumvent the peace, the Ghost Bears had consolidated. Over the past seven years, they had covertly moved virtually their entire population to their Inner Sphere holdings, leaving but a token force in the Clan homeworlds. The Inner Sphere would be their new home.

In those same few years, the leaders of the Inner Sphere discovered the location of the distant Clan homeworlds. In secret, their forces made their way to Strana Mechty itself and challenged the Clans to a Trial to repudiate the invasion once and for all. The Warden Clans, led by Ghost Bear Khan Jorgensson, refused to fight.

In a stunning turn of events, the Inner Sphere forces defeated the Clans on their own soil. The invasion was over, but it was an uneasy peace. The Ghost Bears had settled into their new Dominion, and were growing stronger every day. But there were still threats to their holdings, from both the Inner Sphere armies and their own Clankin.

Star Commander Tseng spoke, breaking into her reverie. "I believe we are being called to form a new Cluster or Galaxy."

Angela frowned slightly at his words. "You listen to gossip as if you were a member of the merchant caste, Star Commander," she chided.

"Neg, Star Captain. I am merely being logical. Consider all the warriors on this ship who are being redeployed. Logic dictates that we are not the only ship of this kind. Forming a new Cluster or Galaxy makes the most sense."

She admired his cool composure in a dispute. "We are Ghost Bears. Ours is not to question the will of our Khan but to know our duty. If Khan Jorgensson wishes to reassign units or form new ones, that is what we will do."

"That goes without saying," Tseng said easily. "But you must be at least somewhat curious."

She ran one hand back through her hair, cropped short to facilitate the contact between her 'Mech's neurohelmet and her scalp. "Of course I am curious. But I know my place as a warrior and keep my thoughts to myself." Again, Tseng simply ignored the slight barb to her words.

"You are more than just another warrior, Angela Bekker. I have taken the liberty of reviewing your record. Your codex is outstanding and you have successfully executed the Clawing ritual. Not to mention what you did on Jarett."

The mention of Jarett stirred a whirlwind of memories in her mind. Jarett was a Draconis Combine world which the Ghost Bears had attacked with full fury in the second wave of the invasion. Angela had been there as part of the Seventeenth Battle Trinary of the First Bear Guards. Trekking through the steaming Solun jungle, the Seventeenth had fought the Ninth Alshain Regulars for a battle that lasted an unprecedented seven days.

Prolonged combat was not the way of the Clans. Combat trials were designed to be quick affairs, and days and days of fighting was a style of warfare unfamiliar to most Ghost Bears. Angela had adapted quickly and managed to pull off the logistical nightmare of moving her supplies along with her force as they tracked the elusive Ninth.

She had won praise for her tactical prowess on Tukayyid, but all that was a long time ago. Besides, Angela did not like to think back on Jarett. It only reminded her of how she had lost all her comrades in later battles of the invasion. So many friends and comrades gone now.

She glanced at the codex bracelet on her left wrist, the same hand that held her prosthetic bionic replacement fingers. A warrior's military record was imprinted on the storage chips of his or her codex, a full accounting of her service in the name of the Clan. Angela's was good, that much she acknowledged. The desire for a bloodname had been a nearly all-consuming passion in her younger days. Now the Bekker bloodname was simply part of who she was. The slightly lighter color of the bionic fingers was a constant reminder of what a Ghost Bear warrior might be called to do.

"Do not be foolish, Constant. For the last few years I have faithfully served the Fiftieth Striker Cluster, but many other warriors can also claim honorable service. Your own codex is strong. As I said, if the Khan decides I am to serve the Clan in another capacity, I welcome the chance to show him what I can do."

"Always stubborn. That is why the others call you 'the Claw.' "

"The Claw?" The very idea filled Angela with rage.

"Aye, Angela. I have heard a number of warriors refer to you that way. Apparently you are well known. Your fighting during the liberation of Jarett was something of a tactical masterpiece, no matter how much you downplay it. That . . . and . . . . your replacement fingers."

She glowered at Tseng, who looked suddenly like he realized he had spoken too quickly and now wanted to bite his tongue. "I do not like this term that others have chosen for me. Nicknames are for members of the lower castes."

Constant Tseng opened his mouth to speak, but before he could say a word a klaxon sounded with a deep, penetrating "whoop" throughout the bay. A yellow light came on and flashed. "They have begun the landing sequence," he said above the alarm. "Perhaps I will see you on the ground, Star Captain."

"Aye," Angela replied, rubbing her artificial fingers together as she often did when in thought. Somehow, she knew that Star Commander Constant Tseng was someone who would not quickly disappear from her life.

2

Ghost Bear Central Command
Alshain
Ghost Bear Dominion
12 January 3062

Angela had obediently gone to the Ghost Bear command center to check in immediately upon arriving on Alshain. The building was massive, a maze of corridors, offices, and security checkpoints, bustling with military personnel and lower castemen. She was rerouted three times in attempting to obey her orders to report, but found nothing strange in that. For Angela, born and bred to be a warrior, following orders was second nature.

Eventually she was directed here, to this office, that of Galaxy Commander Roberto Snuka. The room was similar to every other Clan officer's Angela had ever seen, dull gray and spartan save for the painting on one wall. Delta Galaxy, also known as The Blitzkrieg, did not enjoy the reputation of the elite Alpha Galaxy to which Angela had been assigned until now. Though Delta was a front-line unit of the Touman, it was one of the least favored.

Galaxy Commander Snuka did not look any less the warrior, however, His sleek, short black hair and the scars on his face showed experience in combat far beyond his age in years. Angela had been standing before his desk for some time, but he remained silent while studying her computer file on a hand-held datapad. Every now and then he gave her a sideways glance as if to gauge whether her codex data reflected at all in her appearance.

Angela remained standing, hands clasped behind her back. She maintained her erect posture, but her eyes kept wandering to the painting on the wall behind Snuka's desk. It portrayed a BattleMech, half-fallen in battle, and she assumed that Snuka had painted it. Unlike their fellows in other Clans, the Ghost Bears placed an emphasis on the arts. Every warrior would spend his or her lifetime accomplishing the Great Work in some field of artistic endeavor. Within the rigid discipline of the military caste, the Great Work became a salutary form of release for a warrior. Not surprisingly, talents often followed genetic lines. Warriors of the Jorgensson blood house tended toward sculpture. The Snuka bloodline favored painting and drawing, as did the Vishio. The Bekker line, of which Angela was a member, favored music as their form of expression. She herself had mastered an ancient folk instrument known as bagpipes.

Also present in the room was another officer, Star Colonel Dana Vishio of the Eighth Bear Cuirassiers. She was seated, waiting just as patiently for her commanding officer to digest the codex data. Her uniform showed the insignia of Delta Galaxy, a running blue bear superimposed over crossed golden javelins of lightning. Below that was the patch of the Eighth Cuirassiers, a warrior riding a bear against a background of snow and lightning.

The surprisingly deep voice of Galaxy Commander Snuka finally broke the silence. "Star Captain Bekker, your codex shows a remarkable record of service to the Ghost Bears."

"I am proud to serve, Galaxy Commander."

He leaned forward, setting his elbows on the gray desktop as he steepled his fingers. "So, Star Captain, do you know why you are here?"

"Neg, Galaxy Commander."

He nodded, as if to say that was as it should be. "Delta Galaxy is in the process of reorganizing and expanding. The Khan has decided that you would be well-suited to command a new Trinary. The unit will be attached to Star Colonel Vishio's Eighth Bear Cuirassiers."

Angela was startled by this, but tried to keep her voice perfectly neutral to keep from giving insult. "I am being removed from Alpha Galaxy and assigned to Delta, quiaff?"

Snuka's face darkened in anger. "Aff," he said brusquely. "Does that not meet with your approval, Star Captain? Are you one of those who might say that a posting to Delta Galaxy is inferior to a place in Alpha?"

Angela held her ground. "Many Ghost Bears aspire to be assigned to Alpha, Galaxy Commander. I have not heard the same for Delta. I only wondered if being reassigned was the result of some misdeed of mine."

"I assume you do not intend to insult either myself or my command," Snuka said sharply.

"No, Galaxy Commander."

"Well that you did not," he said. "I would have been

forced to challenge you to an honor duel in a Circle of Equals. The Khan would not be pleased with what I would do to you."

Again Angela held firm. A Circle of Equals was where warriors settled their differences in one-on-one combat that sometimes was fought to the death. "You have read my codex, Galaxy Commander. My record speaks for itself. I assure you I implied no disrespect to Delta Galaxy—especially now that I am assigned to it."

Roberto Snuka nodded. "I am no fool, Star Captain. I know Delta Galaxy's reputation. And perhaps it is true that something you did warranted your reassignment."

"And that is?"

"You are one of the best. A ristar in our Clan. You succeeded in the Clawing rite, and in a manner most striking." As he spoke, he glanced at her right hand with its bionic fingers. "You fought in the invasion and waged a prolonged fight on Jarett. On Tukayyid you proved yourself equally capable in a similar situation. You have shown both courage and tactical acumen. Delta Galaxy needs new blood, on that the Khan and I are in complete agreement. That is why you and many other of our best warriors from every unit have been brought to Alshain."

Star Colonel Vishio spoke up at last. "We need the expertise of warriors like you to sharpen the claws of our units, Angela Bekker. That is why you are being assigned the formation of a new unit under my command."

Vishio's announcement was astonishing enough, but Snuka's next words took Angela totally by surprise. "Khan Jorgensson personally selected you for this assignment," he said.

She did not know what to say and only murmured, "I have never met the Khan."

"That is of no matter. After reviewing the codexes of many of Alpha's finest warriors, the Khan concluded that you were the one who would serve him best in this. His instructions to me were specific and clear."

Angela was stunned. It was odd for a Khan to become involved in assignments at a tactical level. It made her wonder about this posting. Was there something her commanding officers either did not know or were not telling her? "It is both a duty and an honor to serve the Ghost Bears, Commander Snuka. I welcome the chance to command a new unit under you and Star Colonel Vishio."

"Then I welcome you to our command." Roberto Snuka leaned back slightly in his chair. "The Khan has ordained that you be given first choice among the many warriors brought to Alshain for reassignment for your Trinary. You will also have first choice of equipment." He slid a datapad across the desk to her. "This datapad contains the codexes of all Ghost Bear warriors available to you for assignment. The technician caste has also provided you a full inventory of all available BattleMechs and other equipment, as well as the necessary requisition forms."

Angela was surprised all over again. "I am puzzled, Star Colonel. I will be personally selecting the warriors who will serve under me, quiaff?"

Dana Vishio answered. "It is out of the ordinary, but not unheard of." Angela noticed that Vishio sought out Snuka's eyes for a moment, and that he answered with an almost imperceptible shrug. They seemed to be as much in the dark as Angela.

"It helps that we have more warriors than billets at this point," Vishio said. "Select your Trinary members through whatever means you deem appropriate."

Angela thought carefully for a moment. "I met an

able warrior during my trip here. Star Commander Constant Tseng. He would make an excellent second in command, and with his help I believe I can get started quickly."

"Good," Vishio said. "You must make haste in forming up the unit and then be on your way to your new posting."

"Which is . . . ?"

"You depart in a week to assume garrison responsibility for Toffen. Your Trinary will be relieving the rest of the Eighth for redeployment elsewhere."

Toffen. Angela knew of the world. Among the many planets the Ghost Bears had taken during the invasion, it was one of the deepest into the Inner Sphere. Given its proximity to Terra, the world had strategic importance, almost enough to console Angela for being assigned to Delta Galaxy. "What other units will join us on Toffen?"

Vishio caught Snuka's eyes again, as if seeking permission to speak. It was obviously an awkward moment for the two officers. "No other units," she said finally. "Your Trinary will have sole responsibility for defending the planet. Reinforcements will be forthcoming."

What did she mean, forthcoming? Angela wanted to say. Toffen was a front-line world. A Trinary was only three Stars' worth of 'Mechs and Elementals. Sending a unit of that size—and a green unit to boot—to defend an important planet could create a tempting target for an Inner Sphere attempt to take back the planet.

Not to mention one of the other Clans. Bickering and fighting among themselves, the Clans often waged Trials of Possession for each other's worlds. "If I may, Star Colonel, do I understand correctly? Another unit will be joining us in garrison shortly, quiaff?"

This time it was the Galaxy Commander who answered. "Star Captain Bekker, we all have our duties. We are well aware of the importance of Toffen, but you, as a Star Captain, surely realize the need for security and the sensitivity surrounding unit postings. As such, I cannot and will not provide an answer to your query."

He leaned forward across the gray desktop again, bringing his face close enough that Angela could see into his eyes, and not miss the intent of his words. "There are those who do not heed the old adage, 'Beware awakening a sleeping bear.' Those who might misread our Clan's seeming quiescence in recent years, who might take it as a sign that the Ghost Bear sleeps deep in hibernation. You know that this is not the case, as do I. Others may not be so well advised."

She was not exactly sure she understood his meaning, but she did get the message loud and clear not to press him further.

Galaxy Commander Snuka leaned back in his chair once more. "That will be all. Once again, Star Captain, welcome to The Blitzkrieg."

Three hours later Angela was seated at her desk, rubbing at her eyes, which were strained from intense study of the files on the datapad Galaxy Commander Snuka had given her. She had appropriated an office for her use and had been poring over the codexes of the warrior pool from which she would recruit.

Building a unit from scratch was done in one of two ways in the Clans. The first and most common was by simple assignment. Even with the martial upbringing of the typical Clan warrior, it generally took drilling to form such a group of individuals into a fighting unit— drilling and time. The other method was by individual recruitment. Studying the codexes of qualified warriors and selecting those with the skills and the potential to work well together. And like any fresh unit, they would need plenty of drilling, but her new Trinary would have precious little time for that.

A rap at the door interrupted her labors. "Come," she said, standing up to straighten her gray uniform tunic tight against her muscular frame. A man stepped into the room with perfect military precision and closed the door behind him. He snapped a salute and she returned it.

"Star Commander Constant Tseng, we meet again."

"Reporting as ordered, Star Captain," he replied briskly.

"The formality is appreciated but not necessary when we are alone, Constant," Angela said and gestured to the seat opposite her tiny desk.

Tseng sat down with the same military bearing he always showed. "Understood. I just got word that you requested my assignment to a new unit being formed."

"Aye," she said. "Between your record and what I observed of you aboard the DropShip, I believe we two can work well together."

Tseng seemed to relax some. "I appreciate your confidence in me."

Angela gave him a long look. "We do not have much time, Star Commander. The truth is that we must form a trinary from the ground up and then depart for Toffen in a few days. To do that I am going to need help from someone who understands my way of doing things. Someone who knows my thoughts before I do. We became friends on the *Featheringham*. I now must ask you to become something more."

"It sounds like you are describing second in command," Tseng said, and smiled.

"Aye, Constant." She returned the smile. He was

shrewd and perceptive, exactly the reasons she wanted him in the first place.

"What have you got in mind in the way of composition?" Tseng asked.

"I envision the Command Star equipped with heavy and assault class OmniMechs. The Sweep Star must be light and very fast. Our Striker Star should be a mix of 'Mechs, and you will be its commander."

"Elementals?" Tseng asked. Elementals were genetically bred like MechWarriors, except that they were almost twice the size of a normal warrior. They did not pilot BattleMechs in combat, but operated as power-armored infantry. A Point of five Elementals could, in the right circumstances, destroy a BattleMech in a matter of minutes.

"Some, but only in Sweep Star. No more than a Point or two."

"I recommend a single Point," Tseng said. "That is enough to give us the kick we need in battle, unless we are to defend heavily urban areas."

"Agreed," she said.

"The mix sounds good if we can get the necessary OmniMechs, but I must ask—where do you stand on freebirths when it comes to selecting warriors?"

The question was no surprise to Angela. There was always some degree of tension between the genetically bred trueborns and those who were not. It was true that some freebirths managed to win a place in the warrior caste, but there were trueborn commanders who would never accept them in their units unless ordered.

Angela was not one of those narrow-minded officers.

"What is most important is finding skilled warriors who can work together, and quickly. I do not care if they are trueborn or freeborn. What matters is their prowess as warriors."

"I concur," Tseng said. "I would like to review the codexes of available warriors. The sooner we start, the better."

Angela smiled in response. "I have already started, but it will be good to see how well our minds meet. I have annotated the files of the warriors I think we should consider first." She slid the datapad across the desktop, and Constant Tseng picked it up. It was going to be a long night.

3

Angela crossed the 'Mech bay to where a lanky Mech-Warrior stood staring up at a *Fire Moth*, watching intently as several techs swapped out the 'Mech's weapons pods.

"Star Commander Stone?" she said.

The man was built more like a skinny Elemental than the usual compact frame of a MechWarrior. He looked at her from feet to face and nodded once slowly. "Aff," was all he said, then turned his attention back to the techs on the gantry.

Angela cocked an eyebrow at his response. He seemed totally disinterested in anything unconnected to the work being done on his 'Mech. "I am Star Captain Angela Bekker of Delta Galaxy, Eighth Cuirassiers."

Again he turned slowly, almost mechanically, and

regarded her. "I am Star Commander Stone, recently of the Pouncing Bear sibko." Once more he returned his gaze to the technicians.

Another warrior might have been offended at his attitude toward a superior officer, but Angela had reviewed this man's short but colorful codex. Stone had only recently tested out as a full-fledged warrior, but the skill he showed in winning his Trial of Position was enough to earn him the rank of Star Commander. Stone was, according to this instructors, one of the best fast-action commanders they had seen, without being either reckless or impulsive. His specialties were high-speed tactical operations and reconnaissance missions. Often times, when outgunned and outmatched, he had gone in with a lightweight *Fire Moth*, and through speed and skill had managed to take out 'Mechs outweighing his own by three to one.

Despite some quirks to his personality, he had what Angela was looking for. "I am forming a new Trinary, Star Commander Stone. A review of your codex indicates that you could well serve the Ghost Bears by serving under me."

Again, Stone turned slowly to face her. "Those who have trained me will tell you that I am most use at the head of a Sweep or Probe Star."

"It is so noted in your record. That is why I offer you command of my Sweep Star."

"My instructors would be most honorable if they told you that I am a person who desires and requires little direction. I work best in independent actions."

Angela grinned slightly. "That was not in your record, but I understand. Independent action is my forte as well."

"This unit of yours, does it have any chance of seeing action?"

"Aye. Our posting is on the front-line world of Toffen."

Stone nodded and for a moment seemed to be mentally reviewing a map of the Ghost Bear Dominion for the location of Toffen. "Where there is a chance to fight and serve the Clan, there is a chance for greater glory. I am honored to join your command, Star Captain Bekker."

"Excellent. I will cut the necessary orders, Star Commander."

Stone nodded once, then turned back to this Omni-Mech and the work being done it.

The Idle Goose was the kind of bar commonly found wherever there are soldiers. It had been here when the Draconis Combine had claimed Alshain, and now that the Ghost Bears ruled, only the flag of its clientele had changed.

The place was typically dark and smelled of cigarettes, cigars, sweat, beer, and other odors best not identified. Several tables had been pushed back from the middle of the room, and a trio of warriors seemed to be either dancing or squaring off for a fight. In the shadows another warrior had gotten close enough to see and hear without drawing anyone's attention.

One of the combatants, a stout man with a receding hairline, stooped to a fighting stance. "I offer you a chance to take back those words, Star Commander Konti," he said, with a wicked smile.

From the shadows the half-concealed warrior nodded to himself. This was surely the man he was seeking. His name was Gregori, and true to his record, he was obviously the antagonist here.

"Neg, you dung maggot," the other man replied. "And I will not grant you a Circle of Equals. My words, stand, freebirth scum." A grunt of acknowledgment came from another warrior who stood alongside, balling his fists for a fight.

"As you wish, Konti," Gregori said, licking his lips. "You and your friend will eat those words." With that, he sprang like a bolt of lightning at Konti.

Konti attempted to dodge the strike, but alcohol and bad timing cursed his luck. Gregori struck him in the lower chest with a sweeping kick that sent Konti flying back. As he went down, the edge of Konti's fist caught his attacker but only grazed him. In mid-flight Gregori twisted so as to drop to the floor on his side.

Now Konti's comrade moved in for the attack, but Gregori saw him and swept the floor with his legs, knocking the larger warrior's feet from under him and throwing him to the floor as well. Gregori rolled, sweat and hair flying, and landed on the man's back, pummeling his ears with blows to both sides.

Konti got to his feet and picked up a chair as the other bar patrons, oddly silent, moved back to give the combatants room. Konti let go a battle cry as he rushed forward, chair raised over his head, then smashed it down on Gregori, who still sat on the back of Konti's injured comrade.

Gregori kicked off as the chair started downward. It caught his ankles and the back of Konti's ally at the same time that Gregori collided with his attacker's knees. There was a snapping sound as he impacted, a noise as Konti's knee gave way, bending backward. The war cry turned to a wail as he dropped to the floor in agony.

Gregori rose, his breathing ragged. He surveyed the warriors who had been watching the brawl. "Anyone else who wishes to test whether this 'freebirth scum' is worthy to be a warrior of the Ghost Bears?"

He was answered by an angry rumbling from the

crowd, which the man in the shadows recognized as the trueborns preparing to defend their honor. It was time to make his move. He stepped into the dim light of the room and walked over to the brawler. "You are Gregori, are you not?"

"Aff, you truebirth bastard," Gregori spat, uttering the vilest of curses. Trueborns could never be bastards, of course, yet were so by their very nature. "Come and take me, if you can." Clearly his blood was boiling.

"I see that your codex did not lie," Constant Tseng replied evenly.

"What is that supposed to mean?"

"You know what it means," Tseng said. "You have an excellent combat record. You have won a half-dozen Trials of Position, then lost every one of your postings because of your constant squabbling with trueborns in Circles of Equals. Your record for demotions is surely unparalleled in the history of our Clan."

Gregori grinned, no doubt spurred by an excess of alcohol. "I have little use for titles and positions. Or for arrogant officers who have nothing better to do than sit around reading my codex. Come and see what I am made of."

Tseng shook his head. "No, Gregori, but I suggest you drop this fight and leave now. You will not solve this argument today." Tseng wondered if Gregori really believed the age-old conflict between freebirths and trueborns could be resolved in a mere bar room brawl. "Besides, I have come to talk to you."

Gregori shook his head. "I am not in a mood to talk but to fight. Defeat me and I will listen to you."

This was not his style, but Constant Tseng did not hesitate. "If that is the only way you will listen, so be it." He removed his black gloves and tucked them close to the brass Ghost Bear buckle on his belt.

As before, Gregori sprang into the air without warning. The difference this time was that Constant Tseng had not been drinking as had the previous foe. Gregori was already tired from fighting, and Tseng's reflexes were much faster than Konti or his ally's. With perfect precision he sidestepped the leap and brought both of his fists down squarely on the back of Gregori's head.

Gregori staggered and Tseng leapt onto his back to take him down. He pulled the dazed Gregori's hands tightly behind his back and kept them pinned. Gregori moaned slightly, then actually gave a soft laugh. "You have bested me, warrior, Do you have a name?"

"Star Commander Constant Tseng."

The excitement over, the bar's patrons gradually went back to whatever they had been doing before all the fighting began. Against the rising din several warriors went to help Gregori's two victims to their feet. Slowly, Constant removed himself from Gregori's back, standing up so Gregori could do the same.

"What do you want from me?" Gregori asked, using the back of his sleeve to wipe the sweat dripping from his brow and the blood from the corner of his mouth.

"Your codex also indicates that you have the highest kill ratio in our Clan, for a freebirth, that is."

Gregori's eyes narrowed. "I do not want to fight you again, but if that was an insult—"

"No insult," Constant said, cutting him off. "I serve under Star Captain Angela Bekker. She is forming a new unit. From what we see in your record, we think you would be an excellent addition to our force."

Gregori laughed again. "If you've read my codex, then you know that most of my commanding officers think I am a pain in the ass. They say I'm too headstrong, that I disregard orders if tactical situations demand it. In general, Star Commander, they think I'm unmanageable and unpredictable." As if to emphasize his point, he glanced over to where two other warriors were helping Konti out of the bar.

Tseng nodded, running one hand through his straight dark hair. "Yes, but they also say you have a genius for quickly sizing up a tactical situation, and being able to react even as you do so. Your number of combat kills proves that." What Constant Tseng did not mention were the man's non-combat kills, in numerous fights like the one he had just interrupted. Gregori would surely be difficult, but his talents, when channeled, would be worth it.

"And it does not bother you that I am a freeborn?"

"As long as it does not bother you that I am trueborn."

Gregori smiled broadly. "It does bother me if you flaunt your arrogance about your origins. But anyone who beats me so quickly deserves my respect, regardless of where his genes come from. If you'll take me, I am willing to join you."

"Good, then you are now a member of the Eighth Cuirassiers."

"One question, Star Commander." Gregori again wiped away the sweat from his brow and drew a long breath. "How did you find me?"

"Your former commanding officer told me to look for a bar full of warriors, and then find a freeborn either spoiling for a fight or in the middle of one. In other words, Gregori, it was just a matter of time."

The freebirth Gregori smiled broadly. "You I can work with."

The three warriors sat rigidly in the conference room, tension thick in the air. One was a stocky female, with cropped blonde hair worn in a mohawk and a burn scar under the right ear. She wore a typical Ghost

Bear fatigues, but what looked like a Nova Cat tattoo peeked out from under the cuff of her jumpsuit.

The second of the three warriors was a dark-skinned Elemental who dominated the room in sheer size. While that alone would make him stand out, the tufts of gray hair in his short sideburns usually drew even more attention. Clan warriors rarely served into their late thirties, the age he appeared to be. Once past thirty-five, most were destined for the ranks of the solahma, the last refuge for the aged, infirm, or those otherwise considered useless to the Clans. If they were lucky, solahma warriors would give their lives in a suicide attack or in some other way redeem the shame of not having died sooner and more honorably in battle. To see an older warrior among the regular Ghost Bear ranks was an oddity.

The third warrior had short black hair and the hint of a shadowed beard. His skin was pale, as though he had not been exposed to the elements in recent years.

Angela and Constant Tseng entered the room, datapads in hand, and took seats opposite the warriors at the table. They were deliberately silent. Of the three warriors seated, only one of them, the one with the shadowed beard, showed any hint of emotion.

"I will be brief," Angela began, her voice sounding extra loud because the room had been so silent. "I am Star Captain Angela Bekker. At the behest of Khan Jorgenssen, I am forming a new Trinary as part of the Eighth Cuirassiers, Delta Galaxy. This is Star Commander Constant Tseng, commander of the unit's Striker Star. We have asked you here because a review of your codexes indicates potential for serving in this new command." She looked from the fair-haired warrior to the dark Elemental, but not at the man with the shadowed beard. "The real question is whether you are worthy to serve in this new command."

"Worth," the Elemental said, "is often in the eyes of the beholder, is it not, Star Captain?"

"Aye, Dolf," she replied, not needing to check her notepad for his name. "But a codex does not tell the whole story of a warrior. In your case, you are up for rotation to a solahma unit in one of our Periphery holdings. You might only wish to serve in my command to avoid that fate."

Dolf's dark brown eyes locked with hers. "I do not lie, Star Captain. Unless I am reassigned to your unit, I will live out the rest of my life as a solahma. That may yet happen, but if there is a chance that I can still serve and even die with honor in battle, that is the fate I desire the most."

"There is more, warrior," said Star Commander Tseng.

Dolf's eyes seemed to darken. He bowed his head slightly. "Aye, Star Commander. There is more. I have fought in three major battles. Three times I have been the sole survivor of my Star. There are those who say I am cursed. I am not. I need one more chance to prove that."

Angela glanced at her datapad. "I appreciate your honesty, Dolf. Like you, I also fought on Tukayyid. I do not believe in the fates, though. Luck, maybe, but never the fates. Would you serve me well to prove that you are not cursed?"

Dolf nodded. "I will never again be the sole survivor of a unit, Star Captain. Accept me as a warrior and I will prove it."

Constant Tseng looked at Angela and nodded his approval. "Aye, Dolf, we will give you that chance. We intend to create a full Point of Elementals for the Trinary. I would like your help in recruiting them."

The huge warrior smiled broadly. "It would be my honor, Star Captain Bekker."

Angela looked at her datapad again and adjusted the controls to pull up the data she sought. The screen's pale blue-white light danced off her fingers. "You must be Neta," she said, looking at the blonde warrior.

"Aff, Star Captain, I am Neta the Ghost Bear.'

"Formerly a member of the Nova Cats, quiaff?" Constant Tseng said.

"Aff, Star Commander. I was made a bondsman by the warrior Hosek."

"I have seen your codex," Angela said, "but some details were not included. What happened to Hosek?"

"He made me a warrior six months after my capture in a Trial of Possession for my genetic material. Two days later we had a disagreement on the treatment of a member of the technician caste who had damaged one of our 'Mechs. We met in a Circle of Equals and I snapped his neck." There was little emotion in her words, as if what happened had not affected her in the least.

"Was the act deliberate?" Tseng pushed.

"Neg, Star Commander," Neta said. Her eyes glittered as she spoke. "It was an unfortunate accident."

"And since then no unit has accepted you into their ranks, quiaff?" Angela asked.

"Affirmative, Star Captain."

"And why should I?"

Her words seemed to catch Neta off balance for an uncomfortable moment of silence. "Let it suffice to say that I have been made a Ghost Bear but have not had the chance to prove myself. The only time I have ever lost in battle was to my new Clan. I fought with enough skill to merit becoming a bondsman and then a warrior. Now I desire the chance to fight."

"Does the heart of the bear beat in your chest?" Angela asked.

"Once I was a Nova Cat and let my intuition and emotions guide me in the universe. Now I am a Ghost Bear and fight as such. If you are asking if all vestiges of my former Clan have been purged, the answer is no. I, too, will not lie. I still feel the call of the stars as they guide me. But my service and heart are now with the Ghost Bear. My former bondmaster disliked my mystical side, and in the end it cost him his life.

"All I ask is a chance to prove myself to the Ghost Bears, to show that I am indeed a warrior of this Clan." She glanced briefly at Dolf, who nodded. The two of them shared parallel fates with different names.

Angela looked at Tseng, who again signaled his approval. She tossed the datapad onto the table and looked at the third warrior facing her at the table. "And you, old friend. Though we have not seen each other in two years, you look better than the last time we met. I ask if you are willing to fight under my command. We are both of the same sibko and that gives us a bond that is beyond description. But I have a bloodname and rank on you. Would that make it difficult for you to serve under me?"

The man with the five o'clock shadow smiled. "Neg, Star Captain. Not to me. Serving in your unit would be an honor. I owe you a debt that I desire to fulfill on the field of battle."

"Excellent," Angela said, tapping a button on the datapad to shut it off. "I will send the necessary orders to your current commanding officers."

The three new recruits said no more, but their faces

spoke volumes. Angela rose, as did Tseng, and the two left the room.

The three warriors remained silent until the door closed. Neta turned in her chair to the pale warrior and cocked her head in puzzlement. "You know this Star Captain Bekker, quiaff?"

"Aff. That is an understatement. I owe my life to her." There was pride in his voice.

Neta nodded as if she understood, and spoke with the eerie tone of her Nova Cat upbringing. "She is honorable beyond her words and appearance."

"She could have let me die but did not," the man said, rubbing his ribs in memory of the painful injury he had suffered.

"You have served under her before?" Dolf asked.

"Neg. Not served. Something more," the man replied. Slowly Sprange began to tell them the story of how Star Captain Angela Bekker saved his life . . .

In the corridor outside the room, Constant Tseng stopped Angela and gave her a reassuring grin. "You handled that well."

"Adding Sprange to our unit is fortunate. As I told you, I saved his life once. He will tell the others about me, and it will help instill them with some of the same loyalty. We are going to need all the help we can get in shaping up this unit."

Tseng nodded ruefully. "That is so, but I have met with two other warriors we should consider. One is named Sorrentino. He has not much combat experience, but shows a strong grasp of defensive positions and operations."

"Good," Angela replied. "And the other?"

"Her name is Bethany. She is fresh from the Bloodied

Paw sibko." There was a hesitation in his voice as if he was not entirely sure of this one.

"Thoughts?"

"She is hot-headed, quick to the fight. She is impulsive. She lacks the practical experience of a seasoned warrior."

"But she appeals to you on some level, quiaff?"

"Aff. Her marksmanship and gunnery skills are beyond compare. With you or I commanding her, I think she has great potential in our Clan."

"I want to meet her," Angela said. "And we will arrange for Star Commander Stone to join us. He must also be part of this. Sharing these crucial decisions will forge a bond between us as commanders."

Angela massaged her temple for a moment as if it would rub away the tension. "You had better turn in, Star Commander. Star Colonel Vishio is already on her way to Toffen to oversee the withdrawal. We have a long few days ahead of us. Between gathering the final recruits and working with the quartermaster technicians, we have much to do if we are to be good to go in less than a week."

4

Seventh Battle Cluster Headquarters
Altenmarkt
Wolf Clan Occupation Zone
16 January 3062

Star Colonel Dirk Radick sat back in his stiff-backed chair and stared at the hard copy report in his hand as if it contained the words of the great Nicholas Kerensky himself. He pored over the report as if it gave him power—or hope. His dirty blond hair was abnormally long on the sides, but it was shaved to the skin near the temples in MechWarrior fashion. He kept running his hand unconsciously through his hair as he read, searching for a clue, some piece of information that might lead him to the honor he so desired. Most warriors preferred their data electronically, but Dirk Radick read hard copy reports because it was different. Being different was something he strived for in every action he took, even in private. Uniqueness, he believed, instilled fear in the weak.

The past few years had not been the best in the long history of Clan Wolf, the Clan of Dirk Radick. Early on, the Wolves had been at the forefront, outpacing all the other invading Clans in the race for Terra. Then came the battle at Tukayyid and the fifteen-year truce that still dragged on.

Since then the Wolf Clan Touman had been weakened by internal disputes and factional splits. That made it even more important for the hard-line Crusaders like Dirk Radick to be ever on the lookout for any opportunity to advance their Clan . . . and their cause.

Among the extremes of the Crusader Clans, the Wolves were on the bleeding edge. And none was more radical than Star Colonel Dirk Radick. As commanding officer of the Seventh Battle Cluster, he had earned a reputation for ruthlessness. Included among his targets were the freebirth warriors in his own and other Clans. He had killed many freebirths with abandon, earning his unit the nickname the Blood Drinkers, a name he wore as a badge of honor.

Radick especially enjoyed the reputation because it made others believe he was rash, uncontrolled, reacting more from rage than reason. The truth was far from that. Dirk Radick was cunning and calculating. He enjoyed making his enemies and even some of his supporters believe him to be reckless and impulsive. It worked to his advantage in bidding and in the twisted maze of internal Clan politics.

He flipped the page of the hard copy document and continued to study it closely. It was a report from The Watch, the intelligence arm of the Clan. Each Clan maintained its own version of The Watch to keep an eye on friends and enemies alike. Until they had invaded the Inner Sphere, the Clans had no need for deceptive operations and intelligence-gathering. Their bidding rituals brought each side's tactical information out into the open, more or less. But now that the Clans were in the

Inner Sphere, and with so much infighting among themselves, there was a need to know what others were doing.

Radick paused for a moment and re-read one entry that had caught his attention. Then he scanned the data two more times. He was just forming a smile when a knock came at his door. He glanced at his chronometer. O700 hours. As usual, she was on time.

"Enter," he said. The door opened and Star Captain Jergan came through it with the military precision that only genetic selection and breeding could perfect. A large woman with red-streaked dark hair, Jergan commanded the Sword of the Wolf Trinary. He had been grooming her as his second, though he was sure she had no clue to his complexity. Today would be a good test of her understanding.

"Good day, Star Colonel," she said, saluting and then taking a seat opposite his.

"A 'good day' is a matter of perspective," Radick grumbled. Let her wonder what his real mood was.

"Something disturbing in today's intelligence reports, Star Colonel?"

"Perhaps." He pushed the report toward her across the desk. "Read page two. Tell me what you see."

She picked up the document, cast him a suspicious glance, then read it, twice.

"The Ghost Bears are reorganizing, quiaff?" she said finally.

"Aff. That is part of it." Radick took a slow sip of his morning coffee. "Look at the entry for Toffen."

She scanned it quickly. "Apparently they are rotating the Eighth Bear Cuirassiers off Toffen."

"Correct. And look at the replacement unit."

She again glanced at the hard copy suspiciously. "A brand new Trinary."

Radick smiled broadly. "Aye, Star Captain." He rose

from his chair and came around to the front of the desk. "A new Trinary, indeed. A green unit. Untried in battle." He pointed down at the report still in her hands. "Review the next page. Take a look at what we know about that unit and what The Watch says about Toffen."

She turned the page and read the entry rapidly. Radick reached across the desk and activated the holographic desktop unit. It flickered to life over the desk, displaying a map of the Clan invasion corridor, focused on the Ghost Bear Dominion. At the very bottom, highlighted in red, was Toffen.

Jergan shook her head slightly. "A Star Captain named Angela Bekker in command of the garrison."

"Yes," Radick said, staring intently at the map. "I recall seeing her name come up in a report several months ago. She is rather well known in the ranks of the Ghost Bears. A ristar." The word was the Clan term for "rising star," one that Radick knew the more radical Crusaders often applied to him. The fact that he was studying the warriors of another Clan was a testimony to the depth of his character—at least in his own opinion.

He drew a long breath and continued. "One of their ristars is forming a new unit and being posted to a frontline world. And, as you can see, the Ghost Bears have been very busy on Toffen. They have been shipping tons of supplies to their little outpost there."

Jergan turned a page quickly. "Crates marked as repair parts and ammunition," she read aloud. "Interesting, considering that the Bears are a Warden Clan. Toffen's position makes it a perfect staging point for a thrust toward Terra, but that does not fit with the Warden credo."

"So then, what are the Ghost Bears up to?"

"Perhaps they are simply planning to beef up their garrison there. That, or they intend to launch some sort of offensive. What do you think, Star Colonel?"

Radick rubbed his chin thoughtfully. "I do not know, Jergan. Only recently they took three of our worlds. Perhaps they think us weak after such conquests and are gearing up to try and take more. Or possibly they are building up on Toffen in an effort to attack us from a more rimward area of their Dominion, thinking to bypass the buffer created by the Hell's Horses presence on some of our former worlds. I wonder . . . what exactly do we know about Toffen?"

Jergan read from the report. "Three main continents, a wide range of terrain types. Climate is varied, but not by much. Much of the world is covered with either forests or dense, grassy plains. There are also a number of mountain ranges, mostly iron and nickel ore. The Ghost Bears have located and are refitting an old Star League fortress on the continent of Graham. The local population is spread out in small villages and cities. Limited production capability. Mostly a self-sufficient agricultural world."

"If not for the Ghost Bears, there would be no reason to go there," Radick mused.

Star Captain Jergan put the report down for a moment. "A single Trinary to garrison such a forward world, isolated and alone? It seems wrong. We would not do that."

"Aye, we are Wolves and they are merely Ghost Bears," Radick said. "The Eighth Bear Cuirassiers are rotating off in the next month or so. This new unit will be rotating in at the same time, but if our intelligence is correct, there are no immediate plans to reinforce it. It is all very odd, Jergan. A lone Trinary. Green. As a unit, untested in battle."

He watched the glowing red ball that was Toffen. "I am sure there will be freebirths among them too, and you know my feelings about them." Radick understood that freebirths were a necessity. His own Khan had used them to help fill out the Wolves' decimated ranks. But he hated them anyway.

"Yes, an egotistical ristar, with a band of unblooded warriors and freebirths that she has to somehow form into a cohesive unit. A unique opportunity for us, Jergan. They will not realize that the Wolf is on the hunt . . . until it is too late."

Jergan stared at him. "You plan to strike at Toffen?"

Radick smiled broadly, an almost wicked grin. "Neg. I mean to *take* Toffen from the Ghost Bears. Striking is pointless. A Trial of Possession for Toffen would be fitting, given the Ghost Bears' stand during the Great Refusal. Taking this planet from them now sends them a message that we are not weak, but that we are ready and more than willing to strike at them."

"This ristar, Star Captain Bekker," said Jergan. "It would be a mistake to underestimate her."

"I do not," Radick snapped, angry at the insinuation. "She earned a bloodname, and even for a Warden that is no small task. From what we see of her codex, she undertook their precious little Clawing ritual as well. I do not underestimate her. I respect her and will bid accordingly when I take Toffen."

"Time is critical, Star Colonel," Jergan said, looking at the holographic map still hovering in the air above the desktop. "We have only a small window of opportunity. It will take days to get a message to and from the Galaxy Commander requesting permission for such an operation. If she requires approval from Khan Ward, we will never have enough time to get there and initiate the attack."

Radick's smile did not fade. "I concur. Contacting Galaxy Commander Carns would imperil such a plan. And we are Wolves. Wolves are hunters. We do not wait for our prey to come to us. We stalk and kill them."

"So we go without formal permission, Star Colonel?" There was a hint of excitement in her voice.

"Aye, Jergan. I will communicate to Galaxy Commander Carns my intentions, but by the time she gets the message, we will be underway. Issue immediate orders to the entire Cluster that we move out immediately. Contact our transport commanders and tell them to get ready to take us to Toffen."

Jergan rose to obey. "How would you like our Omni-Mechs configured for this Trial?"

Radick answered without hesitation. "The Ghost Bears will be unprepared. Our 'Mechs should go with heavy assault weapons. Heavy concentrations of missile weapons and autocannons."

"Getting the proper supplies requisitioned and moved here, then tested and loaded will take time," she pointed out.

"Unnecessary, Jergan. We should be more than safe with standard loadouts and our emergency supplies. The Ghost Bears will have significantly more ammunition and supplies, but it is all concentrated in one place. That will govern their venue of combat somewhat. We will have to study the terrain around that fortress they are using. It is from there they will most likely have to fight. Supplies will not be much of an issue. We will seize Toffen quickly, and then refit with the spare supplies we rip from the claws of the Ghost Bears."

"Understood, Star Colonel," she said. "I will go now if you do not need me here any longer. There is much to do if we are to get underway immediately."

"Aye, Star Captain. I want the refitting done in the next few hours so we can depart promptly. Soon the roar of the Wolves will echo in the ears of the Ghost Bears and our emblem will fly over Toffen."

5

Bear's Den Training Field
Alshain
Ghost Bear Dominion
16 January 3062

The building was more like an angled tower, jutting into the air nearly ten meters and leaning forward over the massive earthen berm that marked the edge of the training facility. Reinforced and heavily armored, the towerlike structure offered its several occupants an excellent view of the training field as well as protection from any stray shots.

The training field was nearly forty acres square, surrounded by a massive earthwork embankment. Inside it was a mix of terrain, the charred remains of several buildings, mock streets, and even an oddly pastoral-looking stream that ran through the middle of the field.

In its relative confines, Ghost Bear warriors could test their skill and mettle against each other in simulated battle. Weapons were powered down; autocannons and missiles carried only light concussion warheads that did mock damage. The members of the technician caste had also reprogrammed the battle computers on both 'Mechs and Elemental suits to simulate damage. To those taking part in the live-fire drill, it would seem all too real, right up to neurofeedback in their neurohelmets if they were hit.

Angela squinted through her binoculars, ignoring the range information its LED displays provided. Star Commanders Tseng and Stone wee also observing the exercise through binoculars.

"Dolf and his recruits are doing an excellent job," Angela remarked. Dolf had found a number of highly qualified Elemental warriors, who Angela, Stone, and Tseng had easily approved. All five now reported as a single Point in Stone's Sweep Star. The Elementals and a single MechWarrior named Natulson, piloting a seventy-ton *Summoner*, were hidden in a cluster of trees, waiting for their two opponents.

The idea for the simulated battle had been Angela's. If this group of warriors did well, they would be the finishing touch to her unit. Recruitment efforts had gone well, and though some of the personalities were mismatched, she believed they would eventually come together as a combat team. This last group of recruits was on the fringe of acceptability, however. There was something that gave her pause with each one—save Dolf and his Point of Elementals.

Natulson, a lanky, large-handed warrior with a Roman nose and broad grin, seemed more personable than the typical warrior. His record had been spotless until recently, when a mercenary unit named Bert's Bombardiers had attempted to raid the world where he was posted. Dishonorably ambushed, his unit had been severely mauled. According to the offical report, it was because he had panicked and frozen under fire. Natulson had formally protested the charge, but it boiled down to his word against that of a fellow officer, who died two days later from his wounds.

The two attackers who were now hunting Natulson and Dolf's force were Bethany and Sorrenteno. Sorrenteno was a short, almost pudgy warrior who might have seemed overweight except that he was so obviously solid muscle. He piloted a *Mad Dog* OmniMech and tended to be a touch cynical. Despite Sorrenteno's relatively long career as a Ghost Bear, he had somehow managed to avoid any major battle or conflict. Like Dolf, he was along enough in years that he would soon be relegated to the trash heap of solahma duty. But, unlike Dolf, Sorrenteno had never shed blood on the field of honor. Still, Angela saw some potential in him. His scores in simulations and exercises were exceptionally high, and he seemed to have a knack for defensive tactical operations. This simulation would prove his worth . . . one way or another.

Bethany was the black-haired fury who piloted the squat *Nova* OmniMech that was beginning to probe the edge of the woods where Dolf and Natulson lay in wait. Tseng had reservations about her, mostly to do with her temper and her inability to control it. Angela thought that Bethany's piloting and gunnery skills, though not yet tested in battle, were good enough to one day place her among the best. In the interview, however, her cockiness bordered on arrogant. This test would decide whether she would merit a place in the Trinary.

The cluster of woods was sparse, but the hardwood trees obscured some of the view. Almost two acres square, the woods grew along a long, sloping hillside, which gave Angela and her commanders a perfect view of the exercise. Sorrenteno had positioned his *Mad Dog* at the top of the hill, and now descended slowly, trying to maintain the high ground. But not Bethany. She crashed down the hillside, kicking up dirt and plowing through brush and low-hanging vines.

"She is reckless," Constant Tseng said, gazing through the binoculars.

"Wait," Angela said. She, Tseng, and Stone already knew where the ambush was going to take place. In powered-down mode, Natulson and Dolf's Elemental Point would be almost invisible until their opponents were right on top of them. They were showing great restraint, waiting for a point-blank kill.

Reaching the bottom of the hill, Bethany's olive-green *Nova* skidded to a stop and began to move along the lower edge of the woods. Sorrenteno joined her, piloting his *Mad Dog* parallel along the ridgetop. His 'Mech glanced against trees as it went, twisting branches and snapping others as if they were toothpicks.

Suddenly the center of the woods exploded with life as Dolf and his Elementals rose into the air on their leg jets. Their power armor painted in spotted brown and green camo, they blended with the trees, but their jump jets flared with menace. They lifted through the trees at nearly ten meters off the ground, letting go with salvos of shoulder-launched short-range missiles, all bearing down on Bethany's *Nova*.

The missiles exploded against the *Nova* with white puffs of powered-down charges, but the 'Mech's battle computer recorded the damage as if it were real. The Elementals came down the hillside through the woods like a pack of rabid dogs on a wounded deer.

Bethany's *Nova* was equipped in its primary configuration, mounting a deadly pack of twelve medium-range lasers. She opened up with almost all of them, shooting brilliant green beams at the Elementals. Neither Angela nor her two commanders said a word, but all knew that Bethany's cockpit must be a sauna after unleashing such a barrage. It was the drawback of 'Mechs, in general, that they sometimes generated more heat than they could vent. When a 'Mech overheated, as the *Nova* was prone to do given its ratio of heat sinks to lasers, it could shut down and become an immobile, two-story target. Angela wondered for a moment if Bethany might have been over-confident in mounting her weapons pods with so many lasers.

These, too, were powered down, and two of her beams actually hit and downed an Elemental, most likely injuring but not killing the massive warrior. Elemental suits were equipped with life-support systems that sealed wounds and injected the warrior with pain-killers that kept him or her fighting even when hurt. The others dropped into the woods, seeking cover and position to make their next leap. Two more short-range missiles streaked out, slamming into the legs of Bethany's *Nova*.

"Pull back," Angela said, as though Bethany could hear her. It was the smart thing to do. The primary tactic of Elementals was to disable a 'Mech by "swarming" it. Leaping onto its armored hide, they would use their mechanical claw-hands to rip open the armor. Their arm-mounted lasers and flamers could wreak untold havoc on the internal systems of their prey. A Point of trained and skilled Elementals could down a 'Mech as rapidly and efficiently as another 'Mech.

Bethany charged forward.

Angela watched in shock as Bethany rushed up the hill into the woods, her lasers raging through the foliage with wild abandon. From within the woods, the massive shape of a gray-green *Summoner* stirred, moving downhill toward Bethany. Natulson had joined the fray, cutting loose with a silvery dud gauss slug that slammed into the center torso of her *Nova* like a cannonball hitting an ancient knight. His pulse laser spit red beams that danced across her armor, inflicting only small burns but considerable simulated damage. Bethany's battle computer shook her 'Mech so hard that it was visible to Angela from where she stood.

"As I told you," Tseng said, watching the Elementals begin to close on their quarry, "she is arrogant."

Stone broke his silence. "Perhaps not."

As if in a panic, Bethany began to back down the hill the same way she had entered the forest. Coming at her, only meters away, the leaping, battle-armored Elementals sprayed her *Nova* with lasers and missiles. Natulson's almost humanoid *Summoner* also rushed down the wooded hillside, snapping branches as it went. Its laser missed, sweeping wide to the left of the *Nova*, while his gauss slug dug deep into the *Nova*'s leg. The leg went limp as the battle computer simulated shutdown of its actuator. Bethany's speed slowed as the Elementals rose in their final leap.

Suddenly Natulson's *Summoner* quaked as if it were being shaken apart from within. A cloud of smoke rose from behind it. Sorrenteno's *Mad Dog* was descending the hill, pouring more than thirty long-range missiles and fire from several of its massive pulse lasers into the *Summoner's* back, where its armor was thinnest. Natulson twisted his torso to face uphill, but it was already too late. He had taken far too much damage. Sorrenteno blasted his left torso with his pulse lasers as his *Mad Dog*'s missile racks reloaded for another barrage. Natulson lost his balance, most likely from gyro damage, and fell, toppling three trees as he dropped with a screech of grinding metal that Angela could feel in her own body like one of her own bones breaking.

Dolf's force had split in two, three Elementals landing on or near Bethany and two turning to face the new threat coming down the hill. One fired at the *Mad Dog*, and Sorrenteno let loose with a wave of long-range missiles that seemed to envelop the air and the woods. Thick white smoke obscured the hillside as the reduced-power warheads did their deadly work. Angela knew that even the durability of the Elementals would not save them against this wave of missiles.

Bethany's *Nova* was in horrific shape, its right leg and one arm hanging like broken limbs. A *Nova* was a short, hunched-over 'Mech that did not lend itself to sweeping movements, but Bethany made her Omni-Mech shake like some highlander in a wild jig, attempting to fling the Elementals free. Two did fly off, hurled into the woods at the feet of Sorrenteno's approaching 'Mech. The last one, its armored white head identifying him as Dolf, held on like a tick. The dance of death raged for several long moments before Bethany finally stopped. Angela thought she might be exhausted from her efforts, or that the damage was too much.

Without warning Bethany deliberately collapsed her *Nova*'s knees, dropping her 'Mech onto its side in an effort to crush the remaining Elemental. Dolf leapt clear of the fall, landing in a small cluster of cedars with incredible force, yet somehow managing to roll and land on his feet. The act was deliberately dangerous. Had her fifty-ton 'Mech dropped on top of Dolf it would have either killed him or destroyed him as a warrior.

Angela activated the communications panel in front of her. "Shut down the simulation," she commanded. She knew a signal was being sent to the participants as crews from the technician and scientist caste prepared to repair both the equipment, and if necessary, the warriors. "I have seen enough."

"She has no control," Constant Tseng commented, lowering his binoculars.

"You are in error, Star Commander," 'tone said coolly.

Angela waited, deciding to let her two officers have their say.

"The others performed well," Tseng said. "But Bethany is too reckless. Instead of working with her partner, she rushed into the middle of a fight. I am willing to bet that her *Nova* is barely operational after that last stunt. Not to mention that she almost killed a valuable warrior."

"Neg," Angela said, then activated the speaker system in the comm panel again. "Bethany, this is Star Captain Bekker. Tell us why you rushed into the woods to engage both of the enemy. Your actions appear to some to be negligent."

Bethany's voice was hoarse in reply. "Sorrenteno and I planned it that way. I would come from below and rush in to flush them out. He would stay on the high ground and hit them from the rear as I drew their fire. The rules of the scenario permitted us to engage multiple opponents, and it was the best way to take advantage of our weapon configurations and the terrain——sir." Her breath was ragged, and she was obviously worn out but happy at winning the engagement.

Angela cocked a smile as Tseng lowered his head, acknowledging error. "That will be all, Bethany," she said, shutting off the comm system. She looked at Tseng thoughtfully. "I think she will do well with us."

"Respectfully, Star Captain," Tseng said, "I still believe her arrogance makes her an element of discord in our Trinary. Perhaps we should consider another candidate, quiaff?"

Angela looked at the stoic Stone, who stood with arms crossed, just listening. "And you, Stone?"

"She is skilled," he said. "She has a good grasp of tactics. But her personality is abrasive, as we know from her interview. She will be a focus of dissent in our unit."

Angela nodded. "There is always some of that in a unit, and as long as she is part of us, our dissent has a name . . . and it is Bethany. Star Commander Tseng, she will be assigned to my Command Star. If your fears prove true, I want to handle them myself. If you oppose the decision, let us settle it in a Circle of Equals." Her tone was matter-of-fact rather than challenging.

Constant shook his head. "Neg, Star Captain. My opposition is not that strong. But what about the others?"

"Natulson and Sorrenteno should fit in ably with your Striker Star and complete our needs there, Star Commander. Have their transfer orders on my desk as soon as possible. Also inform the shipyard and quartermaster that we depart in thirty-six hours."

She looked out across the training field and then back at Stone and Tseng. "There is still much work ahead of us, gentlemen. We have our warriors. Now we must turn them into a fighting unit."

6

DropShip **Bloodied Paw**
Zenith Jump Point, Setubal System
Ghost Bear Dominion
30 January 3062

The DropShip seemed to pitch around Angela as the JumpShip to which it was docked completed its jump into the Setubal system. Her stomach lurched, and she stumbled over to the sink as fast as her magnetic boots would let her. She pulled a damp cloth from the dispenser and wiped her face in an effort to cool it. The contrast of her hot forehead and the cool cloth was not as soothing as she had hoped . . . then again, it rarely was.

She pushed the taste of bile back down into her throat and felt a tremendous chill rush through her body like a huge wave breaking against a beach. Jump sickness. Not all warriors suffered from it, but Angela was one who did. JumpShips were kilometer-long vessels that used their jump drives to tear a hole in the fabric of space, propelling the ship between the stars in what seemed like an instant. The calculations and the charging of the massive batteries needed to accomplish a successful jump took long and tedious hours. When a jump occurred, however, the ship would emerge almost instantaneously at another star system up to thirty light years distant. And when it did, almost inevitably, Angela felt as if her stomach was going to turn inside out. The spartan life of a Clan warrior did not much lend itself to secrets, but this was one she had kept for many years. She would not let those in her command see any weakness. She did not want to give them any reason to doubt her. Ever.

She looked at the stars through the small viewport of the DropShip *Bloodied Paw* as the "all clear" klaxon signaled that the jump had been successful. Somewhere, ten days or so away, was the planet Setubal, another in the holdings of Ghost Bear's domain. The next jump was home—at least for a while. Home to Toffen.

Angela opened the door and made her way down the narrow corridor to the Tactical Operations Room. A military DropShip like the *Bloodied Paw* often served as a base of operations once a unit landed, and a ground force commander could use the TOR to coordinate and communicate with ground troops. Many newer DropShips did not have a TOR, and operations were coordinated from the bridge. But the *Paw* was an older model *Union-C*, and its TOR had never been converted to cargo space.

As she entered the long, wide room, the gathered warriors, *her* warriors, rose to snap-attention. She saluted, then signaled for them to sit. The room was dominated by a massive communications and holographic projection table. There were no viewports, only the white light of the ship's illumination.

This was their first formal meeting as a Trinary. The fourteen MechWarriors and five Elementals of her command had been running endless drills and exercises on the shipboard simulators under their Star Commanders, but this would be their first meeting as a single group. She knew that they must learn to work together at the Star level before they could even hope to function as a larger unit. It was an old military-training model, and it was still around because it worked.

Angela took her seat at the head of the table. Facing her were the nineteen men and women who would fight, and possibly even die, at her word. They wore pressed gray jumpsuits, and their whole attention was focused on her.

"First off I want to welcome you to Trinary Six of the Eighth Bears Cuirassiers," Angela said. "You have each met your Starmates, but this is your chance to know the rest. Look around this table. These are the members of your Trinary. They will fight beside you for the honor of our Clan. Learn who they are and their strengths and weaknesses. Any one of these warriors might save your life one day." As she spoke, her people began to glance around at the others. Even the tall Elementals, towering over the others at the far end of the table, seemed somehow brought to the same level as the others by her words.

Angela gave them a moment or two before speaking again, watching as they silently appraised one another. "You were each hand-picked for your skills and your service to the Ghost Bears. After this meeting you will take part in a battery of simulations working together as a unit. Once we arrive at our garrison, we will commence another series of drills and operational exercises that will hone our ability to function as a cohesive unit. As I go through this briefing, please feel free to ask questions."

She reached out and activated the holographic display. Flickering to life in front of them was a huge sphere of blue and green, almost luscious in appearance. It was a spinning planet, nearly a meter in size.

"This is our destination. It is the planet Toffen, situated near the Draconis Combine and only one jump from the Free Rasalhague Republic. Of all the worlds the Ghost Bears control, it is the one second-closest to Terra, the homeworld of us all. Our posting there is highly honorable, as I am sure you will agree."

There was an appreciative murmur among the ranks, then she continued. "Toffen has three continents. One is a small, barren wasteland covered with rocks and sand. The second-largest continent, Jacobitz, is the center of industrial activity. The Inner Sphere has tended to make its raids there, but in recent years those have been few and far between. Most of the industrial capacity is civilian in nature, and even the Inner Sphere warriors do not strike too hard for fear of hurting the people they claim to hope to liberate. Almost all the large cities are there, as well as extensive mining operations. Jacobitz is mountainous and has a rough weather pattern, no matter what the time of year." As she spoke, the image of the continent shimmered light green on the holographic display so that everyone could see it.

"That leaves Graham, where we will be posted. Graham is the largest continent." A large oblong shape on the globe shimmered green. "The southern expanses are on the equator and are hot jungles and deserts. To the north, they give way to vast, rolling plains from the center of the continent to the western shores. The plains flood in the spring and are burned off by the locals during the summer."

Angela activated a control on the tabletop. "Our base is located east of the plains in a heavily forested region. It is mountainous, with four major ranges and countless others. The largest body of inland water is named Lake Ishimaru and is almost one hundred-forty kilometers north of our base of operations. Three rivers run near the base, the largest of which is the Rapidan.

"The base itself is an old Star League Defense Force facility that was abandoned after the Exodus and overgrown by the forests. Our scientist caste researchers located it and launched a program to restore the facility. From the reports I have read, they have cleared more than one hundred acres of forest around the base and almost fully reactivated it as a defensible position. Its isolation is perfect for combat trials."

"What about local populations, Star Captain?" asked Gregori. Angela wondered if his question was aimed more at recreational than tactical data, but she did not know him well enough to be sure.

"The largest city on Graham is Pied, which is only thirty thousand strong. There are numerous villages, mostly farming communities, both in the forest where the base is located and near the plains. The closest civilian activity is a small village called Rixleyville, which lies south of our base in the foothills of the mountains. Otherwise we are virtually isolated from distractions."

"What do we know about the base itself?" asked Neta.

Angela stabbed at the controls three or four times, and the holographic image of Toffen disappeared. It was replaced by a revolving schematic of the fort, laid out in amazing detail and moving slowly enough that everyone could take in some of the image. "From the reports I have digested thus far, the facility is built from reinforced granite mined from local sources. Do not let the appearance deceive you. The place was designed to withstand a tactical nuclear attack and is big enough to land upwards of three DropShips, if you make use of the parade grounds inside. There is an HPG transmitter for off-world communications and heavily stocked warehouses and support vehicles. The defensive turret systems have not yet been reinstalled, but there are firing platforms designed for use by BattleMechs, so taking it by force would be costly."

"Bases are a throwback to a different era," Bethany said with a hint of scorn. " 'Mech combat is best served in the open."

Stone turned to her with an icy star. "Bethany, we will be the only unit on the whole of Toffen. That fort might become critical to the defense of the world at some point. What you say is true in some ways, but if that fort was good enough for the Star League Defense Force, it is worthy of the Ghost Bears too."

The sentiment seemed to be shared by most of the other warriors. Anything connected with the great General Kerensky and the Star League bordered on the sacred to most Clansmen.

"How long are we going to be on our own defending this place?" Gregori asked.

"Undefined at this time," Angela responded. "Do you have a concern, Gregori?"

His shrug was almost cocky. "Neg, Star Captain. I just like to have plenty of allies present when trouble comes looking for me." He came close to chuckling.

"You are not so far from the truth, Gregori," said Tseng, his voice ever calm and professional. "All of you should note that we are a lone Trinary. Perhaps the Draconis Combine, mercenary raiders, or another Clan may decide they want to test our mettle. If that is the case—"

"—if that is the case," Angela cut in, "then we must be ready to defend Toffen with every bit of strength we have. Good warriors died to claim this planet for our Clan. I will not see it lost as long as I am able to stand and fight."

There was a murmur of agreement around the table.

Bethany let it die down somewhat before speaking. "Additional forces are warranted. The defense of such a front-line world is usually assigned to an entire Cluster."

"True," Angela said. "But we are not an ordinary unit. You have been hand-picked for this one. I was chosen to command because I have demonstrated my ability to serve the Ghost Bears. If we are to defend this world alone, then so be it. It is not the way of the warrior to question orders but to fulfill them." She directed the last words at Bethany, intending to silence her.

"Victory is the true duty of the warrior," Bethany argued. "If that means questioning orders, then so be it."

Angela made both her voice and her expression stern. "Bethany, my orders are not subject to question. Let that be clear to everyone here and now. Regardless of where or who you have served under before this, my word is what stands in this unit."

Angela cut off any further discussion by returning to the matter at hand. "Star Commander Tseng has prepared a detailed tactical profile and analysis of the terrain on Graham as well as the rest of Toffen. I suggest that each of you download it and study it. Memorize the maps and terrain features. They may save your life."

Star Commander Stone spoke next. "I have also prepared, at the order of the Star Captain, a rigorous schedule of simulations. These will be the first trials of our Stars working together on missions."

He reached out to the controls in front of him, and the holographic blueprints of the fort disappeared, replaced by a schedule spinning slowly in front of them. "Copies of this are in your data directories, along with Star Commander Tseng's tactical analysis."

Gregori leaned forward, staring at the schedule. "You must be out of your mind," he muttered, then caught himself, "—sir."

"Problems, Gregori?" Angela asked sharply.

"You have us down for ten-hour drills, sir. We did not have that much time in the simulators per day when the invasion was on."

Angela did not answer immediately, letting the silence work to her advantage. She would not say what she was thinking, which was that perhaps they *should* have trained this hard during the invasion if they wanted to win. "There is no mistake. The schedule stands, Gregori. A warrior cannot have too much training."

Gregori's mouth opened to speak, but Angela let him know by the look on her face and the aggressive way she rested her fists on her hips that she was not a commanding officer given to suffering long debates over her orders.

"Understood, sir," he said slowly.

"Anyone else have questions?" Angela looked at Bethany, who did not return her gaze.

"Only one more question, Star Captain," Sprange said. "When will we be named?"

The naming was a ritual every newly formed Ghost Bear unit underwent. The members of the unit could choose a name, but only after the unit had survived its first trial of combat under fire would the name be theirs and officially noted in the Ghost Bear Touman.

"A good question," Angela said, relieving some of the tension in the room with a small smile. "A name is needed, one that we can rally behind in battle. One that we can wear on our sleeves in future fights, and one that will be noted in the lines of The Remembrance."

The Remembrance was an epic poem that each Clan maintained, its passages singing the praises of battle and of the greatest warriors in each Clan. To be mentioned in its lines was a mark of great honor, surpassing even a bloodname for many.

"Listen," Neta said suddenly. Her eyes were closed, and when she spoke her voice had an eerie, faraway sound. "We are the Stalking Bears Trinary."

"One of your Nova Cat visions, quiaff?" Bethany mocked.

Neta opened her eyes. "Aye, Bethany, a vision of sorts. Perhaps a glimpse of our future." She looked over at Angela.

Angela could tell from the approving nods and smiles that the members of her unit liked the name. "So be it, Neta of the Ghost Bears. We are the Stalking Bears. Let our enemies hear our roar in the night!"

Pride showed in the faces of the gathered warriors, except for the grim-faced Bethany, who seemed apart from the general good feeling of her comrades.

"Now that we are named," Angela said, "each of you still has much work to do. I suggest you get started now. Dis-missed!"

Then, with military precision, she turned about-face and left the room, leaving her command to disperse.

Gregori waited until the door closed before leaning to look down the table at Bethany. "Nice way to make an impression with the new commanding officer, Bethany," he jibed.

She stared back at him, her eyes hot coals of anger. "Watch your words, freebirth—before I make you eat them."

Gregori smiled broadly. "Perhaps I was wrong about this tour of duty."

"In what way?" Dolf asked from the far end of the table.

"I thought it was going to be boring." Gregori smiled mockingly at Bethany. "But I see that there's plenty to keep me happy. If nothing else, irritating you, Bethany."

= 7 =

Fort DelVillar
Toffen
Ghost Bear Dominion
13 February 3062

Angela could see the gray granite walls of Fort DelVillar outlined by the bright blue sky of Toffen as she walked her *Executioner* down the ramp from the DropShip *Bloodied Paw* onto the tarmac. The fortified ramparts had been restored, and would eventually be painted over, but for now, during the reconstruction, they were still bare stone. The massive walls gave her a sense of security, but blocked her view of the rest of Toffen.

She moved the humanoid OmniMech down the ramp, and the rest of her Star followed almost in formation. Behind her was Sprange in his *Timber Wolf*. Then came Neta in her *Kingfisher*, the 'Mech newly painted in camouflage greens and browns. Bethany followed in her squat *Nova*, its spotted brown and green paint scheme looking older and more worn, despite the age of the warrior at the controls. Bringing up the rear of the Star was Breedfelt's *Kodiak* whose clawlike fingers almost touched the ramp as he descended. The *Kodiak* was not really a front-line 'Mech, but Breedfelt had been on the design test team and had virtually lived inside the 'Mech for over three years. It was the kind of experience Angela could never hope to duplicate with mere training.

As she reached the tarmac, she pivoted the *Executioner* to face the control tower, and the rest of her Star followed with the same precision. Traditions were important to the Ghost Bears, and one of the most important was the change of command of a Ghost Bear holding.

Striker Star followed, led by Constant Tseng, fanning out to the left of Angela and the Command Star. They too pivoted ceremoniously to face the control tower. The giant BattleMech feet made a deep, metallic thudding noise as they moved into position. As Kyle, the last of Tseng's warriors, took his place, the Sweep Star started down. Once they reached the tarmac, Star Commander Stone led his troops slightly forward and center of the other two Stars.

The last troops to descend the ramp were Dolf and his Point of Elementals. Through Stone, Dolf had requested and been granted permission to repaint his Point's battle armor. With the same formalized movements, the Elementals took their places in power suits freshly camouflaged in brown and dark green. Their flat black helmets seemed like a mark of distinction for the newly formed Star. Angela kept the head of her *Executioner* facing forward, observing the movements of her Trinary on the tiny screen of her short-range sensor readout.

The DropShip burn to Toffen had taken a total of nine

days once their JumpShip arrived at the system's nadir jump point. The whole time she had continued to press the Stalking Bear Trinary, her people, ordering them into countless mock battles in the DropShip's cockpit simulators. She had run them through a wide range of scenarios. The team was actually coming together, beginning to operate as a unit, but not as quickly as she had anticipated. They had to learn each other's strengths and weaknesses and the trust that only experience could provide—even if only experience in a simulator environment.

Angela tried not to be too concerned over the frictions created by some members of the unit. Neta was having a hard time fitting in, thanks to Bethany and the occasional taunt from Gregori. Though Neta was a full-fledged Ghost Bear, her origins in another Clan did not grant her the same degree of respect as other warriors. The up side, however, was that picking on Neta was the only thing that kept Gregori and Bethany from killing each other. For the most part, Neta let their verbal taunts roll of her back, a detachment that made her seem almost otherworldly. Sometimes Angela wondered if Neta really did see the future.

Added to that was the fact that word had gotten out about Dolf. Though the Ghost Bears were not generally a superstitious Clan, his history as the lone survivor of three different units in combat did not help the unity of Sweep Star. Stone dealt with it by simply ignoring it, pretending it did not exist. Angela understood that Stone's silence was both his shield and his sword, and he used it when needed. But no one mentioned Dolf's past in his presence. The fact that he stood a meter taller than the others and could crush any of them quickly in a Circle of Equals had something to do with that.

Angela wondered how long it would be before Bethany finally said something to Dolf just to get a reaction.

None of this was unexpected. Angela had been a member of three different front-line combat units in her life as a Ghost Bear and she had seen such tensions before. In trying to build a unit from scratch, however, they often tested her patience. But she kept it to herself. She had to be a leader, not simply a Star Captain.

A Star of 'Mechs emerged from the massive storage and repair bays at the far end of the tarmac and began to march slowly toward where the Sweep Star stood at attention. Angela throttled her *Executioner* and moved some twenty meters forward of her unit as the other 'Mechs approached.

It was an impressive formation. On the flanks were two powerful Warhawks, whose replacement armor plates showed that they had seen action in combat. At the center of the formation were three large *Timber Wolves*. Their boxy, shoulder-mounted missile racks almost touched as they marched, except for the lead 'Mech almost ten meters further ahead. Attached to its right weapons pod was a staff bearing two standards. The top one showed the emblem of Clan Ghost Bear, the white bear's head encircled by six flaying paws. The lower banner was that of Delta Galaxy. The formation stopped a precise eight meters in front of her.

The change of command rite in the Ghost Bears was a simple one, but took on more importance because Angela's was a new unit. The comm system in her neurohelmet crackled to life. She sat up straighter and looked out at the *Timber Wolf*.

"This is Star Colonel Dana Vishio of the Eighth Bear Cuirassiers. By order of Ghost Bear Khan Bjorn Jorgensson and Galaxy Commander Roberto Snuka of Delta Galaxy, I hereby turn over garrison responsibility for this holding, Toffen, in the Dominion of Clan Ghost Bear, to star Captain Angela Bekker." The *Timber Wolf* extended its right arm so that the flagstaff and banners unfurled fully.

Angela reached out with the humanoid hand of her *Executioner* and used her cockpit manipulator controls to grasp the flag staff. "I am Star Captain Angela Bekker of the Eighth Bear Cuirassiers. I accept responsibility for defending this world against all who would test the might of the Ghost Bears." She spoke the words in her best command tone over the microphone in her neurohelmet so that everyone could hear the pride she felt.

"Furthermore," Star Colonel Vishio said, "effective this date and time, your unit is officially activated. Has your Trinary a name, Star Captain?"

Angela smiled, thinking of how the name had come into being. "Aye, Star Colonel. It is my honor to present to you the Stalking Bears Trinary."

There was a slight pause. "Stalking Bears, I welcome you to my den and as members of this family. Cuirassiers, ten-hut!" With that, Dana Vishio and her Star pivoted to open the way to the 'Mech bays from which they had come. The 'Mechs raised their right arms and weapons pods, a tribute salute from warriors to warriors.

Tradition called for Angela to return the tribute to her new commanding officer. Such tributes could be in any form, and Angela had seen many in the years she had served the Ghost Bears. Hers would be personal, but no less a gesture of respect for her new CO. She activated the communications system and tied it to the microdisk play unit.

Over the comm system came the mournful tones of bagpipes, her pipes. She had recorded the song for her new commanding officer. "Stalking Bears," she commanded over the wail of the pipes, "forward march!" Filing past her new commanding officer, Angela Bekker and her Trinary proceeded forward to their new post.

Within two hours she stood outside Star Colonel Vishio's office and noted that Vishio had already removed her rank insignia from the door, since the office would now belong to Angela.

She knocked on the door three times. "Come," said the voice from the other side, and Angela went in.

The sight that greeted her was astonishing, unlike anything she had ever seen among the Clans. The office was almost plush in its design and accouterments. It sat high in the tower at the center of Fort DelVillar, with huge windows offering views of more than half the complex. In the distance, just over the fortress walls, she saw the dark green treetops of Richart Forest, which surrounded the base. The polished black granite desktop shimmered in the light from the windows. Standing behind it was Star Colonel Vishio.

"Welcome to Toffen, Star Captain," she said. "Please sit down and make yourself comfortable. You will find that I do not stand on formality when we are alone."

"Thank you, Star Colonel," Angela said as she sank into a sumptuous leather chair that seemed far too comfortable for her tastes.

"Impressive installation, quiaff?" Vishio said, pointing to the view.

"Aff," Angela said, squeezing the cushioned arms of the chair in amazement. "It is unlike any other posting I have ever seen."

"Soft," Vishio said as she sat down behind the desk.

"Aye."

"The labor caste craftsmen who have been renovating this facility for the last eight years have been painstakingly restoring it with period furniture. I had intended to replace it with more Clanlike items, but they tell me this is the sort of thing used by the Star League three hundred years ago. I felt odd changing it, but you may do so if you wish. This is your post now."

Angela shook her head. "Neg. If this was good enough for the great Kerensky and his people, it is good enough for me."

She reached into her belt and pulled out the tiny silver diskette she had prepared and handed it to Dana Vishio. "I hope you found my tribute appropriate. I recorded it on this diskette, along with the duty roster information for my unit."

Vishio took the diskette and looked at it curiously. "I have only heard the pipes once before. What was the song?"

"The Seventy-ninth's 'Farewell to Gibraltar,' " Angela said. "I thought it appropriate for someone leaving her post. It is a challenging piece for me. The fingering to play a Birl is a stretch."

"It is appreciated," Vishio said, but Angela noticed something in Vishio's expression that puzzled her. "I will be departing within the hour for our new assignment. Chief Technician Luray has been provided your complete TO&E and is preparing the bays for your Trinary. I have also informed the medical officer, a doctor named Drogan, that you are taking command. You will want to meet him."

"May I ask why?"

"He was born and raised on Toffen, and fought in the Draconis Combine military. You will find him to be an irritant, yet highly effective."

"I am becoming used to those of unusual character and backgrounds," Angela said.

"Yes, I reviewed your roster and the unit's codex. You have your hands full, but I believe I see the logic in some of your choices. I do not question the decisions of my officers unless there is good reason. If you can mold them into a unit, they will be impressive."

"Thank you, Star Colonel."

"I assume you have had a chance to review the quartermaster's report on your trip in?"

"Aye," Angela replied, but she was still puzzling over something odd in Vishio's voice and manner. "I am a little surprised at the quantity of supplies and repair parts being stored here, sir. There is enough for an entire Cluster to fight a Trial for two or three weeks. Such stockpiles are unusual, to say the least, and we brought down at least two cargo bays' worth of expendables as well."

"Indeed. The supplies were ordered here by the Galaxy Commander," Vishio told her, not answering the question at all. "Your duty is to protect them and this world. Ours is not to question the strategic moves of our high command."

Angela remembered the words she had spoken to her own Trinary members a short time earlier: *It is not the way of the warrior to question orders but to fulfill them.* The words suddenly took on new meaning.

She realized that something happened inside a warrior when she advanced in rank. She often had to think strategically and forget that, on the tactical level, other warriors fight and die. "I understand, Star Colonel. I was merely pointing out that the supply base seems overstocked."

Dana Vishio hesitated as if she were about to say one thing, then changed her mind to say something else. "We do not know each other, I mean *really* know each other, do we, Star Captain?"

"Neg."

"When I was informed that one of my Trinaries was being transferred to another unit and that the Eighth Cuirassiers would have to create a new unit to replace it, I was a little put back. But then I reviewed your codex and learned that Khan Jorgensson had personally selected you for this assignment. You are well suited to this posting and I believe you will carry it off with honor, but I admit that I sometimes have my reservations concerning orders."

"I am afraid I do not understand, Star Colonel."

"As I have risen in rank, I have leaned that there are aspects of command that I never enjoy. Leaving you here, alone, at this critical juncture of your unit's development—it is not my choice, but a direct order." There was enough reticence in her tone that Angela wondered again if there was more to the Toffen assignment than she knew.

"I take your meaning," Angela said. What else was there to say?

"Neg," Vishio said, waving her hand dismissively. "You do not. That is not the issue. What is important is what you do from this point forward. You are not like many of our Clan's warriors, Angela Bekker. You have shown yourself to be highly adaptable, as circumstances dictate. You do not rush into a battle, but realize the lesson that Tukayyid taught our people."

The mention of Tukayyid as a lesson hit home with Angela. The Clan fighting style had always been short, fierce combat trials with bid resources. They happened fast and furious, and the Clans had been virtually unstoppable in the Inner Sphere. On Tukayyid the forces of ComStar had fought the Clans, but instead of a short combat trial, the battle extended over days and weeks. Some of the invading Clans, like the Smoke Jaguars, did not adapt to the situation and were utterly defeated. The Ghost Bears, including those in the Binary she commanded, had to change their fighting style and were able to win a draw against ComStar's forces. Only the Jade Falcons and the Wolf Clan fared any better.

"I do not understand, Star Colonel," she said for the second time today.

"I know. I am not asking for understanding," Dana Vishio replied. "All I ask is that you do whatever you have to do, no matter how alien to your training, to fulfill your duty of protecting this world and this base from any who might try to take it. Trust your instincts and experience. They have gotten you this far and I think they will take you farther." She slid a pile of paperwork in front of Angela across the glittering surface of the black desk.

"Best of luck, Star Captain," Vishio said, saluting her.

"Aye, Star Colonel," Angela replied, returning the salute. "And to you as well."

8

Richart Forest
Toffen
Ghost Bear Dominion
17 February 3062

"**C**ontact!" Sprange called over the comm system from the cockpit of his *Timber Wolf.* "Stravag! I just lost it." His frustration was heard and felt by anyone on the commline. This had not been an easy engagement.

Angela adjusted the controls for her long-range sensors as she replied. "Give the coordinates of the signal."

"Zero-three-zero, mark two-one-one, but it was just a flicker, Star Captain."

Angela understood his problem all too well. "With all the rock formations and little depressions, we cannot afford to take the risk. Breedfelt, you and Bethany converge on that location in a wide 'V' formation. Neta, take the far right flank three hundred meters wide of them. I'll take the left. If anyone gets a contact of any sort, send the coordinates. Star Commander Tseng, move to the far left flank and sweep to the north of our position by at least a kilometer in case they are pulling us in for a trap."

There was a wave of "Ayes" as Angela piloted her *Executioner* forward into the low-hanging branches of the trees of the Richart Forest. The fusion reactor that powered her ninety-five-ton war machine throbbed with life and energy as she lumbered through the trees as if they did not exist. It was a simple enough exercise that she and Star Commander Tseng had devised, but the terrain made it more challenging. Her Command and Striker Stars were to locate and destroy the Sweep Star in a mock battle.

She had chosen the terrain for several reasons. First was to give everyone experience in the region surrounding Fort DelVillar. They were some eighty kilometers from the fort, but it was important to learn the lay of the land, never knowing when they might have to fight for real. Secondly, the exercise forced her Command and Striker Stars to work together.

"Where is this alleged contact, Sprange?" someone asked sarcastically, a voice Angela instantly recognized as Bethany's.

"Clear the chatter on the channel," Angela barked.

"I have a reading off to my right," came the voice of Neta in her *Kingfisher*. The *Kingfisher* was a newer model OmniMech that had slightly less mass than Angela's. "The reading is fading. Could be a light 'Mech. I picked it up on magnetic scans only."

Angela checked her short-range tactical display for the position of her Star as she swerved the *Executioner* out of the path of a massive oak tree. "Command Star, right flank hold, left flank wheel. Striker Star, take the far edge on the left."

Her plan was simple. Anchoring the right end of their

spread-out line and then sweeping like a swinging door around the left, along with Star Commander Tseng's Star, she hoped to pinch in and crush Sweep Star.

"I have a target. *Fire Moth*, primary configuration. Cutting off to the west," Bethany said. The *Fire Moth* was one of the lightest OmniMechs the Ghost Bears fielded. Weighing in at only twenty tons, it was designed for speed rather than firepower. There were two in the Sweep Star, so it had to be either Stone or Dis.

"Confirmed," came the voice of Breedfelt. "I got the fix for just a minute. It is cutting toward our left flank."

"Hold your positions in the line until Striker Star is in place," Angela commanded, pushing her *Executioner* even faster through the dense trees and overhanging vines. She had to be up there, leading from the front.

"Engaging target," Bethany said over the speakers inside Angela's neurohelmet.

Damn.

The tactical display showed Bethany rushing forward, far too early for Striker Star to be in place. The glowing blue dot that represented her 'Mech on the display advanced from the line and broke off to the left flank, the pivot point Angela had chosen for her wheel maneuver.

"Neg, Bethany," she bellowed, but it was already too late. The blinking short-range display showed that Bethany had fired at the target, marking it as hers. The Clan code of honor demanded that warriors fight one-on-one duels unless a target fired on another warrior. That opened things up.

There was no time to think. Angela splashed her *Executioner* through a shallow bog and up a small, rocky hillside as she reconsidered her options. "New orders. Command Star, advance north. Striker Star, move fast and up on the left flank. Form a battle line running north and south and we will try and drive them into you."

"Aye," affirmed the distant voice of Constant Tseng. "We are the anvil to your hammer."

"New target!" came the almost panicked voice of Sprange. "Elementals to our rear. Say again—" Static cut him off. The simulated damage that his 'Mech's battle computer was running had obviously damaged his comm system.

Angela slowed her gait and looked at the display. Dolf's Elementals, which had been on the far right flank, had moved in behind her line and were now savaging Sprange.

"I have two targets," Neta reported. "A *Viper* and a *Fire Moth* on my forward left."

"Confirmed," came back Breedfelt. "Additional *Mist Lynx* on the far right of our flank."

Tacticians and strategists for centuries had called it the "fog of war." It meant that most commanders could not see the entire battle, were often unsure of either the enemy's position and where they were going. Angela did her best to make her way through that fog.

"Striker Star, move to the east. Move now!" she ordered. "Command Star, engage and begin to fall back five hundred meters. Star Commander Tseng, you are now the hammer."

Reaching the top of the hill, she was greeted by a barrage of powered-down laser fire and the white powder-puff explosions of dummy missile warheads from a *Viper* that had been using the hillside to block its signal. Angela's tactical display showed hits in the left leg and center torso. She knew the warrior more by name than his machine. Hello, Scarry. Not bad damage, but enough.

She slowed and moved to the right, firing a barrage of long-range missiles and a blast from her massive autocannon. Half the long-range missiles missed their mark, peppering the leg armor of the stout little *Viper*. The blast from the massive autocannon on her right arm sprayed the dummy shells into the left arm of her target. The simulated damage was devastating. A glance at her own display told her that the weapons pod on that arm was all but gone, and the way it hung limply at the *Viper's* side told her she had taken out half the smaller 'Mech's firepower.

Scarry dropped back down the hillside, putting some distance between them. Angela brought the targeting reticule in line with the *Viper's* rounded head and toggled several of her target interlock circuits to fire her autocannon and long-range missiles at the same time. The temperature in the cockpit rose slightly as she heard the audible sound of the missile-loading cycle complete its work. Neta's voice shattered her concentration. "I have Elementals here, four Elementals."

"Splash one *Fire Moth*," Bethany practically cheered, seemingly oblivious to the rest of the battle raging under the forest canopy.

Angela fired, this time missing with her autocannon but hitting the *Viper's* center and right torso with most of her missiles. Over half of them were stopped in midflight as the *Viper's* antimissile system barked a roar of fire that ripped up most of the missiles in the air between the two warriors. The autocannon round's impact, even when nothing more than a powered-down explosive charge, still ripped a crater into the dead leaves and pine needles of the forest floor. Scarry fought the controls as his battle computer attempted to tip the 'Mech over from the impact of the weapons.

"Striker Star here, we cannot find targets," Constant Tseng said.

Be careful what you look for . . . Scarry was not intimidated by the attack but moved to the right. Angela saw a glimmer of another 'Mech moving there, a lightning-fast *Fire Moth*. Scarry's *Viper* let go with a small short-range missile attack and two pulse lasers that did simulated damage to her *Executioner's* head, rocking her Omni as if it were a piñata.

When this was all over, Angela decided that she and Bethany were going to need to have a nice little chat.

Her office still felt like it belonged to someone else, bu that did not bother Angela nearly as much as the task before her. The rap at the door reminded her of her responsibilities as commanding officer. Bethany's actions had not cost them the battle, but had made the exchange less than equal. The outcome had been a good boost for the Sweep Star's morale, however. They had managed to take out three Command Star 'Mechs and three of the Striker Star's before capitulating. According to the simulated damage display, Sweep Star still had some Elementals and one operational 'Mech just barely standing. It was basically a tactical victory.

"Come," Angela said and was startled when it was not Bethany but a stranger who entered the room.

"Star Colonel Bekker," the man said. He looked fit in his gray jumpsuit, but the silvery streaks in his sideburns gave away his age. "I was told to report to you when my duties permitted." He extended his hand in greeting, but from the tone of his voice, he was not enthusiastic about the meeting.

Angela took his hand and gave it a firm shake. "And you are?"

"Doctor Drogan Wyrick," he replied. "I'm the garrison physician. By your terms, a member of the scientist caste."

This was the man Dana Vishio had mentioned to her. He was arrogant in insisting he had the right to use both of his names. Apparently he did not totally accept his place in the Clan. His use of contractions was another giveaway. Though the usage was common among the lower castes, he did not try to hide it from her as others did in her presence.

"Yes," Angela said and gestured for him to take a seat. "Star Colonel Vishio told me about you, Doctor Drogan."

"I'll bet," he said and chuckled to himself as he plopped down in the chair as if he had no regard for either her or her office. "Whatever she told you is most likely true. One thing I've found about Clansmen, they don't lie. By the way, Star Captain, I go by the name of Doctor Wyrick."

Angela stiffened slightly, but let it pass. Let the lower castes call him what they would. For her he would still be Drogan. "She seemed to regard you highly, but I take it that was not always the case, quiaff?"

The doctor considered her carefully. "She didn't tell you much about me then. You're fishing for information."

"Actually," Angela said, "if you mean I am unaware of your relationship with her, you are correct."

He laughed, as if the thought was amusing. "Then I'll give you the run-down. I was born here on Toffen. You are the third garrison commander I've served. When the Ghost Bears took this world, they pressed me into service as a base physician. That's fine by me. It's what I do. I've spent most of my life patching together soldiers injured in every petty battle from the invasion until now. Your predecessor pretty much gave me free rein on how I ran my clinic and ward. That was mostly because she knew that changing me was impossible."

"You do not speak like someone addressing a member of a higher caste, Doctor."

"No disrespect is intended, Star Captain. It's just that the only thing that changed for me when the Ghost Bears took over Toffen was that I got a new boss and a new flag overhead. Flags mean little to the men and women under them. They are just symbols. You're my third boss. The first tried to break me. I didn't change. Star Colonel Vishio learned to work with me. You . . . I haven't figured you out yet. But if the rumors about you are true, I know we won't get along."

"And why is that, Doctor?"

"The rumor mill says you are a ristar in our Clan. Sooner or later someone has to test those said to be the best, and when they do, I'm the one left picking up the pieces."

There was more than a hint of truth in his words. "Doctor, I hope you are wrong. But if not, I will rely on you to take care of me and my people." She started to rise, but another knock at the door distracted her. "If you would excuse me, Doctor, I have another appointment."

The doctor rose and nodded. "Yes. I've heard. She's a firebrand all right." He pointed a thumb at the door.

"What have you heard?"

"That Bethany. A real hot-head. Doesn't like to follow orders. Most of us in the 'lower castes' are wagering that you will break her, though."

"Indeed," Angela said, unsure how to take this information. "I was unaware that the affairs of warriors were of such interest to the lower castes."

The doctor smiled. "We are pretty isolated out here, so it gives us some amusement."

"And what is your wager, Doctor?"

He looked thoughtful. "It's too early yet for me to know. But based on the fact that you didn't beat the snail-snot out of me for being a wise-ass at our first meeting, I think you will handle her well." Before Angela could respond, he turned and walked to the door. When he opened it, Bethany was standing there.

The doctor spoke to Bethany, who stood at strict attention. "Don't worry. I've softened her up for you," he said in a stage whisper that Angela had no problem hearing.

She started in amazement at his audacity. He turned to throw her a wink and then was out the door and beyond her verbal reach. It was just as well. She had more important things on her mind.

"Come in, Bethany," Angela said sternly. "We have much to discuss."

Bethany entered, her glossy black hair slicked back with sweat. Angela walked past her and closed the door. The sound of it shutting seemed to reverberate as Angela went to sit down behind her desk.

"That was quite a performance today," she said.

"I was victorious in battle," Bethany retorted.

"You disobeyed my orders and, as a result, I awarded the victory to Star Commander Stone."

Bethany was obviously unmoved. "The loss was not mine to bear but perhaps to the skills of the warriors you have recruited."

"Neg!" Angela replied, slamming her fist against the black granite desktop. "The actions of a single warrior can sway a victory or defeat. You led us down the path to defeat."

"I disagree, Star Captain. My fighting was flawless. Given the same circumstances, you too would have attacked Dis' *Fire Moth*."

"Neg. I would not. I fight for Clan Ghost Bear. You apparently fight for yourself."

Bethany shrugged slightly. "I am my own person. I

have heard all about the other Star Commanders not wanting me under them. I do not care. But you, Star Captain, are worse. Rather than reject me, you are trying to change me into something I am not."

"I was like you when I first became a warrior," Angela said coldly. "I am trying to help you be more than you are."

"Do not!" Bethany spat back. "I did not ask for your help, nor do I desire it. Stop trying to make me into your shadow."

"It is more than that and you know it. Look at what you did today. Your actions cost our Star a clear victory. You rush forward and we are expected to hold the ground you are taking."

"Again, you blame the weaknesses of the others on me. Or is it that your generation has forgotten how to fight? Perhaps the loss of Tukayyid has taken the fire of combat from your heart."

Angela pushed back in her seat. She should strike Bethany down here and now for insubordination, but it was more important to teach her control. She also understood why Bethany did not want to be cast in the same mold. Bethany felt shamed by what had happened at Tukayyid. She blamed the warriors of Angela's generation for the defeat of the invasion.

"I am faced with two options with you, Bethany. One, to meet you in a Circle of Equals and teach you the right of command. Two, transfer you to another unit, perhaps a second-line unit, until you are ready to grow up."

Bethany's face lit as if it were on fire. "If you do that, I will request a Trial of Refusal on your decision. No matter what, we end up in a Circle of Equals."

Angela leaned forward, her face drawn tight. "So be it."

* * *

The warriors of the Stalking Bear Trinary stood in a wide circle on the tarmac in the shadow of the Drop-Ship *Bloodied Paw*. It had taken longer than she would have thought, but Angela now stood triumphantly in the center of the circle, the semi-conscious form of Bethany in her arms. Her body quaked with adrenaline from the fight, and her skin tingled with a mix of sweat, dust, and excitement. There was a streak of blood running from the corner of her mouth and a salty, coppery taste on her tongue when she spoke. In her mind the unaugmented fight was a blur of fists, arms, heads, hair, and feet flaying about in a whirlwind of motion. Bethany had scored several good hits, but in the end Angela's control had won the day.

"Bethany has learned the lesson of being part of a unit. I hope none of the rest of you need such a lesson in command authority and obeying orders in the field."

She dropped Bethany to the tarmac as if she were no more than a sack of potatoes and passed through the Circle of Equals. There was a long silence as Bethany, her face and body bruised and bloodied, attempted to rally the strength to get up. When she could not, Gregori broke from his place in the circle and went to stand over her.

"The Star Captain taught you a lesson, Bethany. The real question is this, truebirth, do you have the capacity to learn?" Laughing to himself, he walked away, and the rest of the Stalking Bears Trinary went with him.

9

Fort DelVillar
Toffen
Ghost Bear Dominion
28 February 3062

The Stalking Bears passed through the massive archway that marked the entrance to Fort DelVillar in two-by-two-formation, led by Angela at the head of the Command Star. For the last few weeks she had pushed her people through countless combat drills and trials all over the surrounding countryside. They had engaged each other on the shores of Lake Ishimaru. They had staged ambushes and firefights deep in the hardwoods of Richart Forest. They had marched out into the tall, thick reeds and grasses of Graham's central plains, waging mock battles, living and dying in fight after fight. The schedule had been grueling even by her standards. Her own muscles ached from being tossed about in her cockpit.

This particular exercise had lasted three days straight

and had taken her unit over a two-hundred-kilometer area in a series of small fights. It had been exhausting, yet satisfying. Her eyes showed bags of sagging flesh under them, for she had not spared herself either. But her unit was now fighting as one. That was a victory she savored more than any mock battle.

Oddly enough the turning point had been the confrontation with Bethany and her defeat in a Circle of Equals. Bethany had grudgingly fallen into line, though both she and Gregori still found plenty of opportunities to strike a discordant note. But no one could deny a real change. Gregori tended to make his comments with an air of jest, which often relieved the tension. Bethany still seemed to ooze discontent, but was not so vocal about it. Her pent-up anger earned her few friends in the Trinary, though Angela believed that would change with time. She had broken Bethany, but only the physical part of her. Another part of Bethany still resented her.

She led them in the 'Mech bay of Fore DelVillar, where she maneuvered her *Executioner* into position. Once she had backed it into an open niche, she powered down the massive fusion reactor. For just a moment the world around her was suddenly quiet and peaceful. She savored it as much as she did the thrill of battle. As much as Angela loved the authority of command, which she had enjoyed for years leading Binaries and Trinaries of the Ghost Bears, there was a weight associated with it. The constant need to project an air of leadership and strength made her tired shoulders sag. In this rare moment she could let herself be simply human, with all the cares, doubts, and frailties that implied. The feeling was a luxury she indulged for a few precious moments.

Then duty called. She removed her sweat-filled neurohelment, then stretched as much as possible in the cockpit and felt her joints ache from the sudden change of position. She fumbled blindly with the hose that pumped coolant into the vest that kept her from blacking out instantly when the cockpit got too hot. A tap of her finger on the control opened the cockpit hatch with a hiss, and she crawled out to the small platform where a technician was waiting for her to power down.

With her 'Mech now in safe hands, she descended the retractable ladder slowly. On the ground she saw the figures of Star Commanders Stone and Tseng waiting for her. Their bodies shimmered with sweat, and their unshaven faces and bloodshot eyes told her that they too were exhausted.

"Good work, both of you," she said, as her feet hit the floor.

"Our people performed very well," Tseng said, running a hand through his cropped black hair. "More than once I thought I had you boxed in, Star Captain, but each time you managed to evade both my Star and Stone's."

"Aye," Stone said. "Our people are no longer individuals or even Stars. They fight as a Trinary. In mock battles, at least."

"How is Dolf?" Angela asked. Dolf had been injured by Bethany in the drill, when Bethany had sent him sprawling onto a rocky outcropping with a blow from the arm of her 'Mech. His power suit was not breached, but his body had been banged about severely inside the armor.

"Drogan is treating him. A concussion and three bruised ribs. If the doctor would stop talking and do his work, Dolf might already be back on duty."

Angela took this as one more sign that the Trinary

was starting to become one. Here was Stone trying to make jokes, a day she never thought to see.

"Excellent. But you did not come here to tell me that, quiaff?" Angela said.

"Neg, Star Captain. We have pushed our people hard and they have delivered. We have not let up since the day we arrived. They have become a unit. The time has come for them to get some rest."

Stone nodded agreement. "If we continue to push them, sir, our work will come undone."

Angela studied the faces of her two officers for a moment. "My thoughts exactly, gentlemen. For the next two days, light duty. Let them recharge their batteries."

Back in her office, Angela dropped with relief into the chair at her desk. Several datapads sat in front of her, each one requiring some degree of attention. These red-tape battles were the part of command no one was ever fully trained or prepared for. Requisitions, shipping manifests, reports from the techs and other lower castes on everything from the structural integrity of roofs to mess menus for the next month. She glared at the datapads and wondered if any of them could wait for another night, another day for her to muster the energy to endure the tedium of reading through them.

There was a light knock at her door. Looking up from the pile of work, she saw that it was the doctor, entering without waiting for permission.

"Star Captain," he said, "you look like hell warmed over."

Angela was too tired to spar with him. "I warn you, Doctor, if you are insulting me, I will kill you with my bare hands."

"No insult intended. Simply an observation."

"Did you come here just to share this 'observation' with me, Drogan?"

"No," he said, taking a seat. "I came to tell you that Dolf is doing fine. He will be ready for service tomorrow, but only light duty."

"Your service to the Ghost Bears is appreciated," she said. "Now, if you will excuse me, I have work to do." Angela pulled the top datapad off the pile as if it weighed like a brick.

"There is more," the doctor said.

Angela closed her eyes for a moment, but it seemed to take forever to force them open them again. "Proceed."

"As your garrison physician, I feel it's my duty to tell you that these people need a break. You're pushing them too hard. Injuries are minor thus far, but they're starting to make mistakes."

Angela narrowed her eyes and clasped her fingers on the desk, letting the bionic fingers ripple slightly without really thinking about it. "You are presumptive, Doctor. It is not your place to tell me when to rest my command." Her tone was not threatening—yet.

"By Ghost Bear standards you may be right. But I am a medical man and answer a higher calling than blind service to a Clan. I am bound to save the lives of my patients and to do no harm. My people are Ghost Bears. That may change, but my obligation will not. You will find that in this area I am uncompromising."

Angela contemplated his words. This was not a man that she could shake or break. He knew his place, but also knew how far he could push. His concerns were not for his own welfare but for her people. "Doctor, I have already ordered a two-day stand-down so that the Trinary can clear some of the fog in their heads."

Drogan smiled. "Excellent, so we agree on this."

Angela did not smile back. "When it comes to my unit, we at least have one thing in common—their well-being."

"You are different than Star Colonel Vishio, your predecessor. She would have argued with me and done the opposite of what I suggested, just to teach me who was in charge."

"You are right about one thing, Doctor, I am different." Angela gestured toward the door. "Now then, if you will excuse me, I have work to do."

The bonfire roared high into the night sky, sparks dancing upward toward the trees. The Fort, over a kilometer away, shimmered in the darkness as the members of the Stalking Bears sat huddled around the flames, relaxing for the first time in many long, hard days. This was not a place for the officers who led the unit, but for the warriors who fought under them.

"I am dead tired," Sprange said, rubbing his neck and craning it to flex his muscles. "One more drink and I am going back to sleep in a real bed."

"You lack endurance," Gregori taunted. "Of course, I did take you out in the simulation. That explains your lack of drive, quiaff?"

Dolf stepped out of the darkness and joined the small party of Ghost Bears. "Gregori, you are still hoping that one of us beats you to a pulp, quiaff?"

Gregori chuckled. "Neg, Dolf. I just think we should enjoy this little bit of free time rather than wasting it in bed. I take it you are fit for duty."

Dolf nodded, rubbing the compression bandage wrapped around his massive chest. "Aye, just in time, it seems, to join you in relaxation."

"You were fortunate," came a mocking voice from

the shadows as its owner, Bethany, stepped forward. "My attack on you could have cost you your life."

Bethany's arrival seemed to throw a somber cloak over the gathering, taking some of the joy out of the evening. Neta was the only one who seemed unmoved. She sat cross-legged on the forest floor, staring into the flickering flames.

Gregori spoke first, for everyone present, "You have a way with your fellow warriors, Bethany," he said snidely.

"Thank you, freebirth."

"I was being sarcastic."

Dolf cut off the war of words. "Bethany did what she had to. It did not gain her victory, but she believed it was necessary at the time."

"It is too bad," Sprange put in, "that she has not learned the importance of fighting as part of a unit rather than standing alone."

"Perhaps if you concentrated more on your own attitude you would be further in your career than you are now," Bethany retorted.

Sprange raised his fist in anger, but Gregori stepped between the two of them to defuse the situation. "Always cheery, Bethany. You generate bad karma. Ask Neta. The Nova Cats surely know all about karma. What do you make of Bethany, Neta?" he asked.

Neta turned her head slowly, her face seeming to glow in the light of the bonfire. "I must go," she said suddenly, rising to her feet.

Sprange reached for her arm. "Gregori meant nothing by it, Neta. He was just—"

"It is not Gregori," Neta broke in. "I saw something in the flames. Something that the Star Captain must know." She moved away swiftly, vanishing into the darkness of the forest, heading toward the fort.

Gregori turned back to Bethany. "You know, there is something about you that sucks all the fun out of a party, truebirth," he cursed.

Angela rubbed at her eyes. The pile of datapads had been cut in half, but the rest would have to wait. Moving wearily, she rose to her feet. Her only thought right now was to get some sleep, but at that moment the door to her office opened abruptly. Standing in the doorway was Neta.

"Star Captain," Neta said in a rush, "I must speak to you."

"What is it, Neta?" Something had to be very wrong for her to pounce on Angela in the middle of the night.

"It is not easy," Neta said as if searching for the right words. "You know that I am loyal to the Ghost Bears. But my rearing as a Nova Cat is part of my nature too. It will always be a part of me. I cannot ignore it any more than you can ignore the fact that you lost your fingers."

"What is it, Neta?" Angela asked again.

Neta drew a long breath. "I was with the others. I was meditating near a fire. In the fire I saw an image."

"Go on." Angela was so tired that she spoke more from lethargy than real interest.

"In the flames of the bonfire, I saw a creature hunting a bear. The bear had only one paw, the other was injured." She glanced down at Angela's right hand.

"Neta, visions have little meaning to Ghost Bears, as I am sure you know. What are you trying to say?"

"It could be nothing. But Nova Cats believe that such visions are glimpses of the future. If that is the case, someone is hunting us. I can *feel* it. You are that bear, that much I know. The hunter is a beast, one that is vicious and deadly."

There was something in her tone that made Angela

sit up and listen. She sensed that this was no mere hunch, but something deeper, more mysterious. Something that might be beyond the scope of her understanding.

"What can we do?"

Neta shook her head in frustration. "Nothing. It may be nothing at all. It might be our destiny. *Your* destiny."

Angela did not know what to think. "I would not have made a good Nova Cat. Such visions would have frustrated me. For now, speak of this to no one, Neta. If, indeed, we are being hunted, the hunter will soon learn the danger of trying to prey on a Stalking Bear."

10

Fort DelVillar
Toffen
Ghost Bear Dominion
5 March 3062

Angela stood in the 'Mech bay watching the technicians work furiously to swap out her weapons pods for the latest training run. They worked the winch and overheard cranes with skill, moving the new pod smoothly through the air and then into place, attaching it to the chassis of her *Executioner*. She understood the procedure enough that she might be able to do it in a pinch, but this was work for the lower castes.

She had just stepped forward to get a better view of where Chief Technician Luray had swung himself in a harness under the armpit of the 'Mech when she felt a tap on her shoulder. It was the communications technician and he silently handed her a message. Angela looked at the printout, and for a moment her heart seemed to bound like a running animal.

She reached for her pocket communicator and spoke into it. "Star Commanders Tseng and Stone, report to the comm center immediately." Her tone betrayed the urgency. "Star Commander Stone, I know you have your force on maneuvers. The training mission is canceled. Recall all personnel to the fort immediately."

"Aye," replied the stoic Stone.

"Problems, Star Captain Bekker?" Constant Tseng asked.

"Perhaps. A JumpShip just arrived in-system. Apparently we have uninvited guests."

The comm center of Fort DelVillar had been restored when the Ghost Bears rebuilt the massive Star League facility. It was linked directly with a wide array of satellites in orbit and at the jump points, those points above or below a star's gravity wells where JumpShips could arrive. More importantly, the room was tied to the hyperpulse generator that allowed Toffen to communicate with other worlds faster than the speed of light. HPG messages still took a long time to relay, but it was a matter of days rather than years for a message to reach other worlds light years away.

The room was well-lit and purely functional, and one of its walls was filled with banks of displays and readouts. Several techs were furiously manning them. The equipment was new, and the information racing across the displays was constantly changing. Even the air had that "new" smell, the odor of fresh paint. The techs seemed oblivious to the arrival of Angela and her two subordinate commanders, but she could tell by the pace of their movements that they were treating news of unexpected company as a potential threat, as did she. She went to the circular podium in the center of the room and activated the wall-size screen opposite the bank of screens where the technicians were working.

The image flickered for a moment, showing the deep blackness of space. The size of the wall made Angela feel, if only for a millisecond, as if they were actually looking out from the far reaches of the Toffen system. She motioned for a young male technician with the rank bars of a senior staff member on his jumpsuit. He stepped up to the podium and pressed several controls.

The darkness was shattered by a shimmer of bright light as a kilometer-long JumpShip appeared at the jump point, dominating the entire wall. Docked along its hull were three DropShips, bristling with turrets which indicated these were military DropShips—not commercial vessels. "Our satellites at the nadir jump point relayed this image to us three hours ago. Transmission time is delayed by almost an hour and a half."

"Combat vessels," Stone said calmly. "Do we know who they belong to?"

Angela turned and nodded to the tech. He adjusted other controls, and the image on the screen zoomed up on one of the DropShips and the emblem of a snarling wolf's head on its hull.

"Clan Wolf," Tseng said out loud, though it was obvious.

"Indeed," Angela said. "And given the size of the ships docked to that JumpShip, they could be carrying as much as an entire Cluster."

Tseng stared at the wolf insignia on the projection wall, then turned back to her. "They may be passing through and simply recharging at the jump point. Do we have confirmation of their intentions yet?"

"Aye," she said. "This came in shortly after their arrival." She gave the comm tech another nod, which was followed by a rapid flutter of his fingers on the keys of his computer console. Now the image of the DropShip was replaced by that of a warrior dressed in the garb of Clan Wolf. His hair was long on the sides, abnormally long. His expression was sullen, almost threatening.

"I am Star Colonel Dirk Radick of Clan Wolf. I command the Seventh Battle Cluster and have come to take Toffen from the weak paws of the Ghost Bears. I challenge you, Star Captain Angela Bekker, to a Trial of Possession for this world and all that is on it. Tell me with what paltry forces you plan to defend this planet." His voice was arrogant and demanding, as if he could defeat Angela by words alone.

"Neta was right," Angela said under her breath.

"Sir?" Tseng asked.

Angela shook her head, not wishing to speak of it now. She stared at the frozen image of Dirk Radick that dominated the room. "I have looked at our datafiles on this Star Colonel and his unit. He is a Crusader in the extreme, and he and his Blood Drinkers Cluster are known to be ruthless in battle. He also has a grudge against freebirth warriors and has no qualms about slaughtering them in battle. The Watch reports that he is dangerously unpredictable and will push for a fast and quick victory, if his record holds true."

"His hatred of freebirths will make Gregori happy. At last, a trueborn he can sink his teeth into," Tseng said drily.

Angela allowed herself a thin smile, but otherwise ignored the comment. "What other intelligence do we have on Dirk Radick? Do any of you know anything about him, anything that might be of use beyond what The Watch reports?"

It was Stone who spoke up. "I have heard of him from my sibko instructor. They once fought each other in a Trial of Possession for some genetic material right after the start of the invasion. Dirk Radick was a dangerous bidder."

"Dangerous?" Tseng said. "What does that mean, Stone?"

Stone shrugged. "I was told that Radick bid away a large number of his forces, and then won the bid. Later he betrayed his honor by bringing in the last group of forces he had bid away, executing a combat drop on my sibko instructor and his unit. The Ghost Bears were defeated in a matter of minutes and my instructor's back was broken. It was those injuries that forced him into the duties of a trainer."

"Useful information. Creative bidding may be a clue to what we can expect from Star Colonel Radick." Angela paced in front of the huge image on the wall, unconsciously tugging at her artificial fingers as if the joints ached.

"There is more, Star Captain," Stone said. "Dirk Radick called you by name."

She paused and considered that fact. "You are right, Tseng. He did. Where were the Blood Drinkers last known to be posted?"

Tseng moved to the podium and watched the small datascreen as his fingers tapped in the necessary search commands. "According to The Watch, they were recently reassigned from Lothan to replace the First Wolf Cluster on Altenmarkt." His brow wrinkled slightly. "I do not understand the significance."

"The Khan only called for the formation of our Trinary in January. It is now March. He called me by name, which means he knew I would be here, and that can only mean his intelligence forces informed him of that fact. Given the time it would take for the information to make it to the Wolf arm of The Watch and then to Star Colonel Radick, and the transit time for his Cluster to travel from Altenmarkt . . . he must have moved very quickly to get here."

Constant Tseng nodded thoughtfully. "He did not have time to load a sound mix of weapons pods and expendables for such a strike. Knowing the Wolves, he probably came with heavy assault loadouts—missiles and autocannons. Nor did he likely have time to get formal permission from his Khan."

"Nor time to custom-configure his Cluster for this Trial," Stone said. "He is counting on catching us unprepared, striking fast, and breaking us."

"And taking Toffen for the Wolves," Tseng added, looking over at Angela.

"Useful information. Very useful." She pondered her opponent's rush to battle and wondered just how to leverage it. There was a way, but as yet she did not see it . . . But, she told herself, Dirk Radick had already made his first mistake.

"Star Captain," Tseng said, interrupting her thought. "We owe him a response."

"Aye," she said, turning to the comm tech. "Open a transmission channel to the Wolf Clan ship." The tech moved to the wall of monitors, and his fingers danced across two different keyboards. Then he turned to her. "You are on, Star Captain."

Angela drew herself erect and faced the projection wall screen. "Star Colonel Radick, this is Star Captain Angela Bekker of the Stalking Bears Trinary of the Eighth Bear Cuirassiers. This world was won with the blood of Ghost Bear warriors, and I and my entire Trinary stand to defend it against you in a Trial of Possession. I will transmit to you codex information on the warriors of my command. I await your bid to take this world, and I will inform you of the venue of our Trial shortly. I look forward to teaching the Wolf the mistake

of entering the hunting grounds of the Ghost Bear."
Then she made a slashing movement with one hand,
and the technician cut off the transmission.

Angela turned to her subordinate officers. "We have
much work ahead of us. We must choose a venue for
this Trial and come up with a way to beat a unit with a
lot more experience than we have."

11

Fort DelVillar
Toffen
Ghost Bear Dominion
5 March 3062

"**P**roject planetary display number 104," Angela told the comm tech. The continent of Graham appeared on the wall display. In the center and slightly to the west were the grassy plains, marked topographically in pale green. Fort DelVillar was located northeast of the plains, surrounded by the deep green that marked Richart Forest. Angela gazed from one location to another and then back again, searching but still not knowing what she was looking for. Two mountain ranges ran from north to southeast, one on either side of the fort. Running parallel to the mountains on the east was the wide blue swath of the Rapidan River. Her eyes drifted further east, past the last ridge of mountains to the blue splotch on the map that marked the inland sea known as Lake Ishimaru.

She knew she had to find a way to negate Radick's advantage over her unit by figuring out how to make the Wolves fight on her terms. Whatever those might be, she thought. Her eyes still glued to the map, she spoke, mostly thinking out loud.

"Stone," she said in a soft tone that was almost out of character. "If you were Star Colonel Radick, what would you do?"

Stone cocked an eyebrow at the question. "Knowing that my opponent was a unit untested in battle, I would strike hard and fast. I would attack with such force and speed that they would have no time to react as a unit but be forced to fight as single warriors. They—we—would be wiped out in a manner of minutes."

"That is exactly what I would do, too," she said, still staring at the map. A seasoned and experienced Trinary or Cluster could operate almost instinctively at times. The warriors knew each other's reactions in a wide range of situations, and often compensated for one other more out of reflex that planned tactics. But the Stalking Bears were still too new to possess such savvy. "Tseng, if you were Radick, where would you expect us to fight this Trial?"

Constant Tseng studied the map, his dark eyes narrowing slightly. "If I were Colonel Radick, there is only one place I would expect to fight you. The fort." He nodded to himself as though becoming more convinced of his own thoughts. "Fort DelVillar is the most logical place for our Trial. Here we could maintain a tight command integrity. It will take the Wolves ten days to arrive on-planet. We could use that time to build some interior defenses. Make them pay for every centimeter of ground they try to take."

"Stone?" Angela asked. "You would also expect me to fight here, quiaff?"

Stone thought for a moment. "It is the most logical choice. Aff, I would expect you to make your stand here, since it is your logistical and supply base. This is where you will be anchored, no matter what. If I were a Wolf, I would take this facility quickly to destroy you."

She fixed her gaze on the square image of the fort on the map. She knew she had to force the Wolves to fight on her terms, on ground of her choosing. Then it hit her. "What if we abandon the fort?"

Tseng shook his head. "Star Captain, with all due respect, that would be a mistake. Stone is right, we need this place. It is where we repair, where we restock ammo, it is our heart. It is also the best defensible position on the continent. Like the legends of the three hundred Spartans, we will hold this ground and make the Wolves pay with each blind attack."

"You forget, Star Commander Tseng, at Thermopylae, the Spartans were eventually defeated. There are other historic precedents as well. Think of the assault on the Alamo or the attack on Fort Diffly on New Vandenburg, where more than a hundred warriors were killed after twenty days of siege. Glorious events to be sure, often lending themselves to strategic victories, but in the end tactical defeat. In a combat trial, tactical defeat can spell the end."

"Not all were failures. The British at Roarkes Drift held off thousands of Zulu warriors," Tseng put in.

"But there was a technological difference there, Constant. Spears against rifles. Here the playing field is level."

"Do you have a plan?"

"Aye," she said. "Application of some of the basic laws of tactical warfare—force the enemy to fight on your terms, seize the initiative and maintain it. Rather than face Radick's Wolves in a short, fast Trial, we will drag them into a prolonged fight. As on Tukayyid, we will hit him where he is weak, his logistics. Stretch him out, wear him down. Time will be our ally."

"What about the fort?" Stone asked.

"The fort would be easy to defend, but it is mainly a symbol of our presence on Toffen. We will strip everything of value from Fort DelVillar," Angela said. "We can move the supplies and spare parts out and take advantage of the terrain to hide them in small caches. Our techs can also set up small repair areas hidden from the Wolves. Let them take the fort. They will find it stripped clean."

"Then they will hunt us down," Tseng said.

"Yes, but we will remain on the move. They will engage us, but we will control when and where. They have experience, but we know the terrain. To track us down, they will have to stretch their supply lines to the limit. They will be pressed harder and thinner. We will separate and operate as independent Stars. When we hit the enemy, we will do so only to bloody him, then withdraw. When we do fight, we will concentrate our forces, strike, then disappear before they can mass. At all costs we will avoid major confrontations that let them concentrate their forces for a fast victory. We weaken them constantly, wear away at them, a war of attrition."

"Any chance of reinforcements?" Tseng asked.

"I will send an HPG message to command. They will most likely send a force to issue a Trial of Refusal should we lose possession of Toffen. Ghost Bears take care of their own. If we avoid a major battle, though, we may still be fighting by the time our kin of the Clan arrive. That, too, will put Star Colonel Radick on edge." The plan was forming even as she spoke, and as it took shape, she saw that it had more than slight merit. She could force Radick to react, take away his initiative. That would be part of the key to a victory.

Stone spoke up. "A fight of the type you are talking about, lasting for days, it will be difficult for our people. They are unaccustomed to such engagements."

"As was I until Jarett. We Ghost Bears do not adapt rapidly, at least not as fast as the Wolves. On Jarett, though, I learned the need for flexibility, and that same lesson will help us here. I fought for a full week against the Combine defenders on Jarett and achieved victory. The battle of Tukayyid also lasted for days. This is the same sort of fight, but even longer. We *can* do this, commanders." She spoke as if a fire burned in her heart. She reached out to the young comm tech, grasping him lightly by the shoulder. "Locate Chief Technician Luray and Doctor Drogan. Have them report to me immediately."

"There is a huge quantity of supplies and parts here," Tseng added. "Just moving them will be a challenge."

"We have 'Mechs. They can be rigged with cargo nets," Stone said. "Even so, Star Commander Tseng has a valid point. We will have to begin immediately if we are to have a chance."

"I would estimate that we could set up upwards of ten supply dumps," Tseng said. "Obviously, the ones furthest away must be established first." Tseng moved to the map and pointed to several logical areas. The wall display unit marked his fingerprints with a bright orange glow.

Thank Kerensky we know at least some of the terrain, Angela thought. She nodded acknowledgment of Tseng's comment and turned again to one of the comm techs working the monitoring controls. "Send a message to Galaxy Commander Snuka and Star Colonel Vishio. Priority One. Authorization code silver. Security code delta, gamma, zeta." The tech activated the datapad to record the information.

Angela cleared her throat slightly. "This is Star Captain Angela Bekker of the Stalking Bears Trinary. As of this date and time the Seventh Battle Cluster of Clan Wolf under Star Colonel Dirk Radick has initiated a Trial of Possession for Toffen. I have bid my entire Trinary in defense of the planet. I have chosen the continent of Graham as the location for this Trial and will deploy accordingly. I intend to prolong the fight as long as possible. Request you send a relief force now to augment and aid or relieve us if necessary." She motioned to the tech to end the transmission, and he shut off the datapad.

"How long before reinforcements can arrive?" Stone asked.

"Unless they have a unit loaded and at a nearby jump point, we are probably looking at twenty-two days or more, and that is if the unit is close," Tseng said. "Even that is optimistic."

Angela reached out and touched the shoulder of the comm tech who had been transmitting her message. "Once you have sent that message, I want you to remove the key transmission circuit and alignment controls for the HPG. They are to be sent to separate supply bases that we will establish. Further information will be forthcoming."

"You are disabling our HPG," Stone said.

"Aye," Angela replied. "If, as we surmise, Star Colonel Radick did not have time to get authorization for this mission, I do not want him to be in a position to call additional Wolf units or to coordinate with the rest of his Clan."

The door at the far end of the chamber opened, and

Drogan and a wiry young man in a dirty jumpsuit entered the comm center. Angela knew him as Luray, the Chief Technician. A unit did not run on supplies and ammunition alone. These two men would help provide an infrastructure that would allow her warriors to operate for a prolonged period.

Angela beckoned them forward urgently. "Doctor, Chief, we have a situation here. Clan Wolf is attempting to take possession of Toffen."

Drogan's usually cocky face seemed to fall.

"What I need from you, Doctor, is to pack up and prepare to move out our entire medical ward. We will be fighting a running battle with the Wolves, and you will have to set up several field hospital operations in the wilderness. We will be abandoning Fort DelVillar and forcing the Wolves to fight on our terms."

Angela half-expected an arrogant answer from him, but the doctor caught her off guard. "Is that necessary?"

"Aye. It is our best hope. For us to beat the Wolves, we must try to bog them down in a battle of attrition. Keeping our warriors alive while we do that is your responsibility."

For once the doctor restrained his tendency to scoff. "It won't be easy, so I'd better get started. How much time do I have?"

"Nine, perhaps ten days," she said.

"Not enough," he returned.

"Too bad," Angela said. "I doubt that Star Colonel Radick will grant you the latitude that I do, especially with his hatred of freebirths."

Drogan frowned. "Ten days—sir," he said, moving to the door. Angela turned and looked at Chief Technician Luray. "You have heard, quiaff?"

"Aff, Star Captain."

"We will be stripping this fort of anything that might be of use to the Wolves. Coordinate with Star Commander Tseng. You will need to dismantle the fort's repair facilities and set up field repair stations to keep our forces loaded and operational. Can you do that?"

Luray was nervous and seemed to stutter his response. "I am not sure, sir. I have never done it before."

"None of us have done this before. You know your skills and those of your people. So, tell me, can you do it?"

"Affirmative, Star Captain," Luray managed. "I will need to start now."

"Go," Angela said, walking over to the young man at the communications station. She rapped her fingers on the console to get his attention. "Open a channel to the Wolf ship." He tapped the controls, then gave a thumbs-up to indicate that the line was open.

"Star Colonel Radick, this is Star Captain Angela Bekker. I have chosen the continent of Graham as the venue for this engagement. I look forward to your bid—and your defeat." With a wave of her hand, the transmission ended. Let him wonder what she was up to. Let him know that he might outrank her, but that she would outclass him.

Angela Bekker turned to her two Star Commanders. "We will not underestimate Star Colonel Radick. Make sure that our supply caches are hidden from orbital scans in case he suspects something. Mask our trails. Each warrior should know only the location of a handful of our supply bases in case he or she is captured and bonded by the Wolves. From this point forward, act as if the Blood Drinkers are on our soil. The battle, gentlemen, has begun."

12

DropShip Houndstooth
Nadir Jump Point, Toffen System
Ghost Bear Dominion
5 March 3062

"Thoughts?" Star Colonel Dirk Radick said as the message text disappeared from the display. The cramped space of his personal quarters was even tighter with three other officers in the room.

The message was from Toffen, and he had gathered his Cluster commanders to view the response from the Ghost Bear commander. It had been delayed by well over an hour, not remarkable given the distance. He was pleased by the bravado Star Captain Bekker had shown in responding to his batchall, the former Clan combat challenge. It was a sign of spirit. Merely to land and take this world from the Ghost Bears was not enough. A true contest of skills—now that was something worthy of a Wolf.

He waited to hear the reactions of his officers, the

commanders of the three Trinaries that made up the Blood Drinkers. Star Captain Jergan stood erect and silent. Star Captain Lark Radick smiled, his expression almost cocky. Star Captain Vaughn shifted from one foot to the other, apparently wishing there was enough room to pace in the small room.

Lark Radick spoke up first. "What kind of venue for a Trial is this? An entire continent? Perhaps the Ghost Bears do not teach their commanders how to bid, quiaff?"

Star Captain Vaughn shook his head. "Neg. She is attempting to mislead us with this choice of location." He reached over with his beefy hand and fiddled with the controls for the small wall display, furiously searching for the right combination. After a few silent moments of struggling, he finally pulled up a map of the continent of Graham. "Here, take a look for yourselves."

Vaughn pointed to the map. "We have studied what is known about Toffen and its geography on the trip here. This Ghost Bear has plenty of choices for where to fight this Trial. But when all is said and done, there is only one place where she must be. Fort DelVillar, the Bears' precious base of operations." He stabbed his sausage-like finger at the map.

Star Captain Lark Radick moved slightly to the side, staring at the image. "As much as I would enjoy disagreeing with my fellow commander, I must concur with his reasoning. Remember what The Watch reported. There are serious amounts of supplies and parts on Toffen, and all of them stored at Fort DelVillar. That has to be where she is operating from."

Jergan was shaking her head slightly. "Then why choose the entire continent as the venue?"

"Star Captain Bekker seeks to mislead us. She is hoping she can buy time to reinforce Fort DelVillar while she sends us running in every direction all over Graham."

Dirk Radick did not comment. Debate was best left to junior officers. He found that he rather liked young Lark, noting that their shared similar genetic material had created more than a slight resemblance between them.

He turned his attention to the map he had already committed to memory days before, attempting to wrestle with what Angela Bekker had given him.

"So, Lark, in your opinion, you believe we should assault their fort immediately," said Jergan.

"Aye," Lark Radick said. "We should attack Fort Del-Villar, not just from without but also drop some units inside its walls. We can disrupt them quickly and reduce their ability to rally and coordinate their efforts."

"I concur," said Star Captain Vaughn. "Even if this Ghost Bear takes to the forests and the mountains, her logistics will still be tied to their precious fort. If we take it from them, we can use their supplies ourselves if it turns out we need them."

Radick spoke at last. "Star Captain Bekker's Trinary is new, still untried in combat. We must strike at them hard and fast, maul and destroy them. It will all be over quickly."

"So where do we deploy?" Lark asked, but Radick knew the real question on the minds of all three officers was when the bidding would begin. With the batchall issued, all that remained was to determine who among them would win the honor of destroying Angela Bekker and her Ghost Bears.

Dirk Radick stared at the map intently, then turned back to his three officers. "I believe that Bekker is attempting to lure us away from the fort. It is the only logical explanation for her choice of a venue. We will drop directly on top of it. We will take Fort DelVillar from her, and Toffen will be a Wolf Clan holding within minutes after we land."

Radick saw that Jergan did not look convinced. "You disagree, Star Captain?"

"Aye," she said. "I fear that we may be underestimating this Ghost Bear ristar. She is too experienced to use such a blatant strategy. There is something we have not seen, some other reason she has chosen all of Graham as the venue for the Trial. I do not know what it is or what advantage it gives her, but I believe it is there."

"And your evidence for this?" Lark prodded.

"None," Jergan said. "Other than my experience as a combat commander and my gut feelings."

"Perhaps you would make a good Nova Cat with such instincts," Lark said.

Jergan's face darkened. "Perhaps a step inside a Circle of Equals will remove that smirk from your face or the impression that I am anything less than a Wolf."

Lark was about to reply when Radick silenced him with the wave of one hand. "We are wasting time," he said sharply. "We must get on to the bidding."

Their faces lit up at the mention of the bidding, like children just given permission to attack a cake. It was another Clan ritual that would decide which of them and their units would attack Toffen.

"Let us settle our dispute by our bidding, Jergan," Lark said. "That is, if you have the testicles to bid aggressively enough."

"You will find that I function quite well as a warrior without needing them to guide my thoughts," she retorted.

Again Dirk Radick waved his hand impatiently. "I have been giving some thought to the matter of the bidding. It will not be resolved through your petty bickering. The Ghost Bears may be a Warden Clan, but that does not mean they lack ability as warriors. They pushed almost as far as we Wolves did into the Inner

Sphere during the invasion. And since the truce, they alone have not suffered at the hands of other Clans—until now."

"Shall I fetch the bidding tokens, Star Colonel?" Star Captain Vaughn asked. Each Clan had its own customs for the rite, and the Wolves used tokens to determine who would start the bidding.

"Neg," Radick returned. "I alone will be bidding for this Cluster."

"What?" Lark asked.

"Watch your tone," Radick warned. "Under normal circumstances each of you would have the chance to bid away your forces to take Toffen. But these are not normal circumstances. I believe that Star Captain Bekker is concealing something from us, but we will not know what until we engage them. I will bid alone to take Toffen, and will bid away your forces as I see fit."

Lark Radick was obviously unhappy with this turn of events. "This is highly irregular, Star Colonel. You deny us our chance to win honor."

Dirk Radick was unmoved. "My choice to bid the entire Cluster is my right as commanding officer. It is unusual, but there are precedents for it among the Wolves. If you wish to challenge me on this, I assure you, Star Captain Lark, you will suffer defeat and my wrath." His head tipped forward and his eyes narrowed, making it clear that he would tolerate no opposition from his subordinates.

Lark's face reddened. "Point taken, Star Colonel."

"We are alone in the lair of the Ghost Bears," Radick went on, "and I do not wish to bid away forces that might have to be called down later to win the fight."

Usually the various commanders vied with one another by gradually bidding away their forces, until only the minimum necessary to win a Trial remained. If a commander were pressed and in danger of losing a Trial, he or she could opt to sacrifice some honor by calling in the forces of his last discarded bid. Bidding was often tight near the end of the ritual, with only a Point being bid away here and there. As the sole bidder, however, Dirk Radick could bid away entire Stars, or even whole Binaries or Trinaries. That way he could later pull down a large number of forces to achieve victory, if that was the only way.

In observance of the rite, Vaughn spoke the traditional words. "With whose forces will you take Toffen, Star Colonel?"

"I bid the entire Seventh Battle Cluster in my opening bid," Radick said. If he stayed there, the odds against Angela Bekker were overwhelming, three to one, of not more. "My counter-bid is to bid away Star Captain Vaughn's Eternal Crusader Trinary." Vaughn's face stiffened as he realized that his only chance of fighting was if matters totally fell apart on Toffen. The odds of that happening against a mere Ghost Bear Trinary were slim at best.

"Next, I bid away Star Captain Lark Radick's Mauler Trinary," Dirk said, watching Lark's face redden again as he tried to suppress his anger. "My final bid is Star Captain Jergan's Bloodied Wolves Trinary, with one modification. I will take my proper place as acting ground force commander." He paused for a moment to look around at the other three officers. "With this, the bidding for possession of Toffen is complete."

"Seyla," the four warriors intoned solemnly, heads bowed, marking the end of the ritual.

Radick turned to Lark and Vaughn. "Return to your DropShips and begin immediately to burn for Toffen." Their departure from his cramped quarters left him alone with Jergan.

Radick went over to the small operations table where he worked. "Your thoughts, Star Captain?"

Jergan stiffened slightly at his words, which pleased Radick. She feared him, yet did not lose her composure. "Your bidding tactic is legitimate, though it borders on the questionable. You too suspect Star Captain Bekker of some sort of duplicity, quiaff?"

"Neg," Radick replied, waving his hand in the air as if to brush away the idea. "I have fought other Trials against Ghost Bears in my time. They are Wardens, but they are not dishonorable. No, this Angela Bekker is not using duplicity, though she obviously has some plan. I am merely taking every precaution to make sure we do not fail, even if it does cost me some honor."

"If I may ask, Star Colonel," Jergan said hesitantly, "why did you choose my Trinary for the final bid?"

Dirk Radick did something that he knew was disturbing to his subordinates. He smiled. There was no pleasure in it, but more an expression of sinister deviousness. "You are not the best warrior or even the best commander I have under me, Jergan."

"I do not understand then."

"Lark and Vaughn both were eager to fight, but only you had the sense to realize that our enemy is not ignorant. You perceived a risk where they were simply too eager to join the battle. You are starting to show some character. We will need that to defeat this Star Captain, that much is evident in her choice of location."

"And of her forces?"

"As expected, fresh meat. From the data she transmitted to us, she has a mix of experienced warriors and new blood. I believe we defeat them soundly in a straight fight. If not, I have set up my bid to ensure a victory for the Wolves."

"I assume," Jergan said carefully, "that you have determined how you will attack and where."

"As Vaughn said, Fort DelVillar is an obvious target. Regardless of any plan Star Captain Bekker may have concocted, seizing that installation has to be a central point in our strategy."

"If Bekker is inside the fort, planning on a prolonged siege, the fighting will be costly for our troops," Jergan pointed out.

"True enough, but we are the Blood Drinkers," Radick said. "You and I both know there are two ways to take such an installation. We will do so using the most aggressive of those approaches."

From the way Jergan's face lit up, he saw that she understood perfectly what he had in mind. "There are risks, are there not, Star Colonel?"

"Aye. But I did not get where I am today without taking such risks. I would rather have Angela Bekker underestimate me than the other way around."

To emphasize his point Dirk activated the communications systems controls that were next to the projection display controls on the desktop. "Communications officer," he said. "Transmit the following to Toffen. 'Star Captain Angela Bekker, this is Star Colonel Dirk Radick. I will attack you in ten days time at the head of the Bloodied Wolves Trinary. I am sending you my own codex and those of the Wolf warriors who I will bring to crush you. I hope you are prepared to fight well enough to be my bondsman when I take Toffen from your grasp.' " He shut off the comm system and turned to Jergan.

"What remains, Star Colonel?" she asked.

He gave her another of his smiles. "Crushing the Ghost Bears, Jergan. Nothing more is required, nothing less is desired."

= 13 =

Fort DelVillar
Toffen
Ghost Bear Dominion
14 March 3062

The activity at the gate leading out of Fort DelVillar was ordered, yet hurried. Watching from the entrance of the command bunker, Angela was impressed to see the Ghost Bears moving, and moving with attitude. She had shut down the aerospace sensor net a few hours ago, having confirmed that the Wolf DropShips were still a day away from Toffen. The net would be totally useless to them now. She had ordered its key circuits removed and shipped off with the last of the technicians.

The past nine days had been busy ones, but time was now running out. There was little left in Fort DelVillar other than the bare buildings themselves. Working sometimes around the clock, her Trinary and the lower caste members of her command had stripped the fort of anything the Wolves might find useful. Every missile, autocannon round, and bullet had been transported to one of the ten supply caches they had set up at various points across Graham.

A Prime Mover transport wheeled past the bunker, and the lone figure of Constant Tseng dropped off and began running toward her. He jogged the short distance to her, then stopped for a fast and furious salute, which Angela returned. "That should be about the last load," he said.

"Status of the repair facilities?" she asked.

"Chief Technician Luray is setting one up now and reports that he should be operational in the next few hours. I have Barthelow working on the other one. He estimates it will take him at least another day to complete it."

Angela tilted her head quizzically. "You assigned the task to your bondsman, quiaff?"

"Aff," Tseng replied. "The rest of our personnel were busy setting up the other supply bases. I made use of what was available. Is there a problem, sir?"

"Neg," she replied. "I know that we are pressed for personnel. I simply had not thought of using your bondsman." The Prime Mover's engines rumbled as it passed through the granite-walled gate and toward the forest surrounding the walled fortress. A cloud of dust rose up into the air, and an odd silence seemed to settle over the place. "What of Doctor Drogan?"

Tseng frowned slightly. "He complains constantly, but has done his part and is as prepared as any of us."

Angela allowed herself a slight smile. "Our medical officer is quite a character. If he were a warrior, I think he would spend most of his time fighting Trials to defend his honor."

"He has a mouth and favors using it," Tseng said. From his tone, Angela guessed that some of the doctor's barbs must have hit home with him.

Angela craned her neck to stretch the muscles, then

rubbed at her brow and her eyes as if that would remove the weariness. "Indeed he does. But honesty can be useful in a subordinate."

"When was the last time you slept, Star Captain?"

"Irrelevant," she replied, suppressing a yawn. "We all have duties to perform."

"True, but we need to brace for what is coming. I need rest, as do you."

She glared at him while giving a single slow nod. "I assure you, Star Commander, I will be fully rested by the time Radick's Wolves drop."

"Good. I have ordered a final sweep of the facilities to be sure we have left nothing behind that the Wolves might find useful."

"I have already cleaned out the command bunker," Angela said, tugging unconsciously at her artificial fingers. "Nothing is left but a message for Radick if he does what I think he will."

Tseng stared at her, and then looked over at the pair of 'Mechs standing near the gate, Angela's *Executioner* and his own *Warhawk*. A small all-terrain vehicle carrying the last of the ground-support personnel and several small boxes of gear swung past the legs of the OmniMechs and sped off after the Prime Mover.

"Star Commander Tseng?"

"Yes, sir."

"Are they up to it?"

"Our people?"

"Aye."

"Yes," he said. "What they lack in practical experience fighting as a unit, they make up for in spirit. Even the firebrands seem to have a place . . . giving us some sort of a balance."

"Bethany," she said softly.

"Not just her. Do not think for a single moment that

Gregori is any less a hothead. The difference between them seems to be control. Gregori is quick with the comment, but knows when to stop. There are times he dances on the edge of the Circle of Equals, but never says or does quite enough to end up there."

Angela nodded. "You have seen his codex. He has been in the Circle far too many times in the past. Perhaps he has grown tired of it."

"I doubt that, Star Captain," Tseng said, drawing a long, deep breath of the afternoon air. "He has been busted in rank many times in challenges of his Trial of Position because people have insulted him as a freebirth. We have not allowed that to be an issue. Bethany, on the other hand, struggles against an inner enemy."

Angela more than understood. "Yes, in her mind, her enemy is me."

Tseng nodded. "She believes you are trying to force her to be the kind of warrior she has no desire to be."

Am I? Angela considered the thought and tried to come to terms with it. "I am trying to teach her the way of the Great Bear, the way of our Clan—our family. She sees herself standing alone, even in battle. But she has to realize that the whole Trinary must work as a team rather than trying to become a ristar all by herself."

"I do not disagree," Tseng added. "But I fear that only one thing will teach her that—experience in battle. My only concern is that we will lose good warriors as she learns this lesson."

Angela suppressed a yawn and again flexed her neck muscles to relieve the stress. Her gaze flicked to the transport in the distance, now growing smaller. "Every family has members that rebel against authority. We have ours as well. We must watch over them and nourish them just as we would those who obey us without question."

"Aye," Tseng said. "And in this fight with the Wolves, all of us will be put to the test. It will be a style of combat none of us are used to."

Angela turned back to him. "You are right. This will be hard on all of us."

"They will adapt, Star Captain," Tseng said quietly.

"And so will Star Colonel Radick," Angela returned. "He is smart, this Wolf. You have seen his record and the codexes of the troops he is sending against us. All are skilled and experienced. And do not forget his bid. Any other commander would have encouraged his forces to bid lower than a one-on-one ratio for combat. Dirk Radick bid an entire Trinary of some of the Wolf Clan's best forces against us." Using less troops to achieve a victory promised greater honor for a Clan officer. Radick's move would bring him less honor, but a better chance of taking Toffen from Angela and her Stalking Bears.

"Perhaps he expects us to fight from behind the walls of the fort, and believes he would suffer higher casualties in a siege."

Angela gave him a knowing smile. "As Crusader Wolves go, Star Colonel Dirk Radick is one of the most ruthless. I may have tipped him off with my choice of location, given him enough of a hint that he will come down more than prepared."

"Do *you* believe we cannot beat this Wolf?"

Angela laughed, though it came out as more of weak chuckle. "No, Star Commander, I am simply pointing out that it will not be easy. Our enemy is vicious, ruthless, but we must not underestimate his intelligence or his cunning. If we forget for one moment that he is one of the best the Wolves have, we are doomed."

"So noted," Tseng said. "We should be leaving soon." He looked around the oddly quiet fort. "I hear it will soon be raining Wolves."

Angela, still smiling, bend down and opened a package sitting at her feet. Tseng watched as she pulled out a leather object with wooden pipes poking upward at odd angles. She held it with reverence, stroking the bag, caressing the smooth pipes. Her mind became calm as she did so. It was relaxing and smoothed away the edginess from lack of sleep.

"What is that?" he asked.

"My pipes," she said softly. "My bagpipes. I do not want to leave them behind."

"I have heard their music, but I have never seen them. They look complicated."

She hefted the bag up and under her left armpit. The three drones rested on her left shoulder and forearm. The chanter, used to play the tunes, hung in front of her and dropped down. "The pipes have taught me much about being a warrior."

"I do not understand."

"Playing the bagpipes requires a number of skills. I must be able to count music, breathe, read, and play all at the same time."

"Coordination seems to be key."

"It is, but there is more to it than that. There is a rhythm that happens when I play, but it is not altogether musical. It begins when all the elements of playing the pipes come together, and then it is as if the music is playing itself. The only other time I have known that rhythm is in the rush of battle. Different events happen, flow, coordinate, and operate in unison despite opposition. My music guides me, it takes me to the feeling of battle." She paused for a moment. "I am sorry. That must sound odd coming from a warrior."

"Neg," Tseng said. "I believe I understand. Sir, we are alone. Will you play something now?"

Angela lifted the mouthpiece and stood tall, holding

the bag in front of her. She blew into the bag and inflated it most of the way. In one fluid motion she brought her right arm around and pressed the bag, blowing and tucking it under her arm—striking the pipes. The drones began their mournful sound and, as her fingers danced across the chanter, music echoed throughout the fort where the two Ghost Bears stood alone. She played for more than a minute, and finally stopped.

"That was very calming. What was it?" he asked.

"It is called 'The Green Hills of Tyrol'," she said, carefully setting the pipes back into their case. "It is a song that has been played by and for warriors over the centuries. It is a kind of music known as a retreat."

"Retreat? Did you choose it to signal our departure?"

"Yes, and no. It is one of my favorites. I will tell you the lyrics sometime and you will understand. It is about a warrior fighting in a far-off land. For me, that has special meaning." She paused and saw that Tseng understood. As Ghost Bears, they were always on different worlds, always fighting distant battles.

"Retreats originally were played to rally troops as they were led from battle. In the last few centuries they were played at night, to lull weary warriors to sleep." She looked toward the gate, where her *Executioner* stood waiting. "But this is not a retreat for us, Star Commander. No. We *will* return to this place."

She began walking toward her 'Mech, the bag in one hand. "Now we go to hibernate for a bit, and the Wolves will not know where we bide. But soon, very soon, the time will come for us to go hunting the hunters."

14

Fort DelVillar
Toffen
Ghost Bear Dominion
15 March 3062

As the morning sun burned off the dew from the ground around Fort DelVillar, it sent a faint mist into the air. Inside the complex all was stone quiet, as abandoned as when the Star League Defense Forces had deserted the place three centuries ago. There was no wind, and the white and blue Ghost Bear flag hung limp over the command bunker, damp with night dew.

The ancient hardwoods of Richart Forest surrounded the fort, mute witnesses to the quiet morning. An occasional leaf dropped. Small animals scurried here and there, little more than furry blurs in the mist. Now and then the sound of a twig cracking or a bird chirping echoed among the huge branches of the trees.

There was no distinct sound at first. Only a murmur

through the forest. A deer ran out from the trees, breaking into a dash across the grassy plains that had been cleared to provide an open field of fire around the fort. Another deer emerged, racing along the edge of the trees as if being chased by something. Then came a pair of groundhogs, and other small forest animals, all rushing out of the woods as if they were being herded by some unseen shepherd. The sound of their stampede increased as larger moose and wild horses joined the rush, leaving their footprints on the dewy grasses as they fled from the unseen foe.

Then came the roar. It was deafening as the massive DropShip *Houndstooth* rode over the tops of the trees. Its 4700-plus tons of mass raced over the trees, its fusion reactors pumped a blasting heat of thrust to hold it in the air. It swung over the treetops, setting fire to some and sending dead branches and leaves fluttering as it sped over the plains toward Fort DelVillar.

The spheroid-shaped *Union-C* class vessel opened its bay doors as it came lower, sweeping like a massive pendulum toward the gray stone of the fort's outer walls. The doors opened with a hiss, the hydraulics and pneumatics holding the large, armor-plated doors wide. Forms emerged, silhouetted by the yellow sun rising over Toffen.

The forms dropped onto the grass, shaking the ground as they hit. As they landed, the BattleMechs sprang into a fast deployment, spreading out, seeking the gate leading inside. The DropShip had now reached the outer wall of the fort.

Some of the 'Mechs moved toward the gate, others scanned the tops of the walls and firing platforms, their weapons aimed upward. In total, five 'Mechs, a full Star, had dropped outside of the fort and were making their way in quickly and smoothly, as if they had rehearsed the operation dozens of times.

The *Houndstooth* just cleared the top of the fort's outer wall, attesting to the skill of the Wolf Clan pilot at her helm. Having cleared the wall, the ship slowed to a full hover and dropped rapidly to the grassy parade ground inside the complex. As it came down, more BattleMechs came from the deployment doors, weapons menacing upward and outward, searching for targets with a skill that came from years of experience and the best of Clan genetic engineering. By the time the DropShip touched softly down on the now-charred grass, the other ten 'Mechs were already out the doors and moving about the interior of Fort DelVillar.

One of the OmniMechs, a ninety-five-ton *Executioner*, headed toward the command bunker. Like the others, its hull bore the insignia of the Seventh Battle Cluster. The black wolf's head with sinister bronze eyes and blood dripping from its fangs marked it unmistakably as a member of the Blood Drinkers. The three red stars painted above the insignia showed that the 'Mech belonged to a Star Colonel, in this case, Star Colonel Dirk Radick.

"Status," he barked over the commline as he moved the *Executioner* into position in front of the command bunker.

"Star Commander Digorno, Slasher Star. Perimeter and gate secured," came back a calm voice.

"Star Commander Biffly Ward, Assault Star. Outer walls secured. No sign of enemy activity."

"Star Captain Jergan, Command Star. Interior secured. Apparently the Ghost Bears are not here, Star Colonel."

In his cockpit, Dirk Radick pounded angrily on the reinforced control panel of his targeting system. Part of him had expected to find the fort empty. Part of him hoped it would not be, that there would be a fast and furious fight. He barked out a rapid barrage of commands. "All commands move to secondary objectives. I want every building searched and secured. Assume defensive positions on the exterior walls in case of attack. Move quickly." He did not expect duplicity. Neg, there would be no booby traps. They lacked honor. Such was not the way of the Ghost Bears or of this Bekker.

Several MechWarriors dismounted their 'Mechs and began to deploy among the nest of buildings inside the fort. He swung his *Executioner* into a slow walk up the roadway leading to the central gate and saw Slasher Star already moving to the elevated firing platforms from which they would unleash a barrage of laser or missile fire if the fort were attacked. The sound of his own racing heart still pounded in Dirk Radick's ears. His soul craved a fast fight.

As the minutes passed, he came to the central command bunker. The thumping in his ears faded with each passing minute as he realized he was not going to get the fight he desired. His sensors, both long- and short-range, showed nothing. No magnetic anomalies common to fusion reactors. No large-scale motion traces. Even reflective scans did not tell him or his Blood Drinkers where Angela Bekker and her Stalking Bears were. One thing was for certain, they were not in Fort DelVillar.

He powered down his fusion reactor to a low setting and removed his lightweight neurohelmet, then opened the hatch and climbed down the footholds along the torso and leg of the *Executioner* to the grass below. His lungs strained to get enough of the lighter, thinner Toffen air, but that did not slow him down.

Wolf warriors rushed about everywhere, alert, ready for battle, but Dirk Radick knew it was not to be. He walked over to the command bunker's huge reinforced door and was met by Star Captain Jergan.

"Our fears were well-founded," he said bitterly, his hand still throbbing from being slammed against the console in his cockpit. "But at least we have denied the Ghost Bears control of this facility and the logistical support it provides."

"Neg, Star Colonel," Jergan said.

"Neg?"

"I just spoke to Star Commander Biffly. His people have completed their sweep of the repair and warehouse facilities and found them empty."

The words stung, and Radick felt a rush of anger heat his face. "Empty. That is impossible. According to The Watch, the amount of supplies and parts here was so great they could never have moved them out in so short a time."

Jergan spoke in an even tone, as though not wanting to rouse his ire. "Either The Watch was incorrect or they moved much faster than we anticipated." She averted her eyes momentarily, a sign that she was withholding something.

"What else, Star Commander?" he demanded.

"The repair bays have been stripped to the bare walls. Every crane and tool has been removed as well. We have secured nothing more than the shells of buildings. No supplies, no parts, nothing."

Dirk Radick did not speak for a long few seconds, but his eyes seemed to burn with anger. Then he turned quickly and went into the command bunker. Jergan was right behind him, following as he stalked down the reinforced entranceway to the heart of the structure. Wolf

Clan techs carrying tools and gear hustled in and around the hallways and rooms, but Radick ignored them.

Inside the bunker were several rooms, all with doors open, each one telling the same story. He looked into what had been the communications control room and saw all of the equipment panels open. Technicians, sleeves rolled up, brows covered with sweat, were already into the internal guts of the hardware, checking and rechecking systems. Lights flickered from some controls, sending different colors dancing off the walls and across some of the dead screens. Radick reached out for one of the passing technicians and spun him around. "What is the status of this equipment?" he demanded in a tone so threatening that the tech turned pale.

"Well, Star Colonel, sir, apparently the gear is undamaged. However, the Ghost Bears have removed some of the key circuit boards from almost everything."

"Replace them," Radick said slowly through gritted teeth. He tightened his grip on the tech's shoulder to inflict a slight amount of pain.

"It is not that easy, sir." The technician's voice trembled slightly. "We do not carry parts for most of this equipment, especially the hyperpulse generator."

"Make new parts," Radick ordered as if mere words could make the command a reality.

"It is simply not possible, sir," the tech said, straining away from his commanding officer's grip.

"Sabotage," Radick growled, tossing the nameless technician back as if he were an inanimate object.

"Not sabotage," Jergan said. "Bekker simply disabled the place. There is a difference."

"Not in my eyes," Radick said.

"She is within the bounds of honor. If she had destroyed the equipment, she would have been dezgra in our eyes. Instead she has taken away parts that would be of value to us."

Radick wanted to scream, to attack someone or something, but held himself in check. Without the HPG, he could not contact his Clan. Now more than ever victory must be his because he had brought his Cluster into enemy territory with no way to call to the rest of the Wolves. Just then another tech came forward, holding a small, circular device that was obviously a portable holographic projector.

"Star Colonel, we found this in an office upstairs. The note attached to it has your name, sir." The tech handed him the device, and Radick gestured impatiently for the man to return to whatever else he had been doing.

He took the small black device in his hands and used his thumb to turn it on. The holo image flickered to life as a small, doll-like figure standing on the surface of the device, facing him. Dressed in a gray jumpsuit, the figure was that of a woman with a warrior's trim body and blonde hair. On her sleeve was the emblem of the Ghost Bears. As he held her in his hands, it was as if she were some sort of toy a freebirth child would play with. Slowly she began to speak.

"Star Colonel Dirk Radick of the Seventh Battle Cluster, I, Star Captain Angela Bekker, welcome you to Toffen. By now you know that I have left you nothing of value in Fort DelVillar. All you have won is a building, a virtually bare structure, nothing more. Its loss means nothing to me or to my clan.

"No doubt you are angry and looking for a fast battle. This I deny you, as I denied you the contents of the fort. Know this, Dirk Radick, you are where I wanted you to be, when I wanted you to be. I have controlled the situation thus far and will continue to do so. What you have done, you have done at my bidding. You are on Toffen now, in the territory of the great Ghost Bear. And when we meet, and when we fight, I will always be in control of the situation.

"In other words," she said with a sly smile, "I have already beaten you." The image flickered off.

Radick stared at the portable display, then threw it at the wall, smashing the black casing and sending pieces flying at several nearby technicians. What remained of the device landed in a jumble on the floor. As the technicians scattered out of the way, Dirk Radick pulled out his small laser pistol and leveled it at the remains, destroying them with a searing burst of ruby red light. White smoke and the sweet smell of ozone filled the room. Holstering his weapon silently, he spun and glared at Star Captain Jergan with such fury that it seemed he would never be able to control himself, yet somehow he did. "Angela Bekker is arrogant if she thinks she has already beaten me."

"Aye," Jergan said quietly. "She has simply seized the initiative. We shall take that from her."

"Yes," Dirk Radick hissed. "We shall hunt her down."

"They will have the advantage of the terrain. They know this place better than we do."

Radick was unmoved. "We are Wolves, born to the hunt. We can learn the terrain. We will seek her out, concentrate our forces, and destroy them."

Jergan seemed about to speak, but then did not. "What is it, Jergan?" Radick demanded.

"This day, the Ides of March, I wonder if it is an omen," she said.

The reference was not lost on Radick and only served to fuel his anger. "You imply that she is Brutus to my Caesar, Jergan?"

"I was not implying anything, Star Colonel. It just dawned on me what day this was, nothing more."

"Rest assured, Star Captain Jergan, I will break her, crush her, and leave nothing but a bloody smear on whatever rock she is hiding behind." He would give no quarter to his enemy, who had gone so far to taunt him.

Just then another warrior, big Star Commander Biffly, appeared. His face was almost cheerful, and he held out a length of cloth to Radick. "Star Colonel, a gift for you."

Radick ripped the cloth from Biffly's hands and held it up. It was the Ghost Bear flag, which had been hanging over the command bunker. Enraged, he tossed the flag into Biffly's face and pushed him back against the wall, as if he would shatter his spine with the thrust. Then he was gone.

Star Captain Jergan did not follow. She went over to the stunned Biffly and held out a hand to him, pulling him back onto his feet.

From his vantage point among the limbs of a huge oak, Dolf squinted through his enhanced binoculars, peering across the grassy plains. Hidden from view, he studied the figures of the Wolves taking over Fort DelVillar. He saw a slight breeze ruffle a new flag waving over the fort. It showed the growling head of a wolf in profile, announcing that the uncontested siege of the fort was over.

Dropping to the ground, he turned on his small portable communicator, then checked to make sure he had the right frequency. "Sweep Two to Command."

"Go," came the clear voice of Star Captain Bekker.

"Phase one complete. The Wolves are in the box."

"Good. Tomorrow they will begin to hunt. When they do, we shall teach them to be careful what you search for—you might find it."

=== 15 ===

Supply Cache Gamma, Richart Forest
Toffen
Ghost Bear Dominion
16 March 3062

The leafy shade of the forest cast a green glow over the Stalking Bears gathered there. They were nearly seventy-five kilometers from Fort DelVillar, their previous home. Now the Wolf Clan flag over it—a Wolf flag on her world, a world she had sworn to defend in the name of the Ghost Bears. Angela Bekker had faced many tricky situations in her time, but this was one of the most difficult. She and her enemy were evenly matched numerically—but not in experience and skill.

She stood on the foot of her *Executioner* to address the members of her command. Surrounded by the forest and their BattleMechs were her warriors, a handful of technicians, scientists, and laborer castemen, and a small squad of freebirth infantry that had been assigned to provide security for Fort DelVillar, though their slung rifles and needlers seemed puny in the shadow of the 'Mechs towering over them.

They waited patiently, all eyes on Angela. She loooked at them, one by one, to let them know she understood what they needed from her right now. She must be more than a military commander. She must be a leader. To Angela Bekker, the distinction was as deep as an ocean at that moment.

"Members of Stalking Bear Trinary," she began in a loud voice almost swallowed by the surrounding woods, "you have worked hard over the last ten days. The work has paid off. Star Colonel Radick and his Blood Drinkers have landed and won nothing but empty buildings and non-functional equipment.

"Now he will try to find us and destroy us. We have shamed him, and his honor is impugned. He will be the wolf on the prowl, hunting us, hoping to crush us in a quick and furious battle to soothe his injured pride." She could see in Bethany's eyes that she too craved such a fight, a swift conclusion to the Trial of Possession. She knew that others were surely feeling the same way. It was their nature as Clansmen. Now she must ask them to change how they fought, to try something new.

"I seek to deny him this release. We will split up into our respective Stars. All non-warriors will report to their assigned caches and remain hidden there. Each Star Commander will operate independently until we encounter the Wolves. When we find them, we will strike—but only when the terrain and circumstances are to our advantage. We will move to concentrate our forces if at all possible, injure and bleed our enemy, and withdraw in good order. This will wear them down. Time will be our greatest ally in this Trial."

Angela knew she needed to drive the point home, to make sure everyone understood. "In numbers we are equal to the Wolves, but the Blood Drinkers have the advantage of experience. They are veteran and elite. We, too, have strong skills, but even more than that we have heart. We have been given the solemn duty to defend and keep this world in the name of our Clan. Experience will come, earned one battle at a time. This strategy is our best hope of defeating the Wolves who dare to attack us. Strike, hit them hard, then pull back. As Clan warriors our instincts and training tell us to fight it out once and for all. But this time a stand-up fight will not serve the greater interests of the Ghost Bears on Toffen. Any warrior who does not follow these rules of engagement will answer to me personally." She glared at Bethany, who returned the look with a cool stare.

"You each know the locations of some of our supply dumps, but not all of them. Put nothing in writing lest it fall into the hands of the Wolves. When you engage the enemy, do not fall back to nearest supply base. The Wolves will most likely be tracking you. Use the terrain, split up, choose a more distant rendezvous. Likewise, you all have various command frequencies for communications. Avoid general broadcasts unless absolutely necessary."

Angela put her arms behind her back in a perfect parade-rest stance so none of her Trinary could see her nervously pulling at her bionic fingers. "This will be the last time for a long while that we will all be together, face-to-face. When we have worn down the Wolves, bloodied them time and again, they will either leave Toffen or be in a condition where it is to our advantage to engage them in a stand-up fight. Until then, we must become one with the landscape. I wish you all good luck, and good hunting."

There was no general cheer, but from the expressions on the faces of her command, Angela saw they were buoyed by her words. Then the group broke up as each one went off to complete his or her final tasks.

She walked over toward her own Command Star, but Stone and Tseng intercepted her first. Both looked worn and tired, yet she could tell they were ready for whatever lay ahead. The stillness of the forest was broken by the throbbing sounds of BattleMech fusion reactors coming to life, making the floor of the forest vibrate.

"We are ready to move out for the Rapidan River," Tseng said. "I have located several fords where we can cross."

"Good," Angela said. "I want you to keep in range to support Sweep Star." Then she looked to Star Commander Stone. "You should be the first to encounter the Wolves. Rixleyville is prominent enough to draw their attention and is in your operations area. Heed my words, Stone. Hit them and get out of there."

"Aye, Star Captain," Stone said. He had checked out the area near the small village several times, and conferred with Angela more than once on their plans. In fact, she and her Star Commanders had located several dozen probable locations for staged battles against the Wolves, locations where if Radick pressed, he would find the rocks and trees fighting against him as well. Each had been carefully mapped and studied. When possible, Stars had walked them to make sure they knew the terrain better than the enemy would.

"I am a mere Sweep Star," Star said. "Speed is my greatest ally. Star Colonel Radick will pay the price of his Wolf arrogance if and when we do engage him."

Tseng crossed his arms over his chest. "Our people are ready, Star Captain, as ready as we can get them. Perhaps we should ask Neta if she has any visions of what the fates might have in store." His tone was part mocking, part serious.

Angela cut him off coldly. "Say nothing ill of Neta and her beliefs, Star Commander. I trust them, no matter how odd they seem. Even before we knew of the Wolves' arrival, she predicted that they would come. Say what you will about the mysticism of the Nova Cats, her intuition is correct and I for one trust it."

Tseng stood speechless for several awkward moments, then said, "If you trust her, that is enough for me."

"Each of our people brings something different and special to our unit. Soon we will find out how all of this uniqueness works together," Angela said. She shook their hands, using both of hers to clasp theirs. First Constant Tseng, then Stone. "Good luck to you both."

Stone said nothing but bowed his head in respect. Tseng said softly, "And to you, Star Captain." The two men then turned to join their own Stars, which were already mounting up and preparing to deploy.

Angela's own Command Star had stood waiting for her and she went over to them now. Neta and Sprange seemed the most relaxed. They had fought in battles before, just not together. To them, all that was different about this Trial was the manner in which it would be fought.

Breedfelt seemed apprehensive, the look on his face somewhere between tired and worried. Angela caught his eye as she approached, hoping to reassure him. She ignored Bethany, who stood there, her dark eyes sharp as knives, her arms crossed defiantly. There were times, Angela told herself, when the rebel is appreciated, and times, like now, when it seemed more bother than it was worth.

"Are there any questions before we begin?" she asked. Most shook their heads. Sprange smiled, and that was reassuring. Bethany shifted in place, then opened her mouth to speak. Angela tried not to roll her eyes as the novice warrior began to speak, but she was sure the others saw it.

"I have a request, Star Captain."

"Proceed," Angela replied, though she dreaded hearing it.

"I request point position as we patrol, Star Captain."

Angela was surprised by the request. "We will rotate assignment of point. However, you shall have the honor of first assuming that role." Bethany nodded with satisfaction. "If there is nothing else, everyone saddle up and let us be on our way." As the warriors began heading toward their 'Mechs, Angela reached out to touch Sprange's arm.

"Sprange, if I may," she said softly, so that none could hear.

"Aye, Star Captain."

"Bethany. Her request to take point. I do no understand."

He smiled. "We spoke with her, the entire Star. She is against your strategic premise in this operation. We convinced her it was the key to victory. She understands, but believes that if she takes point as we patrol, she is more likely to engage the enemy first."

"How does that resolve her problem?"

"If she is the first to fight, she may get in a kill before you order our disengagement. We understood her logic. If you had not chosen her, we would have volunteered our assignments to her."

"You helped her through this, quiaff?"

"Aff. It is a start, little more. As you helped me years ago. Another warrior might have let me die to achieve her goals. You did not. I do not consider my debt of honor paid to you, but this a step in that direction."

Angela smiled and chuckled slightly. "I was right in choosing you for my command, old friend."

"And I am glad you did so."

"Thanks to you, Bethany is learning to adapt. That is the lesson I hoped to teach her."

"In a way," Sprange said, "you did."

She smiled at the notion. "She has found a way to compensate for her instinct to stand and fight it out versus what I demand of her . . . and you."

"She is hard to control and does not respond well to reason," Sprange said. "But we were all like that at one time. The difference is experience."

"Aye, old friend." Angela patted him on the shoulder. "Now let us share another experience—the pleasure of driving the Wolves off Toffen."

Sprange nodded and Angela started toward her *Executioner* for the long climb up the handholds to the cockpit when a shadow fell over her. Turning, she saw the towering form of an Elemental standing behind her. Somehow the warrior had come up on her without her noticing. Through the open face plate of his power armor she saw the rock-like features of Dolf.

"May I have a word, Star Captain?" he asked.

"If it is an operational issue, you should do it through the chain of command. If it is a personal matter, I would be more than happy to discuss it with you."

"It is not something I can talk about with Star Commander Stone, since it would involve his death," Dolf said.

Angela tipped her head to look up at him, unsure of where the conversation was going. "I do not understand."

Dolf moved a little closer and leaned forward and down so that his voice would not carry far. "You know my past, Star Captain. I am old by Clan standards. Our upper command would surely have assigned me to solahma duty had you not recruited me into the Trinary.

You also know of my past, that three times I was the sole survivor of my Star, the only one to live through the battle."

She remembered his codex all too well. Some might call it bad luck, some might call it good. To Dolf it was bad. It meant that he had not won the glory of death in combat before he became too old to be a warrior. "I am more than familiar with your past. But it has no meaning to me. What matters is not what happened elsewhere, but what you are now. You are an excellent warrior, Dolf."

He nodded his head inside of his power armor. "Thank you, Star Captain. But what I come for is to ask a favor." With those words Angela knew instantly what he wanted, but did not interrupt.

"I do not wish to repeat my previous fate. If my Star is wiped out and I am the only survivor, I desire that you kill me so that I do not have to live with the deaths of the others on my head."

"Dolf," she said, struggling for words, "what you ask borders on dishonorable action for a Ghost Bear."

"Neg, Star Captain. You will lose no honor. I do not desire to be an old warrior unable to achieve honor in death. If my Star is wiped out and I alone live, do not let me suffer that disgrace again. Kill me so that I may be granted some release."

Angela said nothing. She knew she would feel the same way in his place, and she herself was not so far from him in age. "Dolf, if the circumstance demands it, I will do what is right." It was the truest answer she could give him.

"Thank you, Star Captain," he said, satisfied for the moment.

Angela only hoped that it would not come to that for any of them.

PART TWO

Stalking Bears

And now this soldier, this Scottish soldier
Who wandered far away and soldiered far away
Sees leaves are falling and death is calling
And he will fade away, in that far land.
He called his piper, his trusty piper
And bade him sound a lay . . . a pibroch sad to play
Upon a hillside, a Scottish hillside
Not on these green hills of Tyrol.

And so this soldier, this Scottish soldier
Will wander far no more and soldier far no more
And on a hillside, a Scottish hillside
You'll see a piper play his soldier home.
He'd seen the glory, he'd told his story
Of battles glorious and deeds victorious
The bugles cease now, he is at peace now
Far from those green hills of Tyrol.
—"The Green Hill of Tyrol," traditional Scottish song

16

Village of Rixleyville
Toffen
Ghost Bear Dominion
19 March 3062

The stride of the *Mad Dog* was slow and careful as it moved through the center of Rixleyville. The town, even at its peak, had never consisted of more than four or five buildings, small concerns that barely made a living for their owners. However, for the many hundreds of families from the surrounding farms, this small village was their only link to civilization.

The approach of the Wolf Clan's Advance Star was no surprise to Star Commander Stone as he sat watching from the cramped confines of his *Fire Moth*'s cockpit. He had the 'Mech running at minimal power levels to keep down its heat signature, but the real work of concealment was being done by the nickel and iron deposits in the rock formation that was hiding him from view. Rather that turn on his active sensors and track the approaching Star, he opted for a more traditional method, eyeballing.

The five Points of the Advance Star had patrolled through Rixleyville at the same time very day for the last three days, searching for the Stalking Bears. Stone knew the 'Mechs on sight. He was even familiar with their "V" sweep formation as they came through the village. Everything was going as it had before.

Except that in a few seconds the Wolves would be under attack.

Rixleyville would not be the battleground in this first major clash with the Wolves. Stone did not want the lower castes living there to pay the price of combat between warriors—that lacked honor. It was not the way of the Ghost Bears. The site Stone had chosen was the terrain *near* the village, where he was hidden. He had checked it carefully, and it would give his Star the advantage they needed. All he had to do was to wait patiently, until the Wolves were where he wanted them.

The lead *Mad Dog* stopped as it exited the small intersection that was the heart of Rixleyville. It pivoted at the torso, swinging to the right and left as if searching for a target. Stone noted calmly that this was new behavior. The *Mad Dog* pilot seemed to sense something. Stone's hand hovered over the throttle control for his *Fire Moth*'s fusion reactor as he considered revving the engine to life, springing the trap. He resisted the temptation and hoped that the rest of his Star would too.

The plan was simple. Behind him was a lightly wooded area running down the long slope of a hill. At the bottom, a bog. This bog, however, was well-hidden. The Wolves would not know it was there, but Stone had already made several trial runs across it. His *Fire Moth* and Dolf and his Elementals, also hidden among the rocks, were fast and light enough to get across. The heavier 'Mechs of the Wolf Star would not fare as well.

On the far side of the bog, waiting in the low hills, was the rest of his Star, all equipped for long-range combat. Stone and Dolf would attack the Wolves, then fall back to the bog. The Wolves would follow. They had no choice, it was their nature. And when they did, they would become mired and grind to a halt. Sweep Star would pummel and bleed them, then retreat before the rest of the Wolf forces could converge on the area.

The *Mad Dog* pilot stopped his sweeps of the area and walked his 'Mech forward, very slowly. The rest of his Star followed at the same pace, carefully scanning every building around them as if they expected the Ghost Bears to be hidden in the centuries-old structures, preparing to strike. Stone waited, watching as every step brought the Wolves closer to his trap.

Opening the comm channel, he spoke into the microphone in his neurohelmet. "Striker One to Striker Two."

Dolf's voice replied almost as a whisper. "Striker Two, go."

"Engage on my mark. Wait for my signal to fall back—just as we planned, quiaff?"

"Aff," a static-filled whisper came back.

As the *Mad Dog* continued methodically forward along the road, which ran only a mere hundred meters in front of the rock formation, Stone gripped the handle of the throttle control and pulled it back. The 200 XL engine throbbed to life. Lights burst on in the cockpit as the *Fire Moth* powered up, ready for battle. The *Fire Moth* was the lightest of the Clan OmniMechs, designed more for speed than for fighting. He had chosen to configure it with weapons pods that gave him significant punch. Against so much firepower, speed alone might not be enough.

"Striker One to all units. Execute phase one," he said in his usual calm voice, despite the excitement he felt.

He watched as the *Mad Dog* stopped dead in its tracks. He knew why. Suddenly its sensors were picking up his fusion reactor and the enemy 'Mech it powered. Working the foot pedals and the directional control, Stone pulled back and then to the right of the rock formation, bringing him in perfect line of sight of the Wolf 'Mechs. The *Mad Dog* turned to face him, but before it could fire, Stone used the joystick to swing his own targeting reticle onto the bird-like form of the 'Mech.

He had rigged a pair of extended-range medium lasers in his Omni's left-arm weapons pod to one target interlock circuit, and the pair of short-range missile racks in the right arm and torso to another circuit. He triggered the SRMs first. The *Fire Moth* tugged as they launched, the gyro straining to compensate for the attack. The missiles roared out of the right arm and torso, ten in all, streaking toward the left side of the *Mad Dog*.

The warheads burst all over the *Mad Dog*, the ugly black and orange explosions shattering the ferro-fibrous armor plating as most of the missiles found their marks. The Wolf 'Mech shuddered under the impact, but answered instantly with its large pulse lasers, sending short, sputtering bursts of red light into the space between the two 'Mechs. Both shots went wild, missing their mark, mostly due to the impacts of Stone's weapons. The other Wolf 'Mechs began to fan out when another wave of short-range missiles suddenly raced out at them from the far side of the rock formation. That was Dolf's Elemental Point firing a salvo of warheads at an unlucky *Adder*, mauling its torso and leg armor, leaving it pockmarked and blackened.

Stone processed the image instantly as he dropped back and moved further to the left. Speed was all his *Fire Moth* had in such a fight, being outmassed three to one and outgunned nearly four to one. He juked to the right and locked on with his medium lasers. One missed its mark, the brilliant emerald beam lashing out at the forest behind the *Mad Dog*. The other hit the 'Mech's already damaged arm armor, slicing into several armor plates, and sending one flying into the air as it heat-popped free from the 'Mech chassis.

The Wolf 'Mech began to move as well, closing the distance. Stone knew he would soon be dead if he tried to stand and fight. As it was, he may have overstayed his welcome. The *Mad Dog* fired its pair of medium pulse lasers. One hit the *Fire Moth*'s right torso, and the 'Mech pitched hard as armor plating exploded off. A light ripple of heat washed over the cockpit. Stone knew that at least several of his heat sinks had been reduced to scrap-metal in the attack, which meant his 'Mech could start generating more heat than it could vent if it took more damage as it moved.

Fighting the controls and using his own neurofeedback to compensate for the adjustments to his balance, Stone revved the gyro to stay upright as he turned his *Fire Moth* toward the bog.

"Execute Phase Two now!" he barked into his microphone, his voice raspy.

At a full run he raced for the bog, swinging his torso around enough to let go another wave of missiles at the pursuing *Mad Dog*. He did not see whether they hit their mark. All that mattered now was the second phase of the plan.

His secondary tactical display showed that Dolf and his force were having a harder time pulling back from the injured *Adder*. It was closing on the Point of Elementals faster than they could fall back. There was nothing he could do, not now. The display also showed that the other Wolf Clan 'Mechs, another *Adder*, an *Ice Ferret*, and a *Mist Lynx*, were moving in on the flanks and starting down the hill he was now descending. They were searching for new targets, other Ghost Bears.

As Stone reached the bog, his *Fire Moth* shuddered and moaned around him as internal structure crumbled under an unseen assault. *Missiles.* The fusion reactor under his cockpit began to roar, and another ripple of heat seemed to turn the cockpit into a pressure cooker. Sweat stung his eyes inside the neurohelmet, and his coolant vest suddenly became something between inadequate and worthless. Checking the damage display, he saw that his rear armor was gone, and if the data was accurate, most of his 'Mech's internal structure was shredded and probably hanging out, either exposed, burned, or reduced to worthless, ruined bits of technology.

He turned slightly and swung his torso the rest of the way around as his 'Mech stepped into the bog. He saw the approaching *Mad Dog*, further away than he expected, but still racing down after him. He locked on with his missiles and let go another twined salvo of ten, their white trails marking the air between the two 'Mechs as they streaked toward their targets. Four missed, but the others slammed into the *Mad Dog*'s head, peppering away armor as they impacted.

The ground under his *Fire Moth* gave way, but not too much. Stone would have to keep the 'Mech moving if he was going to make it across. He continued at a run despite the steady rise of heat in his cockpit from his loss of sinks and engine damage. On the far side of the hill he saw the rising forms of Dolf's Elementals, or at least some of them, the flames of their leg jets blocked every other instant by leaves and branches as the *Adder* still tried to close with them.

Suddenly a flash filled his mind and vision, and everything went white. He felt a giant lurch, and heard a crunching noise almost like the sound of a bone breaking, but it was all around him, in every direction. There was a sudden pressure on his chest as the cockpit straps dug into his shoulders. His head slammed to the side and he felt something, cockpit glass perhaps, rain against his faceplate as his head bobbed about madly inside the neurohelmet. In his mouth he tasted something salty, blood.

Stone's mind raced to process the sensations into some form of reality. He had experienced the feeling before, during warrior training in the sibko. *Neurofeedback.* His 'Mech had taken severe damage, and the link between his neurohelmet and brain and the Battle-Mech's gyro had taken a hit, feeding back some of the energy to him in the cockpit. Opening his eyes he saw sky, and knew instantly that his *Fire Moth* was down. In his heart, he was sure it was dead. He moved his head slightly, and felt his neck muscles ache as he did. The damage display, flickering on and off on emergency power, told him the story he did not want to believe.

His 'Mech's left leg was gone, according to the damage readout. Not just damaged, but severed. Apparently the *Mad Dog*'s lasers had finally found their mark. He still had armor on his center torso, but not much. His gyro was not working at all, but the sensors indicated that, if he dared, he could restart his fusion reactor. His 'Mech was dead. Was his command gone as well?

Instinct and training kicked in, even if his body didn't. He punched the release to the restraining straps and tried to sit upright, but his body seemed to lack the strength. His movements were clumsy and awkward as he removed the neurohelmet and pulled himself upward to the cockpit hatch. With a reassuring hiss, the emergency release worked, and the hatch cracked open. With what energy he had left, Stone crawled through the half-open hatch, cutting his left knee on it as he pulled his body through.

The cool wetness of the bog greeted him as he fell free from his smashed BattleMech. He heard the roar of missiles overhead as he rose on all fours, his fists sinking slightly into the black muck. All around him were the sounds of battle. Lifting his head, he saw, in the distance, a thick, hissing cloud of green and white smoke rising from what had been a Wolf Clan *Adder*—the 'Mech that had been pursuing Dolf. Stone had no idea how long he had been out. A wave of dizziness swept over him as he rose enough to lean on a small sapling in the bog to steady himself.

Nearby was the *Mad Dog* that had lashed into him, kneecapped and bent head-first into the bog. It must have fallen in and then been finished off by another member of his force. The other Wolf 'Mechs were on the far side of the bog, and showed signs of varying amounts of damage. Above his head and on both sides, missiles streaked past, heading in both directions.

He lifted the personal communicator that hung on his belt to his lips. "Sweep One here. Status report," he said with difficulty. His ribs ached as he tried to take in more air, to put more energy in his voice.

"Sweep One, this is Sweep Two. What is your location?"

"At my 'Mech," Stone said, wiping his face. "Status."

"Sir," came the voice of Dis, his Star's other *Fire Moth* pilot. "We have inflicted projected damage on these Wolves. We are tracking sensor signals to our rear. I am moving to investigate."

Readings to the rear? That was not in the plan, not at all. He saw a pair of Elementals drop on their jets near him. They lashed out with their shoulder-mounted short-range missiles at a distant Wolf Clan *Ice Ferret*, mangling its legs with a series of small explosions that ripped at armor and the myomer muscle fibers that powered the BattleMech's movements.

Stone spoke into the communicator again. "Negative, Sweep Five. Execute Phase Three. All Sweep Star forces, pull back and out. Move," he said, losing his grip on the small tree and falling to his knees.

The small communicator, now reading the command frequency, hissed to life. "Sweep Five. Wolf Clan 'Mechs to the rear. Enemy to the rear. We are turned." Suddenly the sound of an explosion came over the line, then a long, almost painful hiss. Then nothing. Stone knew that sound, he knew what had happened. Dis was gone, either dead or crippled.

Stone stared down at the mud and felt the sticky sting of blood in his mouth. *I am to die here. It was a good plan. Somehow they got behind us. It was a good plan . . .* He stopped fighting the pull of the gravity and started to drop face-first toward the mud. He never impacted, though. He felt a tug around his waist and seemed to hover over the mire for a moment, then rose into the air. He reached out with his hands and felt metallic ferro-fibrous armor, the armor of an Elemental suit.

In a foggy daze, he looked up and saw the opaque faceplate of Dolf, holding him by the waist. His armor was badly dented and torn in one place on the chest, but Dolf was still operational.

Stone looked up at the faceplate weekly. "We must withdraw."

Dolf's voice came through the small speaker in his

power armor. "We are pulling back now, Star Commander." Then Dolf began to move back, raising his left arm and firing a bright red blast of laser energy at a far-off enemy.

"Leave me. I will just slow you down," Stone said, coughing. "That is an order."

"You will have to face me in a Circle of Equals later, sir," Dolf said, jumping over a fallen and rotting log with his commanding officer tucking under one arm. "We need you more than ever. The Wolves have two Stars coming at us."

"Leave me to die," Stone stammered.

"Neg. If I do, I might be the only one to survive," Dolf said. He jumped again and they rose into the air, this time augmented by the built-in leg jets in the Elemental suit. The dizziness came over Stone again, and this time he gave in to it, closing his eyes and letting the seductiveness of sleep take him. He never felt the landing or what followed . . .

17

Supply Cache Lambda
Toffen
Ghost Bear Dominion
20 March 3062

Angela felt the eyes of the various technicians, laborers, and warriors following her as she left her BattleMech and approached where they worked. The morning dew on the low brush and vines wet her bare legs as she reached the cave that had been designated as Supply Cache Lambda.

The cave was a large, roof-like shelf of rock jutting out the side of a steep hill. Under it, the Ghost Bears had hollowed out adequate living and storage space, rough, but enough to survive. The rocky overhang was nearly as tall as her 'Mech. A damaged *Mist Lynx* stood along the far left wall, with technicians working furiously to re-plate its armor. The blackened scars showed where it had taken damage, even though the armor had already been repaired. She gave it more than a casual glance. Was this all that was left of Sweep Star?

Inside the cave she saw several open spaces partitioned off, mostly by crates of parts, foodstuffs, and ammunition. She walked in, and tension seemed to spike. A figure moved toward her in the thin light, and she made out the face of Doctor Drogan. His eyes showed the same bags of weariness under them that hers did, and his movements were sluggish. Angela stopped and spoke first.

"What is the condition of my warriors?"

The doctor looked bitter, tired, drained, and angry all at the same time. "Those who made it here will live."

Angela could just as easily have gotten a report via the communications channel, but it was important that she come there. She knew that one part of leadership required really being there for her people. Another figure emerged from the shadows, a giant shape, and she saw that it was Dolf. He wore the same kind of shorts she did, albeit larger for his massive, genetically engineered frame. He towered over her, stooping slightly to keep from hitting his head on the rocky projections. As he came forward, Drogan stepped back.

"Star Captain Bekker, our losses were severe," Dolf said grimly.

"Report," she commanded.

"Dis was killed," he said. "As were Drake and Dole." His face tightened as he named the Elementals who had served under him. "Kate is uninjured, and our technicians are repairing her 'Mech. Scarry's *Viper* is five kilometers from here, disabled from battle damage. It too will need repair." He cast a glance at the doctor. "Scarry is injured."

"What of Star Commander Stone?"

Drogan spoke up now. "He suffered a severe concussion, neurofeedback damage, two broken ribs, and a light dose of radiation from a hit to his engine. He should live."

"Should?"

"Affirmative—if there are no complications."

"Tell me what happened, Dolf."

The big warrior drew a deep breath and let it out with a sigh that revealed his exhaustion. "Our plan was working flawlessly except that Star Commander Stone was downed before he could get across the bog. From the hills, Kate, Scarry, and Dis laid down a barrage of long-range fire that seriously hurt the Star pursuing us. Two of the Wolf 'Mechs were also downed in the mire. The other suffered a variety of damage.

"Dis picked up a signal to our left rear flank and moved to check it out. Apparently one of their other Stars, Slasher Star, was in the vicinity and literally stumbled into us. It was an unlucky encounter, to say the least. Dis drew them away, but his 'Mech was far too light to survive the engagement. None of us could track his ejection pod and we believe he was killed. I assumed command and extracted our forces in a full retreat from the area. We continued for several hours before coming here."

"Enemy losses," Angela asked, almost stunned at the BDA, the battle damage assessment.

"One *Mad Dog* and one *Adder* downed and assumed destroyed, though the *Mad Dog* most likely could be repaired. An *Ice Ferret* took heavy damage in the legs. Another *Adder* took major armor damage. A Wolf Clan *Mist Lynx* lost one of its weapons pods and took some damage as well."

The had lost two 'Mechs, two Elementals, and the surviving 'Mechs of this Star had been hurt bad but might be repairable. Angela knew they could ill afford more losses like these. "That's all, Dolf," she said, dismissing him. Drogan remained.

"He did well," the doctor said.

"Aye." Angela did not say to Drogan that a person of his caste did not speak to an officer of military matters, but she knew he was right. "In our first clash with these Wolves, we fared equally. We should have done better, though."

"The arrival of the other Wolf Star was not expected. The Wolves got lucky."

"How long will these warriors be out of commission, Doctor?"

Drogan rubbed his chin in thought. "Scarry has some minor leg burns but could be back in his 'Mech in a day's time. Kate is uninjured. Dolf and his Elementals are fine. Stone will be out of action for at least three days."

"Very well," Angela said. "You may return to your duties, Doctor . . ." Then, after a moment, "And you have my thanks."

Drogan waved her thanks away. "This is only the start, Star Captain. Bring this to an end quickly. I don't want to have to patch together you and the rest of your command over and over again, each time losing more of you." There was concern as well as more than a hint of insubordination in his words. Angela was too tired to reprimand him.

She sent him back to work, then walked over to where some technicians were trying to repair the *Mist Lynx*. She managed to get the attention of one of them, then realized it was not a tech at all but Barthelow, Constant Tseng's bondsman. His jumpsuit was covered with black smudges and smears of green coolant, and his face showed the sweat and dirt of hard labor.

"Barthelow, you are the tech in charge here, quiaff?"

"Aff, Star Captain. Chief Tech Luray is too far away. He sent me here to assume command of the situation."

"Very well then," she said, nodding her approval, "what is the status of this unit?"

Barthelow was somewhat nervous at first, then seemed to find a source of calm in dutifully giving his report. "We have effected repairs on the Elemental armor from spare parts. Two of them are on patrol, per Dolf's orders. This *Mist Lynx* will be fully operational in two hours' time." He jerked his thumb over his shoulder at the light 'Mech standing under the overhanging rock. "I have a tech working on Scarry's *Viper*, and she reports she will have it mobile in an hour, and here in three. She says it will require at least three days to fully repair and get it working. Extensive damage to the gyro, and even with a proper repair facility, that is a difficult piece of machinery to align."

"Aye," Angela said. "Do we have a reserve 'Mech here or nearby?"

Barthelow nodded. "Our only reserve 'Mech is an older model *Viper* at supply cache Bravo. That is well over two hundred-fifty kilometers from here, though."

Angela mulled over what she had heard. "Barthelow, are you required here?" she said finally.

"Neg, Star Captain. I can assist the teams, but I have less to contribute than the current technical staff."

"Then I want you to go and recover our reserve 'Mech and bring it here. One of the techs can transport you there. By the time you get there and back, Star Commander Stone might be able to make use of it."

His mouth hung open for a moment. "Aye, Star Captain, and thank you!"

Angela understood. Barthelow had been a Mech-Warrior before becoming a bondsman. Being asked to pilot a 'Mech again was something any warrior would live for. Now, she was not just asking him to do it, she was ordering it. "I will inform Star Commander Tseng of your disposition."

She turned toward the battle-worn *Mist Lynx* as the technicians worked a hand winch and pulley to adjust the position of an armor plate on its torso. Her unit had been hurt, but they could recover some of what was lost. She only hoped they was faring better than the Wolves.

Star Colonel Dirk Radick stood on the side of the fallen Ghost Bear *Fire Moth* and surveyed the surrounding terrain. Some trees in the hills across the swamp were scarred with laser and charged-particle burns. The ground was uprooted and pockmarked with craters from missiles and autocannon fire. His small group of technicians worked furiously on Star Commander Biffly's mired *Mad Dog*, attempting, from what he could see, to get the 'Mech upright.

He had to admire Angela Bekker for choosing this location to fight. The lay of the land suited her forces. It had been only blind luck that his Slasher Star had been nearby when the battle erupted. They were converging on the site when they encountered a picket of Stalking Bears. The *Fire Moth* had rushed them, then moved away, slowing the advance of Slasher Star for several precious seconds. Just enough that some of the Ghost Bears were able to leave the field of battle. Radick's forces had destroyed the small 'Mech so utterly that there was little left of the MechWarrior other than a charred corpse, its mouth open in an eternal scream.

Star Commander Biffly Ward waded through the bog and then climbed up onto the fallen form of the other destroyed *Fire Moth*. "The technicians report that they can recover and most likely have my 'Mech operational within twenty percent of its norm."

"And the *Adder*?" Radick asked, pointing across the lowlands to the mangled remains of another Wolf 'Mech.

"That one is a total loss, thanks to the Ghost Bear Elementals. And there is not enough left of the 'Mechs the Ghost Bears lost in the fight to salvage."

"And the losses to the Ghost Bears?"

"We recovered two dead Elementals and two destroyed 'Mechs. Some were seriously hurt, as were our own, and we know that at least one of the downed warriors is unaccounted for." Biffly wiped his large brow of sweat, leaving a dark dirt smear in its place.

"You let the others get away, Star Commander," Dirk said coldly.

"I did not have a choice in the matter. The terrain was formidable and did not permit me pursuit, sir." He was obviously nervous, and Radick saw through his meaning. Biffly was trying to shift the blame on to Star Commander Digorno for not pursuing, yet it was this fool who had stumbled into the trap to begin with.

"I do not blame you entirely, Biffly Ward. We were not fully aware of the intentions and capabilities of the Ghost Bears until you allowed your unit to fall into their hands.

"Star Captain Angela Bekker is a skilled commander. It was pure luck that our Slasher Star prevented her from inflicting further damage on you. Their withdrawal can only be interpreted as confirmation of her strategy."

"Sir?"

"She is refusing to face us in a direct engagement. This Bekker seeks to force us into a drawn-out battle and wear us down rather than try to beat us honorably.

Otherwise she would have stayed to fight. We have had less subtle hints thus far, but you have confirmed it."

"Aye, Star Colonel," Biffly replied.

Moving suddenly, Radick stepped across the surface of the fallen *Fire Moth* and grabbed Biffly by his collar lapels. He lifted him into the air, and brought his face only centimeters away from the other man's. "I recommend that you do not confirm anything else regarding the Ghost Bears for me, Star Commander. Do this again, and you will suffer my wrath. Do you understand?"

Biffly was not so much scared as preparing himself for further physical attack. "I hear and obey you, Star Colonel," he replied in a strangled voice.

With less warning than when he had grabbed him, Dirk Radick let go of Biffly and smiled. "Good. Now see to the refit of your unit."

As Biffly Ward climbed back down to the ground, Dirk Radick returned his attention to the problem of Angela Bekker. He activated his personal communicator, then the channel for a broadband transmission, which covered a wide range of frequencies. He did not want to miss this chance to address his little Ghost Bear.

"Star Captain Angela Bekker of the Ghost Bears, this is Star Colonel Dirk Radick of the Wolves. We have engaged, and you have shown that you can fight. How long can your green unit hope to attack my veterans and survive? You have paid dearly in our last fight. I will continue to press you. Your best chance for survival is to come and face me in direct combat. Otherwise, it is you, not I, who will be worn down."

He shut off the device and returned it to his belt. *I must defeat this Ghost Bear,* he told himself. *I must do it before she does it to me.*

18

Lake Ishimaru Shoreline
Toffen
Ghost Bear Dominion
25 March 3062

Star Commander Constant Tseng snugged his back-side into the cockpit seat. It was only days that he had been in the cockpit of his *Timber Wolf*, but it felt more like a lifetime. He slowly surveyed the area, making sure everything was in order. Behind him, nearly two kilometers away, were the shimmering waters of Lake Ishimaru. Its blue surface reflected the setting sun. All around it, except for the shoreline that he faced, were dense forest, rugged rock formations, and almost im-passable terrain. The shoreline was the only clear, open area where someone could actually reach the lake.

He swung the torso of the *Timber Wolf* around the road stretching into the wilderness of the forest. The road was the only means of travel in this area, the only place where a 'Mech could easily navigate. Though it was possible to move through the dense, old trees, it was difficult even with the power of a BattleMech. Between the road and the shore of the lake was a flat, open glade. He had studied the terrain during their exercises, and had done the necessary research on every aspect of what he saw. Now came the waiting, and that was always the hard part.

Star Captain Bekker had conveyed to him the extent of the damage Stone and his Star had suffered. It was not devastating, but they had been hurt more than the Wolves, which had certainly not been the plan. They had arrived at the same conclusion, that the arrival of the additional Wolf Star at Rixleyville had been a fluke, an unlucky twist of fate. Things will be different this time, Tseng told himself. Checking the digital chronometer in the cockpit, he saw that it was nearly time. Days of planning were going to be put to the test.

Reaching out, he activated the *Timber Wolf*'s active sensors. Instead of simply taking in data, they were now transmitting outward in an attempt to draw a signal. In this game of cat and mouse, such a move made his 'Mech stand out as a target for long ranges. Anyone in sensor range would detect him and be able to home in on his signal. And that road was the only way in or out.

He adjusted the seat strap and checked his sensors. He had been monitoring the Wolf Clan Star that had been searching this area for some time. This Star varied its schedule of patrols, but he knew it was only a matter of time before . . .

A light lit on his long-range sensors. Then another small blip of light appeared. Fusion reactors. Magnetic anomaly signals. Four . . . no, five. The entire Star, moving single file, heading this way. He throttled his own reactor to life and switched both sets of his long-range missile racks, a total of forty missiles in a single salvo, to the same target interlock circuit. As the signals approached, he turned and started sweeping the area where the road reached the clearing where he stood. Licking his lips, he watched carefully as his enemies closed in.

The first 'Mech to enter the clearing was a massive *Gargoyle*, its man-shaped head painted to look like a rabid wolf with bronze eyes. He saw the image at the same time as the audible tone of weapons lock hummed seductively in his ear. The Wolf 'Mech was raising its right arm, its autocannon and missiles readying to fire, even as Tseng let go with his own long-range missiles, followed closely with a blast from his large lasers.

There was a rush and a pitch in balance as the *Timber Wolf* let go its barrage. The majority of the missiles slammed into the legs and lower torso of the *Gargoyle*, while a few missed and hit in the woods behind it, shaking the massive trees as if a ground quake struck. His large lasers, bright red coherent beams, sliced into the missile-impact area, sending armor plate flying from the right leg and the left arm of the *Gargoyle*, staggering it back under the assault.

The Wolf warrior let go his own attack, his LB 5-X autocannon firing a blast of depleted-uranium slugs into the center and right torso of Tseng's 'Mech, ripping off armor plates and sending shrapnel from the impact spattering against the cockpit glass. A spray of short-range missiles followed almost instantly, hitting the right-arm weapons pod with such force that the *Timber Wolf* almost lost balance. The 'Mech seemed to groan under the strain of the impacts.

The other Wolf 'Mechs appeared but did not fire. That was as it should be, according to the Clan ritual of combat. Until Tseng fired at another Wolf 'Mech, it would remain a one-on-one fight between him and the *Gargoyle*. He swung his targeting reticle low and triggered his medium pulse lasers, the bright green beams savaging the already mangled armor plates of the Wolf 'Mech's legs. He felt a ripple of heat rise in the cockpit but ignored it as he began to move backward, putting some distance between him and the Wolf MechWarrior.

The Wolf let go with his autocannons again even as Tseng heard the load cycle engage and the distinct metallic click of his long-range missiles preparing to fire. One of the shots missed by only a few meters, most of its force shooting past his *Timber Wolf*, most likely into the waters of Lake Ishimaru. The other shot reverberated in his ears and brain as his 'Mech's right arm quaked under the impact of the slug-like ammunition. The Wolves advanced, albeit slowly, as once again the missile lock purred in Tseng's ears.

Again came the recoil as the missiles cleared the boxy shoulder-launched compartments. He didn't wait to see the impacts, but instead turned and sprinted in a zigzag pattern toward the lake shore in the distance. Then he swung the *Timber Wolf* around toward the *Gargoyle*, which opened up again with another blast of its missiles and autocannons.

A few of the missiles hit his 'Mech's right leg and left arm with a vengeance, but most of them missed. The autocannons, on the other hand, were shredding his armor away with each blast. Having put some distance between himself and the *Gargoyle*, he saw the blackened pockmarks where his last missile storm had torn into the torso and hip of the other 'Mech. Now the entire Star of Wolf 'Mechs was bearing down on him. Should his current target fall, any one of them was ready to step into his or her place.

He fired his large lasers, spiking the cockpit tempera-

ture enough that he tasted his own salty sweat when he
licked his lips. One laser missed totally, almost striking
a Wolf *Linebacker* that was near his intended target. The
other beam cut deeply into the already-blackened left
arm of the *Gargoyle,* this time mangling not only ferro-
fibrous armor, but severing some of the myomer bundles that performed as a 'Mech's muscles. Strands
snapped and hung out of the open holes as the menacing machine continued to pursue him.

Tseng checked his short-range sensors and saw that
he was near the shore of Lake Ishimaru. It was behind
him, and the Wolves were closing in. It was time to engage them all. He checked his commline and made sure
he was on the desired frequency.

"Striker Star, Phase One, green," he said.

He did not look at what was going on behind him,
but he knew what the Wolf warriors were seeing. Rising from their hiding place in the water were two more
BattleMechs. Their legs still hidden by the cool waters
of the lake, they fired at the advancing line. The Wolves
seemed stunned by this unexpected maneuver, if only
for a heartbeat.

Tseng did not hesitate to take advantage of their surprise, and fired another vicious missile salvo that
seemed to devour the legs and torso of the *Gargoyle* in a
horrific impact. The giant machine staggered. A Wolf
Summoner was pummeled by fire from Natulson's
Summoner, and the air came alive with missiles and the
crackling cobalt blue of a PPC blast. Another 'Mech on
the far left flank, a *Warhawk,* sagged under the missile
blasts from Sorrenteno's *Mad Dog.*

The *Gargoyle*'s pilot attempted to fight the kinetic impact of so many missiles, but could not. Like a staggering drunk, it drifted to the right, then the left, then fell
as Tseng poured another burst from his medium pulse

lasers into its legs, flaying armor plating onto the ground all around the fallen 'Mech.

Tseng squinted as he advanced forward toward the Wolves. "Striker Star, Phase Two, green," he barked into the neurohelmet microphone. Now, while the Wolves were in the midst of a fight.

The air cracked next to him as the Wolf *Warhawk* fired its massive array of particle projection cannons past him and into Sorrenteno, somewhere behind him. In the distance, he saw the woods also come alive as the remaining members of his command emerged from hiding in their powered-down 'Mechs. Gregori's imposing *Grizzly* let loose a withering barrage with its gauss rifle, a pulse laser, and a handful of long-range missiles, stabbing a Wolf *Linebacker* in the rear where its armor was already dangerously thin. Most of the missiles did not hit, but the other weapons did find their target. The *Linebacker* seemed to quake in place, shuddering as its internal ammunition cooked off under the assault. It turned to face Gregori, slowly, showing Tseng the horrible rips in its now all but evaporated rear armor. Sick green coolant leaked like blood from the wound, sizzling on the blasted hot armor remains.

Kyle in his *Cauldron-Born* raked the Wolf Clan *Mad Dog* as it reeled and pivoted to face the new assault. Kyle pressed forward, closing the distance to mere meters. His primary weapon, a massive autocannon, missed the mark, gouging a crater to the left of its target, while the red beams of the large lasers ate away at the *Mad Dog*'s thin rear armor. Tseng watched in shock as the *Gargoyle* pilot attempted to stand the 'Mech upright, clumps of sod dangling off the cratered armor as it labored to its knees. He did not hesitate, but fired another blast from his medium lasers, ripping away at the Wolf 'Mech's armor as it attempted to rise and fight. The pulse laser struck the cockpit-head of the 'Mech, burning off the wolf visage painted on it. One of his beams missed totally. Another scarlet lance dug deep into the torso of his target, this time not impeded by armor. Smoke, black, oily, sick smoke, billowed from the hole, and for a moment the *Gargoyle* seemed frozen in place, locked in a silent seizure.

The warrior somehow managed to get the 'Mech on its feet, smoke still venting from the gaping hole in the side torso. It fired wildly at Tseng's *Timber Wolf*, sending short-range missiles into his 'Mech's legs, shaking him violently in his command couch. Both of the autocannons missed their mark by a staggering distance, telling the Ghost Bear commander how much damage he had inflicted. Switching to his large lasers, he cut loose again into the sickening torso of the *Gargoyle*. Both shots found their mark, burrowing and burning deep into the internal guts of the 'Mech. Black smoke was joined by green and white as the massive *Gargoyle* fired its short-range missiles again. Half hit Tseng's center torso while the others disappeared past his cockpit into the unknown.

He reached his right thumb up the joystick and pressed the top trigger, the target interlock circuit for the long-range missiles. The missiles thundered out from both sides of his cockpit, a sound he heard as a roar of honor. The warheads hit the *Gargoyle* from top to bottom, some missing, but most rocking the massive OmniMech with incredible force. The Wolf pilot again tried to fight the impact, but this time it was too much. He fell forward, hitting the ground hard. Constant Tseng was sure that this time the Wolf 'Mech would not be getting up.

He checked his tactical display and saw that Sorrenteno in his *Mad Dog* was almost destroyed. He had lost almost all his armor, yet he still stood in the blue water of the lake, blasting with everything he had. Kyle's *Cauldron-Born* grappled at point-blank range with the Wolf *Mad Dog*, both 'Mechs almost invisible to the naked eye for all the smoke billowing from them. In front of him, the *Linebacker* crumbled as Gregori's *Grizzly* advanced on it, its right arm and side badly torn and barely operational, according to the data readout.

Tseng activated his broad-band frequency. "Wolf Clan Commander, this is Star Commander Constant Tseng. Your force is decimated and faces destruction. Surrender now and do not waste the lives of these warriors."

A static snap and hiss, then a voice. "I am O'Connel of Slasher Star. You have already destroyed Star Commander Digorno. I hold rank here. We will never surrender, not to the likes of—" His message was cut off as Kyle's *Cauldron-Born* exploded at point-blank range with the *Mad Dog*. The *Cauldron-Born* went off in a flash as its fusion reactor dumped. The *Mad Dog* bore the brunt of the blast, its armor flying off nearly thirty meters under the impact of the explosion. It turned to face Tseng, and he saw the 'Mech's charred front. Myomer bundles were exposed, severed, and the vents of fire ripped up its sides. With Kyle gone, Tseng chose this as his target and fired his large lasers. In a second, the lasers severed the spine of the *Mad Dog*, sending it toppling onto the ground only two dozen meters from the remains of the *Gargoyle*.

Suddenly it was quiet, an eerie silence that would have shaken the souls of most warriors, but not Constant Tseng. He scanned the smoke and debris and saw that there was no more fire or lasers in the air. On the ground, the remains of the entire Wolf Star were all around him. He pivoted his *Timber Wolf* and saw Sorrenteno's *Mad Dog* standing up in the water, its torso hardly recognizable as belonging to a BattleMech. It was an odd vision, the war machine, still smoking at the hip actuators, standing in a lake of calm blue water as the light of early evening reflected off its surface. Natulson's *Summoner* had taken heavy damage, but was full functional. Gregori's *Grizzly* had lost some armor almost everywhere, but was otherwise still operational and ready for battle.

Kyle was gone. Sorrenteno might be dead or may have ejected. "Gregori, take a position to cover the road in case they have additional forces converging here," Tseng commanded coolly.

"Aye, Star Commander," Gregori replied.

"Natulson, attempt to track any sign of Sorrenteno or his escape pod."

Tseng did not wait for the other warrior's acknowledgment. He switched to the command frequency in his cockpit. "Striker One to Command One. Operation went as planned. Losses are light. Request clean-up immediately."

Star Captain Angela Bekker's voice came back quickly. "Recovery crews are on their way. And Star Commander," she added, "good work."

19

Lake Ishimaru Shoreline
Toffen
Ghost Bear Dominion
27 March 3062

The Command Star of the Bloodied Wolves Trinary moved off the road in a spread "W" formation, with Star Colonel Dirk Radick's *Executioner* in the lead. They fanned out with military precision, covering the woods and the distant lake. At first glance, in the light of the yellow sun, there was little evidence of a battle. Dirk Radick saw the mangled remains of Slasher Star's Battle-Mechs first, crumbled heaps of battle technology left abandoned where they fell. Other signs emerged as well, including the occasional crater where a missile or autocannon round had missed its mark. Several trees at the perimeter of the clearing bore the telltale carbon scars from stray laser fire.

"Deploy your troops, Star Commander Jergan," he commanded, sweeping the trees with his weapons.

Jergan, seating in her *Warhawk* just behind him, moved forward so that the rest of her Star, still moving in the trees at the edge of the road and forest, could fan out faster. "Command Star, secure this area. Watch the treeline, Fletcher. Patton and Helenica, take forward positions, keep yourselves trained on that lake."

Her words were not idle ones. The data dump Star Colonel Radick had shared with her told the story of how the Ghost Bears had lured in the Slasher Star, hitting them from the deep-water lake and the forest. It was brief, and the final results of the battle were unknown. What was known was that Slasher Star had been trapped by the Ghost Bears, then nothing.

Dirk Radick moved his *Executioner* forward almost casually. He did not feel the same tension that his junior officers did as they entered the glade and moved toward the lake. When he had not heard back from Slasher Star, he had assumed the worse. It had taken a day and a half to reach the shores of Lake Ishimaru, but by the time they arrived, Radick was sure that not only was Slasher Star gone or crippled, but that the Ghost Bears would not be there waiting for him.

That was not the strategy she was employing, this Angela Bekker. No, she was up to a bigger game, one which he was going to have to adapt to quickly or die. But in this defeat he had still won something, an insight about her strategy and the need for greater caution in dealing with her.

He stopped his BattleMech and set it for low-power operations. Lying near his 'Mech's feet were the remains of what had once been a *Gargoyle*, its internal structure ripped open like an animal laid out to be cleaned and gutted. When he opened the hatch of his cockpit, he was blasted with the smell of charred insulation and fried myomer bundles, mixed with spilled coolant. Dirk knew it well, the scent of battle. As he climbed down the footholds set into the torso and leg of his *Executioner*, he saw the fallen forms of several other 'Mechs, each one just as mauled.

Radick walked over to the fallen 'Mech and stared at the cockpit. It had been painted with the symbol of his Blood Drinkers, but all that showed now was charred and peeled paint from the horrific struggle the 'Mech had endured. He knew the 'Mech and its pilot, Star Commander Digorno of the Carns bloodline. The dried blood smear inside the cockpit told him the fate of Digorno. He had died with honor, even if in defeat. Radick vowed silently that he would win this Trial so that the loss of good warriors not would be in vain, their honor tainted.

He stared at the brownish stain a long time, then off toward the lakeshore where the 'Mechs of the Command Star moved about, making sure the area was totally secured. Radick stood there for nearly ten minutes, looking at the terrain, clearing his mind, attempting to recreate what had happened here.

He heard footsteps behind him and turned to see Star Commander Jergan approaching. "Battle damage assessment, Star Commander," he said calmly.

The expression on her face told him more than any words. "We have found the remains of four of the Slasher 'Mechs, sir." Her eyes drifted for a second to the fallen *Gargoyle* lying on the ground. "The remains of two of the Ghost Bear 'Mechs are present as well."

"What about the fifth 'Mech of Slasher Star? Is it possible that it is in the lake?"

She shook her head. "I spotted the tire marks of a Prime Mover. From what I can tell, the Ghost Bears removed all of the ammunition from our Star and at least one of our 'Mechs that was damaged in the engagement, warrior Lucian's *Summoner*."

A pair of warriors approached from across the clearing. Radick walked over to meet them, and Jergan had to jog several steps just to keep pace with him. One of the warriors was in her Command Star, Patton Ward. He was helping an injured warrior, Kevin Carns of Slasher Star. He was limping, and his arm was in a sling. The contrast between his dirty and bloodied uniform and that of the pristine Patton Ward's was stark. He rose to weak attention as Radick approached, then nearly collapsed onto a small stump.

Jergan spoke first. "Kevin, what happened?"

He raised his head, and Radick saw that his once black mustache had been almost totally singed off. Small black crater marks dotted his face from a burn. His eyes were tired, red, and he was obviously exhausted. Patton Ward offered him a canteen, but he did not drink, just held it feebly in his dirt-encrusted hands.

"One of their warriors engaged us as soon as we came out of the forest. A single *Timber Wolf*. It hit Star Commander Digorno. We all advanced. It had nowhere to go. Then some of them rose from out of the lake. The water and the rocks must have obscured their reactor signatures. Just as we were about to take them on, the rest of their Star hit us from the rear. They had been hidden in the trees all along. We must have passed only a hundred meters from them and never saw them." His voice was a mix of despair and exhaustion.

"A *Timber Wolf*," Jergan said. "What other 'Mechs did you see?"

"A *Mad Dog*, a *Summoner*, a *Cauldron-Born*, and a *Grizzly*," he said, finally succumbing to the lure of the canteen and gulping down a long drink of water. A rivulet ran down his face as he drank, streaking the dirt and grime.

Radick looked at Jergan. "From what we know of

their unit, he must have faced Star Commander Tseng and his Striker Star," Radick surmised.

"Any other survivors?" Jergan pressed as Kevin Carns finally lowered the canteen.

"Neg. We were destroyed. They lost two 'Mechs in the battle, and the others were badly damaged."

Dirk Radick leaned forward, getting in the face of young Carns. "Tell me, what happened then?" He was angry, enraged at what had happened here. This was not what he had anticipated, not what was planned. Someone was going to have to pay, and pay dearly.

"Star Captain Bekker arrived with her technicians only three hours after the fighting. They stripped our 'Mechs of everything of value—gyros, actuators, ammunition, everything they could take. They even took the remains of Lucian's *Summoner*."

Jergan stared at him hard. "And they did not find you?"

The question was an important one for a warrior. To be defeated by the enemy was dishonorable, but it was even worse if the enemy did not take you as bondsman, making you part of their Clan. "They found me, Star Colonel. They gave me medical aid, and left me here."

"They judged you unworthy to be made a Ghost Bear," Radick said, leaning even closer to Kevin Carns.

Carns was shaken, but seemed to draw from some reserve of energy, and his voice rang with passion. "She, this Angela Bekker, told me that normally she would have made me a bondsman. Star Commander Tseng said that I fought with honor. She said she was leaving me behind for a reason."

"And that is?" Jergan pressed.

"To deliver a message to you, Star Colonel." Carns licked his lips, blinking under Radick's glare.

"And that message?"

"She said that we have already lost to her. She led us here, and beat us here. She said to tell you that she controlled you, just as she did the day we landed here. She told me to say that we can withdraw now, and save our honor. If we press her in this Trial, you will share my fate."

Dirk Radick said nothing for a moment. Then, without warning, he struck Carns in the face with a slap that nearly knocked the younger warrior off the stump. The canteen flew from Carns' hands, and its contents gurgled onto the grass. Kevin Carns bore the attack, too dishonored to do anything more.

The audacity! Radick spun to face Jergan. "You see her strategy in motion now, do you not?"

Jergan nodded. "The Ghost Bears think to wear us down, drain us logistically, weaken us, then destroy us."

Radick's eyes flared wide for a second. "What is our expendables and repair parts status?"

Jergan pulled a small datapad from the thigh pocket of her jumpsuit and punched several of the controls. "We are almost out of missile and autocannon ammunition. We have some armor repair plating and myomer repair kits, but in terms of critical systems parts, we are almost bone dry after the refit of Aggressor Star." Star Commander Jergan looked about, and from her expression, matters were now made worse by the demise of Slasher Star.

"Her strategy will fail," Radick growled.

"Aye, Star Colonel," Jergan said carefully, obviously trying not to further ignite his anger. "To defeat her, we will have to keep our remaining forces under tighter control, operating much closer together so that we can concentrate rapidly when engaged."

"Not only that," Radick said. "We have to send our people out to try and locate her base. Locate that base of operations and we can inflict the same logistical damage on the Bears that they are trying to inflict on us."

"That could be a problem," Jergan said. "What if she is using multiple supply bases?"

Again Radick's eyes opened wide, if only for a second. "If that is the case, we can take them from her piecemeal and use them to refit ourselves." He stepped back, casting an angry glance at Kevin Carns, then at Jergan. "Twice now she has lured us into a fight on ground of her choosing. The first time, we were fortunate to have two Stars in position and so forced her from that ground. This time we were not. Pass this to all of the warriors. When we engage the Ghost Bears again, pursuit must be accomplished carefully. Make sure they scan the terrain, and do not take the most obvious approach to engage the enemy. Doing so will avoid her entrapments and her plans."

"Aye, Star Colonel," Jergan said.

Radick glared down at Kevin Carns again. "And get these remains of a warrior out of my sight. If we lose this Trial, he will be nothing more than a member of the dark caste, a mere bandit. Anyone not worthy of serving as a Ghost Bear bondsman is unworthy of being a Wolf." He had chosen his words carefully. Being removed from the warrior caste was a fate worse than death for a warrior. It was a path of no return. Radick's threat had been genuine, aimed at sending out the word so that the rest of his command would understand what would happen to those who failed.

As Patton Ward led the wounded Kevin Carns away, Jergan moved closer to her commanding officer and spoke in a low voice that no one else could hear. "Star Colonel, I understand what you are doing and why you say what you do, but sometimes, our warriors, they do not. Most are fanatically loyal to you, others see you as the next Khan of our Clan. When you berate them, you risk losing their support."

Radick shook his head. "How they feel about me is not important. Let them know fear. I see it in your eyes now and then, Jergan. Not just of the Ghost Bears, but fear of me. Fear alone is the greatest motivator ever devised. And I will use any weapon at my disposal to win this Trial."

20

Near the Rapidan River
Toffen
Ghost Bear Dominion
1 April 3062

From her position standing on a huge boulder at the top of the hill, Angela Bekker surveyed the bend in the river down below. The Rapidan was a fairly fast-moving river, almost eighty meters across and deep and treacherous enough to make crossing in a Battle-Mech as dangerous as it would be slow. On the far side of the river, her Command Star was in position, having crossed via a series of fords further upriver. They were moving along the high buffs, locating the appropriate terrain, positioning themselves for combat.

Her *Executioner* was only a few meters away from where she stood, its shadow stretching back toward the thick forest. She liked the terrain here. It was good for the type of operation she was planning. Not perfect, but as good as any for another damaging attack on the

Wolves who had dared to desecrate Toffen. Performed properly, this operation could again inflict more damage and wear the Wolves down further.

Angela looked back at her *Executioner* almost longingly. It was a war machine not a home, but it often served as one for her. It was an extension of her, and thus far in this campaign, it had been spared the damage of battle. She looked past the BattleMech and up at the sky. Her HPG message regarding the Wolf attempt to take Toffen must have reached her commanders by now, perhaps even the Khan himself. Would they send additional troops, and if so, when?

Angela glanced down and saw Constant Tseng standing on the ground with arms crossed, waiting for her to notice him. She climbed down the gray stone, kicking up dust on the way. "It is as good a place as any," she said, jumping down next to Tseng.

He nodded. "Crossing the river at the crook is impossible. Anything on this side with the Wolves will be trapped, or so it would appear."

She gave him a slight smile. "I refuse to underestimate Dirk Radick. From what we know of him, he is ruthless, but not stupid. Two times now I have lured his forces in and damaged them, the last time seriously. He will not want to fall into the same trap again."

"I agree, but the terrain will work against him here," Tseng said. "He can try and skirt the flanks thinking he has avoided our ambush, only to find that he is equally as trapped."

"I should be satisfied that he believes he is defeating my plan, then?"

"Aye. His warrior's instinct will work against him. As we have found, disengaging from a battle is more difficult than starting one."

Angela checked her wrist chronometer and then

glanced over at her *Executioner.* "I received a report from Stone," she said. "His Star has determined that the Wolves are leaving only a handful of their most damaged BattleMechs at the fort for its defense. Their patrols have been limited as of late and have kept close to their base of operations. Their Command Star is headed this way, however, patrolling along the river banks. In a day or so, we will be facing them."

Tseng nodded. "This tells us something. They are not as bold as when they landed. Some of their forces cannot be fully repaired. We are most likely pressing their reserves of parts and expendables to the breaking point."

"Perhaps," she said. "Again, I refuse to underestimate Dirk Radick. His Blood Drinkers are known as some of the best of Clan Wolf. For all we know, he is aware of Stone shadowing him, and is making him believe he is seeing what we want to see." The thought brought a shiver that raised goose bumps all down her arms.

"What is our status?"

"Sorrenteno is still under the care of our doctor. Chief Technician Luray has managed to get the isorla *Summoner* mostly operational. We still have ample supplies of ammunition and parts. Though Sweep Star is operating at roughly half efficiency, having Stone back in the field again has been a boost for morale."

"Have you chosen yet who will lead the upcoming attack?" Tseng asked.

"We have several 'Mechs and warriors who fit the mission specifications for this side of the river," she said. "Gregori and his *Grizzly,* Kate and her *Mist Lynx* come to mind."

"And," Tseng said, "Bethany's *Nova* also happens to fit the operational parameters."

"We only need two warriors for this, and Kate is with

Sweep Star at present," Angela said with a slight shrug. "That leaves us with Bethany and Gregori."

"Together?" Tseng chuckled. "That is something that could be, for lack of a better word, unstable."

"Perhaps a better word would be 'entertaining,' " she countered. "You helped me develop this plan, Star Commander. We need two 'Mechs that fit the mission specs, and they are the only two available."

"We are taking a risk by making unstable elements key parts of this plan," Tseng said.

Angela was unshaken. "War is comprised of unstable elements, Star Commander. I have faith in these two. But do not think for a moment that I will not be monitoring them."

"I will inform Gregori and have him report here in the next two hours or so," Tseng said. "I will meet you on the far side of the river."

"Very good," Angela said, casting another glance back toward the river. "Inform him, as I will Bethany, that they are being called together for a reason, and not to kill each other. Save something for the Wolves."

"I hate you," Bethany cursed into her neuro-helmet mike.

"And I have nothing but love for you, trueborn," Gregori replied.

"Our Star Captain must hate my very soul to post me with you," she muttered.

"What a terrible thing to say," Gregori taunted. "What will our children say?"

The idea of a trueborn bearing children was not just insulting, but disgusting to a trueborn warrior. The Clan genetics program was designed to create an engineered, superior breed of warrior. Random breeding—which was how free births were created—was looked down upon and considered taboo. Future generations of Ghost Bears came from the genes of the best warriors, mixed together carefully by the members of the scientist caste. Gregori's hinting that the two of them might procreate was a shot as well placed as a missile barrage. Bethany's temper flared hot and hard. She powered her weapons pods, swinging her stumpy *Nova* around to face Gregori's towering *Grizzly*. "One more insult, Gregori, and I will take care of you myself."

"And face the Wolves alone?"

"Aye," she said. "I would rather face them than listen to your drivel."

Suddenly their comm systems hissed to life as someone overrode their conversation. "This is Star Captain Bekker. I have been monitoring your communications. You two act like surats in heat. Both of you, kill the chatter or you will answer to me in a Circle of Equals."

"Understood, Star Captain," Gregori said.

"Aye," Bethany returned. "But when this is over, Star Captain, I ask that you let me teach this freebirth the meaning of honor."

"This is proving to be even more fun that I thought," Gregori mocked.

Angela wanted to make sure they knew that the time for bickering was over. "If we survive this, you two have my permission to beat each other to death. But for now, back to your stations, watch your sensors, and be ready to engage the Wolves," she commanded.

Angela stood in the dark, surveying the same hill where she had stood earlier in the day from the opposite bank of the river, high on the rocky buffs overlooking the rippling waters of the Rapidan below. Using her electronic binoculars, she saw the faint electromagnetic signatures just over the rise where the two 'Mechs were poised. On the hillside, near the rock where she had been earlier, they would stand out for any Wolf Clan 'Mechs that happened to be in the area. Two hours had passed since she had been forced to referee her two warriors. A fire burned in both their souls. If they could only channel it, what havoc they could wreak against the enemy.

She sensed someone's presence nearby and lowered the binoculars, turning to see the figure of Neta standing in the darkness, visible only by the small wrist-light she wore. "You crept up on me, Neta," Angela said. For an instant her heart had begun to race that someone could get so close without her noticing.

"I am sorry to startle you, Star Captain," Neta said softly. "I brought you some juice. It is not so cold, but quenching." She held out a small cup, which Angela took and sipped from.

There was something about Neta. Angela had felt it when they had first met, but more so after Neta had predicted the arrival of the Wolves. All her life she had heard jokes about the soothsaying of the Nova Cats. Now that she had experienced it firsthand, Angela found herself in awe. "I am surprised that you are still awake. Tomorrow may prove to be a busy day for us."

Neta nodded once slowly. "Tomorrow *will* be a busy day for us," she said with full confidence. "I went to sleep two hours ago, but I awoke. I felt the need to come to you."

Angela felt a shiver run down her spine. "Is something bothering you, Neta?"

"Neg, Star Captain. But something is bothering you—the decision to put Gregori and Bethany out there together."

Angela raised her eyebrows. "I would be lying if I said I did not have my reservations."

"No need, Star Captain. You have made the right choice," Neta said calmly.

"You saw something in your dreams, Neta?"

"Aye, Star Captain."

"Can you tell me more?"

"Sometimes getting a glimpse into the future is as much a curse as a blessing. I just have a feeling, that is all."

"I wish I shared your calm," Angela said.

"Remember, Star Captain," Neta said, "it is fire that forges iron into steel. No fire burns brighter than the fire of battle." Before Angela could press her further, Neta turned and slipped back into the darkness.

For the first time in hours, Angela knew that finally she would be able to sleep.

=== 21 ===

Near the Rapidan River
Toffen
Ghost Bear Dominion
2 April 3062

Gregori surveyed the hillside for at least the four-hundredth time since the sun came up. Thus far there had been no sign of the Wolves, but he knew they were near. His only company was a silent communications channel and a fellow warrior who would be just as happy as any Wolf to kill him. Bethany had taken a position almost a hundred meters in front of him, further down the hillside toward the river. Her stout, short-legged *Nova* was facing away from him, toward the far end of the forest that covered much of the slope. In the direction from which the Wolves would come.

Ever since the dressing down from Star Captain Bekker, Gregori had held his tongue with Bethany—a task he found far from easy. It wasn't that he hated her. If anything, irritating her provided him with much entertainment. What he did hate was her contempt toward his status as a freeborn warrior. It was the same feeling that had cost him more than his share of promotions, standing as almost a record among the Ghost Bears.

That was what made this fight personal. When they had received the codex information on the warriors the Wolves had bid, Gregori understood the true nature of the enemy. The Blood Drinkers and their Star Colonel were insidious in their dealings with freeborn warriors. They did not try to capture and make them bondsmen. In fact, they would rather kill a freeborn savagely than ever have to deal with one as a peer. Radick had built his and his unit's reputation on this ruthlessness. If Gregori failed against them, he knew his fate was death.

His *Grizzly* was a second-line 'Mech, a far cry from the refittable and modular OmniMechs that most trueborns piloted. He did not mind. At seventy tons, the *Grizzly* was geared for long-range combat with a deadly gauss rifle, three pulse lasers of various sizes, and a ten-pack of long-range missiles. He scanned the area, adjusting the filter controls on his long-range sensors, and in response got an audible alert in the earpieces of his neurohelmet. Glancing down at the readout, he saw several unidentified targets, all moving toward them.

"Bethany, confirm my readings," he radioed.

"Of course I confirm," she said. "I show four 'Mechs approaching."

"Make that five," he countered. "They will be in visual range in a minute or two."

Bethany did not wait. "Command One, this is Command Two. I have one Wolf Star closing on us from the south."

Star Captain Bekker's voice came through clear and crisp. "Does Striker Two confirm?"

Gregori heart raced with excitement. "Aye, Star Captain."

"Stick to the plan," Bekker admonished. "Get them on the hill leading down to the river, and we will take care of the rest."

Gregori cracked his knuckles, then wrapped his fingers around the firing joystick and the throttle controls. All around him the *Grizzly* seemed to come to life. The low hum of the gyro some four meters under his cockpit, the throbbing of the fusion reactor—now revved to full power. Yes, this was going to be a dangerous fight, but he intended to survive it.

"Contact!" Bethany yelled out. A Wolf 'Mech emerged from the light forest, a *Stormcrow* sweeping toward her *Nova* with clear intent. Its arms were elevated and bent, as was the norm for the *Stormcrow,* giving it an odd appearance as it brushed against the lower limbs of some of the trees. Bethany swung her arms to fire, but Gregori swung faster. Even as he heard the sound of the target lock, he let go with his gauss rifle and long-range missile rack. At the same moment, the *Stormcrow* let loose with its weapons, firing at the closer 'Mech with its autocannon. Somewhere, in the middle of the barrage, Bethany had opened up with half of her deadly wall of lasers as well. In the distance, Gregori saw a *Warhawk* and an *Executioner* move forward, both ready for battle as well.

The moment he and Bethany had fired at the same 'Mech, regardless of timing, freed the enemy from the constraints of the Clan's formal rules of engagement and turned it into a free-for-all. "You idiot," Bethany screamed as the *Stormcrow* rocked back under the assault.

"Too late for debate," Gregori stammered out as he triggered another of burst of his weapons.

The silvery slug fired from his *Grizzly*'s magnetically

charged gauss rifle slammed with full fury into the *Stormcrow*'s side, shooting armor plating into the air just in time for his missile salvo to arrive. The white trails of the long-range missiles spiraled in and around the Wolf 'Mech, hitting the cockpit and center torso, and sending up a series of gray and black explosions as they pummeled the armor plating there. Bethany's wall of horrific laser fire laced the smoke and hit the legs and lower waist of the oddly shaped OmniMech, though the smoke kept Gregori from seeing what damage had been done. Most of the Wolf's attack had hit Bethany's right side, where the armor was blasted away.

The *Warhawk* brought its weapons to bear on Bethany, its large lasers and long-range missiles creating a barrage of light and death. The large laser beams raked her right torso and weapons pod/arm. The squat *Nova* reeled back under the assault as the missile salvo hit her in almost every location save the cockpit.

"Bethany!" Gregori barked. "We've got to get out of here."

She did not respond but fired another blast into the *Stormcrow,* this time with all of her lasers. The *Nova* packed a deadly wallop, twelve extended-range medium lasers. When fired all at once, they could rip almost any BattleMech apart. The cost to the *Nova* pilot, however, was a wave of heat that would be unbearable, one that might start shutting down systems or injure the warrior.

She must be toasting, Gregori thought as he watched the lasers hit the *Stormcrow.* The emerald bursts of destruction raked the Wolf 'Mech with such force that it quaked visibly, armor evaporating and blasting off in every direction. Some of the shots found their marks in the 'Mech's internal structure, burrowing deep like worms, spilling out sick green coolant from blackened holes.

The *Stormcrow* teetered back a step or two as the *Executioner* and the *Warhawk* moved all too slowly toward the wide flanks of the light woods on the hill. It should be falling, Gregori thought. Even the best pilot lost control when a 'Mech suffered that much damage, but somehow the Wolf pilot was staying upright and operational. For a moment, Gregori realized just how good the Blood Drinkers were, and what risks they were taking. The other Wolf BattleMechs also fanned out, taking the line of enemies even wider. They were not advancing wildly, apparently having learned something from their last two encounters. Gregori did not like that at all, and the pounding of his heart drummed faster in his ears.

To show that it was not dead, the *Stormcrow* let loose a blast from its long- and short-range missiles, raking the area where Bethany's *Nova* stood, nearly immobile from its heat-spiking barrage. For a moment it was bathed in smoke, shrapnel, debris, and the orange flashes of explosions. Armor plating was shredded, as was the ground around her from the missed shots, the sod cratered with little mushroom clouds as the warheads went off.

"Bethany, pull out now!" he commanded as her 'Mech reeled under the impacts.

"Neg, that *Stormcrow* must drop first," she hissed.

He was tempted to leave her, but he understood exactly how she felt. Bethany would not move until the Wolf 'Mech was destroyed. Instead of waiting, or rushing to her side, he swung his own gauss rifle on the staggering *Stormcrow*. The targeting reticle of the tracking system toned in his ears as he locked onto the center of the oddly formed 'Mech. It made a perfect target with its arms held upright, forming an "X" in his targeting and tracking system. He triggered the weapon and felt the tug as the silvery rifle slug zipped at supersonic speed into the heart of the Wolf 'Mech. He did not see the damage it did. Instead he saw the *Stormcrow* tip backward under the force of the hit, its torso seeming to collapse in on itself as if its spine and ribs had shattered under the impact.

He heard a howl over his headset, the deafening sound of Bethany wailing in anger and frustration. The *Executioner* let loose with its long-range missiles at Gregori, drowning out her complaint under the roar of the impacts. The missiles hit his left side, ripping apart armor on his arm, leg, and torso as he began to back up the hill toward the crest. Bethany's *Nova* turned just in time to catch only a partial attack from the *Warhawk*, her torso armor mangled by the electrical arcing of the charged particle blast. She lumbered slowly, still bleeding off her heat, moving diagonally up the hillside, bellowing as she moved. Ripples of heat exhaust rose from her sink vents as she moved.

"You surat spawned freebirth suckling idiot!" she cursed. "That kill was mine!"

Gregori held off rebutting until he reached the top of the hill. "Nothing but love for you as well, Bethany, but we've got to get out of here." Swinging his 'Mech around, he fired his large pulse laser at the *Warhawk* to buy her some time. He took a hull-down position, hitting the *Warhawk* hard with a stream of laser fire that stitched along the leg, melting armor plates with each hit.

As soon as he was out of line of sight, Gregori swung down the hillside toward the bend in the river and broke his *Grizzly* into a full sprint. He watched his tactical display as Bethany rounded the hill, an orange blossom of explosion following her as she too began to race down the hillside. The *Warhawk* was the first to reach the top of the hill, just as he turned to face it. The Wolf pilot returned Gregori's previous attack with an immediate burst from its particle projection cannons.

The PPCs sent their man-made lightning ripping toward him as if Zeus himself was hurling the bolts of lightning. One struck his right torso, the other slammed into the left. He was tossed forward in the command couch as his *Grizzly* jerked back hard under the hit. A spike of static electricity in his cockpit made his hair stand on end for just an instant, and he tried to compensate for the sudden loss of over a ton of armor plating in the assault. Through clenched teeth and narrowed eyes, he kept his focus on the *Warhawk* even as he saw the *Executioner* and a *Dire Wolf* still moving for flanking positions on either side of the hill.

Bethany stopped some forty meters away, turning and firing half of her ER lasers up the hillside at the *Executioner*, wrenching away armor plating but otherwise not doing much damage. The situation on the tactical display was not good. Behind them was the swift-running Rapidan River, too deep and fast to cross. In front of them, on the high ground, moving to the flanks, were four Wolf 'Mechs, each one slowly, almost methodically descending the hill toward them.

His gauss rifle recycled another round, and he heard the audible metallic snap of the long-range missiles completing their loading. A maroon and sand-brown spotted *Hellbringer* came along the low side of the hill near the *Executioner* as the Wolf forces moved in for the kill. Gregori had been in many battles in his life, but he had never felt like he did right now. It was a sick feeling, one that rose like bile from the pit of his stomach. A feeling of helplessness. Still locked on the *Warhawk,* he let go with a blast of his long-range missiles and gauss rifle again.

Not without a fight . . .

22

Near the Rapidan River
Toffen
Ghost Bear Dominion
2 April 3062

Angela watched from her cockpit, heart pounding. The bend in the river thrust toward the high bluffs where she and the rest of the Command Star were poised. Down on the opposite bank, Gregori and Bethany, their backs to her, unleashed a punishing salvo at the Wolves descending the hill. In a wide line of battle, most of her unit's fire poured into a *Warhawk* and an *Executioner* that were very slowly moving down either side of the hill, assuming flanking positions.

She knew her warriors would not last long. Worse, from the way the two Wolves had poured their fire into Gregori, it was obvious that the time-honored rules of engagement had somehow been breached in the twists and turns of battle. Gregori's bulky *Grizzly* was bathed in explosions, turning as if to shake off the attack, when in fact he was shaking off over a ton of his protective armor. Time was running out for them, unless she acted. She had hoped the Wolves would rush forward, get a little closer than this. Dirk Radick had become cautious. He was adapting.

"Command Two and Striker Two, pull back," she barked. With their backs to the swift and deep Rapidan River, such a retreat would normally be out of the question, disastrous for even the best warrior. Then Angela saw the flanking maneuver of the Wolf *Hellbringer* moving along the hill. It unleashed a vicious attack against Bethany's *Nova*, which had lost far too much armor to stay in the fight.

"Command Star, attack at long range as soon as they light up," she ordered. Suddenly her seemingly trapped 'Mechs lit their jump jets and rose into the air, turning and lofting across the rushing water as missiles and lasers swept the air in a vain effort to drop them.

Angela had chosen Gregori and Bethany for this action more for the capabilities of their BattleMechs than for their warrior skills, just as she had chosen the location because she knew that the only jump-capable 'Mech the Wolves had was Dirk Radick's *Executioner*. When her 'Mechs cleared the river on their jump jets, she doubted that not even Radick would dare to jump across the river alone.

As they cleared the river, Angela took her Executioner forward from the rock outcropping that had protected it and dropped her targeting reticle on the Wolf *Hellbringer* that was rushing down the riverbank to fire off another shot at Bethany. The rest of her Star also advanced from their hiding places, drew their targets, and triggered their long-range weapons at the Blood Drinkers.

Her gauss rifle let go its polished slug at supersonic

velocity, while her extended-range large lasers swung on line and pumped a microjoule of energy into their pre-heat sequence. Her aim with the gauss rifle was good, its half-meter titanium sphere hitting the *Hellbringer* in the left arm. The limb was bent back as if broken, twisting the entire 'Mech under the savage impact. The arm was still attached, but there was no armor on it, and sparks snapped and crackled from its damaged shoulder actuator.

Attacks rang down from her high ground overlooking the river and the opposite long, sloping bank. Sprange in his *Timber Wolf* had switched out weapons pods so that he too was armed with long-range weapons. His own gauss rifle round missed the *Dire Wolf* that fired back at Bethany on the low ground near the opposite bank. His large pulse laser stitched a series of armor pits across the chest of the Wolf while his long-range missiles plowed into the legs of the massive 'Mech, denting and ripping the protection. Angela's large lasers missed their target by a mere meter, but her forces were scoring numerous hits along the hillside. The *Warhawk* stopped its advance under the impact of Neta's extended-range PPCs. One missed its mark, searing the grass next to the 'Mech into a circle of black; the other bright blue electrical burst exploded at the left knee joint of the Wolf machine.

The Wolf *Executioner* on the far shore fired at Gregori's *Grizzly* as it made its way slowly up the bluffs, mangling leg armor enough that Gregori lost his balance and dropped face-first against the muddy hillside with a ground-shaking thud. Breedfelt's *Kodiak* stayed near the top of Angela's hill, using its only long-range weapon, a large laser, to fire down at the *Hellbringer* she had already hit.

Moving instinctively, she switched her gauss rifle

and large lasers to the same target interlock circuit and targeted the *Dire Wolf* that had stopped in place on the opposite hillside. The pilot of the *Dire Wolf* let loose a barrage that shot past her to where Breedfelt stood at the top of the hill. She locked onto the *Dire Wolf's* center torso and triggered all three of her weapons, which bathed her cockpit in a wash of warm air as the weapons churned out their deadly dessert. One laser missed, but another struck at the heart of the *Dire Wolf*, right below where the gauss rifle had gored it. The *Hellbringer* had contorted under the impact of her assault, but the *Dire Wolf* seemed to merely shrug it off. Its front armor plating was further scarred by Bethany as she backed up the hill, her medium lasers doing their work before she got out of range.

The *Hellbringer* hung into the battle despite the mauling of its left weapons pod, which still sparked from the damage. It swept its good right arm into line with Breedfelt's *Kodiak* and fired. The lightning blast slammed up the hillside, and Angela saw on her display that the massive *Kodiak* took a deep and penetrating hit in its right leg.

The PPC blasts lit up the hillside as the *Warhawk* joined in, bringing Neta into line. Her *Kingfisher* rocked back near where Angela stood as one of the shots tore off a large portion of the armor on her chest. The other shot missed short, sending a blast of rocks, dirt, and tree roots spinning down the hillside to where Gregori still struggled. The thin wisps of smoke from the weapons of war filled the air like a low-hanging fog.

Dirk Radick's *Executioner* fired its large lasers, lancing blood-red into Bethany's *Nova* as if to stab the squat 'Mech to death. Angela did not have a view of Bethany, but her secondary display showed that the legs of Bethany's 'Mech had lost all their armor and that one of her weapons pods was either shot off, blown up, on fire, or simply hanging in place. The heat Bethany was giving off revealed that she had either taken a hit to her fusion reactor shielding or had lost several heat sinks. Either way, Angela felt in the pit of her stomach that Bethany was not long for the battle.

And the Blood Drinkers guaranteed that.

The *Warhawk* snapped off a shot at Bethany with one of its PPCs, the azure beam searing into her 'Mech's already weakened legs. Then Angela saw a series of explosions from the spot on the hill where the *Nova* had been, though her vision was somewhat obscured by the rocks and the smoke of battle. Checking her tactical display, she saw that the *Nova's* fusion reactor was off-line. She bit her lower lip and moved forward slightly on the hill, deprived of the attack she wanted to make by the distance and the river that she used to her own defense. *Do not die, Bethany. I savor the revenge you will take on these Wolves.*

Gregori fought gavity and mud to bring his *Grizzly* to its knees, then to a standing position as missiles cratered the hill around him, missiles from the Wolf *Executioner*. Angela turned to face that 'Mech, knowing full well who was at the controls. Then, without warning, the Wolf *Executioner* pivoted precisely in place and began to move back around the hill.

She fired, but only her lasers were recharged as she thumbed the target interlock on the joystick. Of the two lasers, only one made its mark, slagging the armor off the leg of Radick's 'Mech, which left behind melted globs of armor in its deep footprints on the hillside. He turned at the torso to face her, long enough to let go a wave of missiles in her direction. She saw them coming, but there was nothing she could do to avoid them. Most hit her right-side leg and torso, and her *Execu-*

tioner groaned slightly under the impacts. Then, Dirk Radick turned and simply walked away, rounding the hillside and moving out of sight.

Angela did not need her sensors to see what was happening. The Wolves were withdrawing. The *Warhawk* backed up the hill, firing its PPCs to cover the *Hellbringer*, which was closest to the river. The *Dire Wolf* also retreated along the flank of the hill, taking hits from Breedfelt and Neta as it went, almost dropping under the force of the attack. From the wisps of white smoke belching upward, it was obvious that the Wolf 'Mech had lost a heat sink in its left torso.

The *Dire Wolf* was not out of the fight and, like a true Clan warrior, let Angela know it. Locking onto Sprange, the 'Mech unleashed a horrible blast with its three large pulse lasers and gauss rifle. Sprange's *Timber Wolf* caught the gauss slug in the torso with a crunching sound that Angela heard even in her sealed cockpit dozens of meters away. The grinding and moaning of the metal sounded like bones breaking, and she winced in sympathy. The lasers raked the hillside, some of the small bursts missing her old friend, but others hitting his legs and grating armor plating into small, worthless bits of metallic souvenirs.

The *Hellbringer* was too close to Angela's Stalking Bears to hope to withdraw in good order, no matter what the *Warhawk* did to try and draw fire. Sprange locked onto it and fired his gauss rifle and long-range missiles. This time fate was with him. The gauss rifle slug, a mere blur in the air, hit the Wolf 'Mech's center torso, and its chest seemed to cave in. The missiles followed two instants later, their wispy smoke trails spinning and weaving around each other as they flew. The *Hellbringer* leveled its weapon just as the warheads exploded, hitting the cockpit canopy and the gaping hole from the gauss rifle impact. Explosions went off inside the sixty-five-ton 'Mech, the flames roaring skyward from the hole in its chest as it fell onto its side, half-splashing into the river and the soft sand on the embankment.

Neta squeezed off the final shot of the battle at the *Dire Wolf*. As if cursed, one of her twin PPCs again missed its mark, but the other slammed into the massive right thigh of the behemoth, snapping and popping off armor plating as it scored its target with arcs of electrical discharge. Then, silently, it moved out of her line of sight, along with all the rest of the Wolves.

Angela checked her secondary short-range display, surveying her forces. Feedback signals from Gregori's 'Mech showed that it was seriously damaged, but still operational. Bethany's *Nova* was down, and even now Angela was sure that at least one of her warriors was attempting to pry Bethany from the wreckage that had been her 'Mech. Sprange's *Timber Wolf* looked much worse than her sensor readout indicated. Though it had suffered mostly armor damage, the *Timber Wolf* looked like it had waded through the mill-tailings of hell itself. Breedfelt's damage was minor. Her own *Executioner* had taken some damage, but she would have been ready to press the fight—if that had been the plan.

It wasn't.

The plan had been the same from the start. Injure the Wolves, bloody them, and withdraw. She had chosen this location because she knew that only one of the enemy 'Mechs could not follow her jump-jet equipped force across the river. She and her team, along with Chief Tech Luray, had made sure that their weapons pods were geared for long-range combat except for the bait—Bethany and Gregori.

Several things had not gone according to plan, but

such were the vagaries of battle. She had hoped that Dirk Radick's forces would have rushed forward more aggressively, giving her long-range fire more time to do more damage. She had also been unprepared for Dirk Radick to withdraw his forces. Good as he was, however, two of his BattleMechs were destroyed and the others had suffered damage the Wolves could not repair.

She was preparing to hit the transmit button and give orders to her Star, when a voice came over the broadband channel. She saw the frequency lit on her comm panel and knew that all of her Stalking Bears would hear what came next. She also knew who was signaling even before she heard the voice. "Star Captain Angela Bekker of the Ghost Bears, this is Star Colonel Dirk Radick of the Wolves."

"Yes, Star Colonel. I assume you are signaling to bring an end to this Trial?"

There was a slight pause. "Yes, Star Captain. I am. Such battles, hiding behind a river and so on, are unworthy of the honor for which the Ghost Bears are known. Rather than fight like Inner Sphere scum, let us put an end to this. Name the location and I will bring my forces, you yours, and in a matter of minutes, your unit's ordeal can be over."

Angela was not sure what was behind this. Perhaps the Wolves had been hurt worse than she saw. Or, perhaps Radick was trying to mislead her. Either way her answer would have been the same. "I appreciate your concern for my honor, but by choosing this venue for our fight, I have lost no honor. You, however, have lost much today."

She eyed the ruined remains of the *Hellbringer*, and the smoke rising from the other side of the hill told her that the *Stormcrow* she had never seen was never going to take part in battle again.

"You underestimate our capabilities, Bear," Radick said coldly.

Angela was sure he was bluffing, trying to make her think he was less damaged than she thought. "And you underestimate our determination, Wolf," she replied.

"Neg. I know this much, though. When I am done, you will be my bondsman, and the trueborns in your command will be driven from the warrior caste, ending up as filthy bandits. You have seen my codex, so you know what will happen to your freebirths. Do them all a favor, Star Captain, and yourself. End these nights of sleeping in the forests and creeping about like vermin. Come and face me like a real warrior."

His taunts told her much. "Neg, Star Colonel Radick. Crawl back to your base, but watch your back. Remember, I still have forces out there that might make your trip to the fort less comfortable than you might imagine." She cut off the signal, ending their public conversation. It was a partial bluff. Only Sweep Star was in the area, and they were under order to shadow the Wolves, taking on their stragglers as targets of opportunity on the journey back to Fort DelVillar. Angela knew that despite Radick's bravado, he would be looking behind every rock, every tree, searching and bracing for an attack that might never come.

For now, her own people were waiting for her, listening for her next word. Switching to her Star's frequency, Angela smiled broadly inside her neurohelmet. "Breedfelt, signal Doctor Drogan to send in his team. The rest of you Stalking Bears, let us fall back by the numbers and get something the Wolves cannot—repaired and refitted."

23

Fort DelVillar
Toffen
Ghost Bear Dominion
19 April 3062

Dirk Radick strode toward the gate of Fort DelVillar, not hiding his anger. At his heels was Star Commander Jergan, attempting to match his pace if not his fury. Gone was the eager expression she had worn at the start of the Trial of Possession for Toffen. Her eyes had dark rings under them. Her hair was shaggy and untrimmed. Her uniform was faded and stained. Replacements would have to come when the Trial—no, the campaign, was over.

Coming through the gates were the remains of Star Commander Biffly's command. The 'Mechs seemed sluggish, as exhausted as the warriors at their controls. There were only two of them, mere shadows of the war machines they had been upon first coming to Toffen.

The spotted brown and green camouflage painted on

the lone *Mist Lynx* was only visible in a few places. The rest was flat gray replacement armor, where armor existed at all. Its legs were totally without armor, and all that was left of one arm were a few myomer strands dangling like shredded muscle. A massive rent in its chest showed a glimmer of silver. The gauss slug that had gouged the hole was wedged into the 'Mech's internal structure so deeply that Jergan doubted the techs could remove it with the gear they had.

The other surviving 'Mech was an *Ice Ferret*, though the word "surviving" was questionable in this case. One of its arms was no longer operational. The extended-range PPC barrel was so twisted that it would never again be more than scrap metal. The short-range missile launcher in the other arm looked functional, but the ammunition had exploded, shredding the armor from the inside out in a blossom-like pattern. Laser scars ran from the 'Mech's chest to the cockpit. Trailing vines from its trek in the forest, the *Ferret*'s cockpit glass had been blasted out, yet somehow the pilot had managed to survive. Jergan came up next to Dirk Radick at the feet of the Battle Mechs and noticed a puddle of green coolant oozing onto the ferrocrete around the *Ferret*. The pilots of those 'Mechs wearily climbed down to join their commanding officers.

"So, this is what is left of the Aggressor Star?" Radick snapped when the two warriors walked up to him and saluted. One of them, Drew, had her head wrapped in a field dressing, and the burns on her arms would surely leave her scarred for life.

The warriors said nothing but remained standing at attention. There was not much to say, especially given the mood of the Star Colonel. It had all begun when Star Commander Biffly Ward had gone out to raid one of the Ghost Bear supply dumps, traced by a seemingly accidental transmission. Though the details of the fiasco were not known, one of the survivors, Vaul, had signaled Fort DelVillar to tell them that Biffly was dead and that the rest had barely survived an ambush by the Ghost Bears. All that remained was to get the details of their losses. The details of defeat.

"What about the Bear's supplies, Drew?" Radick ranted. Biffly and his battered Star had carefully monitored the enemy's radio signals and tracked them to their source. The mission should have been fast and easy, a swift strike. Seize the much-needed supplies, and withdraw.

"We were able to locate what we thought was their base. Everything of value had already been removed, sir," she said, still at attention despite her wounds. "Star Commander Biffly had us check out some crates sitting there, and we found a small transmitter on a trip-wire. The Bears knew we were there. They were already attacking while we were still running for our 'Mechs."

"How did Biffly die?" Jergan asked. Biffly Ward had served under her for over a year. He had a talent for strategy, though she had never much cared for him personally.

Vaul answered, his voice almost mournful. "He died with little honor, at least not the kind of honor he would have hoped for. They came at us with a *Viper* at first, then a *Mist Lynx*. Their Elementals were hidden in the tree tops and dropped right on top of us. Star Commander Biffly fired at the *Mist Lynx*, but one of his shots winged an Elemental. It was a free-for-all by the time we reached our cockpits. The Elementals tore his *Mad Dog* apart while the *Viper* fired at us. The *Mist Lynx* finished him off at point-blank range."

The loss of a warrior seemed not to affect Radick at all. "And then you let the Ghost Bears get away?"

Vaul was obviously offended by the comment, but did not dare rebut. He cast a fast glance at Jergan in hopes that she might take his defense, but that was not to be. Jergan had seen Dirk Radick in this kind of mood often enough to know that he was, at the moment, beyond logic and reason. Vaul returned his gaze to Radick. "We did not retreat, Star Colonel. We fought. Once they knew they had hurt us enough, they retreated."

"Did you at least hurt them back?"

Vaul's eyes narrowed. "We did. The *Viper* took considerable damage, and we injured two of their Elementals."

"You let them escape rather than crush them?" Dirk Radick's voice was almost booming with rage.

Despite the risk of adding fuel to the flames, Jergan decided it was time to intervene. "Star Colonel, if he had pursued them, the Bears might have led them into another one of their traps. Vaul's action may have saved what was left of that command."

Dirk Radick spun on his heel to face her, full of fury. This was not the only sniping attack that had occurred since the battle at Rapidan River. In a previous attack the Wolves had taken more damage they could not afford in an exchange of missile and PPC volleys in a narrow mountain pass. Theodore Kerensky's *Adder* had been mangled to the point of being barely operational. Even Radick had suffered damage, but by the time the Wolves rallied, the Stalking Bears had disappeared into a mountain pass. Pursuing them into that terrain was just too risky. Dirk Radick was starting to show signs of the stress all of them were feeling, but in him it came out as fiery anger. "Do not press your luck with me, Star Captain. You will find my mood dark as the night on this hellhole of a planet."

Matters were grim, that much she knew. Her Trinary

of BattleMechs had started out fifteen strong. Now there were only the two mauled 'Mechs from her Aggressor Star, Radick's *Executioner,* Patton Ward's *Dire Wolf,* and her own Warhawk. The *Dire Wolf* was missing almost half of its armor plating, and her *Warhawk* bore more replacement armor than original. Theodore Kerensky's *Adder* had lost one of its weapons pods and all the armor on its legs at the same time. Radick's *Executioner* had also lost a lot of armor and two of its precious heat sinks. Just over a Star was all that was left of her Trinary. And even that was a shadow of its former glory.

Ammunition was another matter she and Radick had pondered seriously only a few hours before, and that situation was just as grim, if not worse. Their stores of expendables were exhausted. What ammunition they did have was divided out among the functional 'Mechs, but that was only a few rounds to each of them. They had configured themselves too heavily with autocannons and missiles. None of them had ever expected this Trial to drag on for weeks.

"I understand how you feel, Star Colonel, but our anger is best channeled against the Ghost Bears," she said in hopes of cooling him off some.

"You must understand, Star Captain, that I am faced with limited options. Given the damage we have taken, the most logical course is to remain here and let the Ghost Bears lay siege to us. But realistically, we only have a week's worth of foodstuffs remaining. Given enough time, they will starve us to death. This Angela Bekker seems content to do just that.

"Or we can go on the offensive and abandon this base. We know, however, that the Ghost Bears have almost two Stars' worth of force to throw against us, and that they have ample supplies and repair capabilities, so that course seems equally futile."

Radick's hopes of convincing Star Captain Bekker to face the Wolves on an open field of combat and end the Trial quickly were long gone. Pressing for such a fight now would leave the Blood Drinkers dead and destroyed in a matter of minutes, no matter what their prowess.

"Which leaves me with an option I had hoped not to employ," he said slowly, his voice dropping off at the end.

Jergan understood. "We can withdraw," she said, but saw the fire start to burn again in his eyes at mention of the word.

"And tell Khan Ward I sent a Trinary of his best troops to their deaths with nothing to show for it? In a Trial of Possession that did not have his blessing. Neg," Radick said.

Jergan nodded. There was more than honor at stake on Toffen. It had become a matter of political as well as military survival.

Radick shook his head almost sadly. "What is left is an action that will cost me honor, but guarantee me victory."

Before she could say anything more, Dirk Radick had turned and was already heading toward the command bunker.

Angela entered the small tent and leaned over the body of the injured Elemental. The air stank with the pungent odor of the Newark swamps, but by now she was used to it. Doctor Drogan threw her a glance that told her the seriousness of the Elemental's wound, and then Angela saw with her own eyes that his right leg was missing from just below the knee down. The Elemental, Krane, was only semi-conscious but seemed to recognize her.

"We succeeded, Star Captain," he said feebly.

"Rest, Krane," she said, giving his massive hand a reassuring squeeze. "Our good doctor will make sure that you continue to serve the Ghost Bears for many years to come."

He nodded and drifted off into a hazy sleep. Angela turned and left the tent, the doctor hot on her heels. "Star Captain Bekker," he said in a demanding tone that, as usual, was ill-suited to a member of the lower castes addressing a superior.

She turned toward him. "What is it, Doctor?"

"He will live if we don't move him for the next few days," Drogan said coldly. "Unless you have other plans."

Again, Angela did not appreciate his tone, but she was more concerned about other matters. "Take care of him, then. We all have our duty, Doctor. That is yours."

"I want you to know . . . I had to perform an amputation on Bethany. The infection on her wounds got worse. We also had to do a last-minute transfusion." His tone was grave.

"Amputation?"

"Yes. Three fingers. Her hand is badly damaged and it will take a lot of therapy before she can handle a 'Mech again."

Angela looked down at her own bionic replacements, and for a few moments her mind was not on Toffen but back in a dimly lit cave on Strana Mechty light years and standard years away. Was the sacrifice worth it?

"When will she be able to pilot a BattleMech again?"

"She has been weakened by the infection. Both she and Krane will serve your Clan again in combat, but not any time soon. Both will need either artificial replacements for the limbs or digits they lost or we will have to bud their wounds and grow them new limbs. Either way, they will not be ready for combat for some time."

"Doctor, I do not tell you how to treat the injured. Do not presume to tell me how to fight another Clan. Perhaps you would like this world to fall into the hands of the Wolves, quiaff?"

He shook his head. "You know I don't want that. But at the same time, I am tired of treating good men and women who are near death. Everyone, yourself included, is starting to show signs of combat fatigue. Most of us are operating on four hours sleep at max, and it's wearing us out, dulling our senses. This madness has to end soon."

His words were cut off by the beeping of her personal communicator. From the readout she could tell that it was a broad-band transmission. "This is Star Captain Bekker," she said, unable to keep the apprehension from her voice.

"Star Colonel Dirk Radick here," came the reply. "I applaud your strategy thus far, Star Captain. You have worn down my Bloodied Wolves Trinary quite effectively. Any other warrior would withdraw at this point, but as you have seen, I am not just any warrior."

"Aye, Star Colonel," she said smoothly.

"In the bidding for this world, I alone executed the bid rather than having my subcommanders do so. While unorthodox, you will find precedents for it in my Clan. As such, I have decided to pull down my last bid or at least a part of it, in order to end this Trial." The gloating of his earlier communications was gone. What was left was bitter determination, the drive to destroy her.

"I am hereby bringing back my last bid, the Mauler Trinary of Star Captain Lark Radick. Normally I would commit the entire Trinary against you, but you have shown yourself to be resourceful. Use of blatant, overpowering force would be wasteful and lack honor. I will remove one of the Stars from the Mauler Trinary and deploy it as a Binary. I do not do this lightly, Star Captain, but out of respect for the honor you have shown thus far. I will send you the data on this unit and, according to the rites of our people, give you time to plan. Though you did not bid any aerospace elements, I am required to formally ask safcon for my Binary's landing in two days' time." His invocation of safcon, safe conduct, ensured that Angela would not attack his DropShip as it tried to touch down. Of course, he was right. She did not have the firepower to do that anyway.

It was his other announcement that hit her like a salvo of missiles. A new Binary! Fresh troops, with ammunition. She felt her energy drain away. She saw the doctor's face go pale as he, too, grasped the implications. "You lose much honor in such an action, Star Colonel," she said.

"Aye," he conceded, with some reluctance. "But in the end, victory is the ultimate honor. You have done well, Angela Bekker. But it is time for this Trial to end."

The commline went dead, leaving nothing more than an evil hiss in its place. Angela closed her eyes and drew a long breath. If she faltered now, everything they had fought for would be lost. She could not let the deaths of her warriors be for naught, not even for the honor of a fight to the finish.

She opened her eyes and activated another frequency. "Star Commanders Stone and Tseng, bring your forces to my coordinates. I want everyone and anyone who can pilot a 'Mech. The time has come for us to finish this fight, one way, or another."

24

Newark Swamps
Toffen
Ghost Bear Dominion
19 April 3062

"So there you have it," Angela said as she shut off the recording of Dirk Radick's message. "Another Binary of fresh Wolf warriors." The Stalking Bears of her command looked as shocked as she felt, but they were silent, waiting for what she would say next, for the words that would decide the fate of Toffen and their lives.

It had taken almost ten hours for them to arrive at the Newark Swamps. Gathered around her were the battered but now seasoned survivors of her command. They were standing on a small, dry hilltop, lit by field lamps her techs had managed to hook up quickly. A handful of her lower caste personnel were also present. Chief Tech Luray was there, covered with so much dirt, lubricant, coolant, and grime that he might never appear human again. Doctor Drogan stood in the back, arms crossed and looking as ornery as ever.

"You have all fought well. In fact, you are some of the finest warriors I have ever had under my command. We have fought and crippled one of the best Star Colonels and units ever bred by Clan Wolf. The Blood Drinkers have years of experience fighting together, but you have brought them to their knees, to the point where they must sacrifice their honor if they hope to take this planet from us."

Angela made sure she met the eyes of each one as she spoke. For what was to follow, she had to be more than a warrior. She held their lives in her hands. She must be more than a commander. She must light in them the fire necessary to win.

"I have considered our options. We can concede this world to the Wolves or we can fight them. I must be honest with you, though. As good as you have shown yourselves to be, we are now facing fresh troops, not worn down like those we have been fighting."

"We must not give up," Stone said, his face gaunt from his earlier injuries and the long nights of patrolling. "Otherwise everything we have endured and all we have lost will be for nothing."

"I agree," Gregori said. "These Blood Drinkers are rumored to kill freebirths and anyone else they deem less than worthy. I cannot speak for Neta, but she and I both stand to lose our lives should they prevail. Rather than concede Toffen, I would rather fight and take some of them with me." Neta nodded agreement as he spoke.

"Our upbringing teaches us to avoid unnecessary waste," Constant Tseng said, rubbing the deep blue bruise his arm had taken during a rough encounter with the Wolves days earlier.

Angela cut off the discussion with a wave of her hand. "You misunderstand," she said. "This is not a democracy, this is a military operation. This matter is not up for debate. I have already decided—we will fight these Wolves. But once again we may have to change how we fight. New troops may call for a new strategy, one that will again catch our good Star Colonel off guard."

Their faces seemed to glow in the dim light of the floods around them. Again she looked at them one by one. "Now all that remains for discussion is where and how."

There were several moments of quiet before Stone spoke up. "The mountains extend to the north of the Rapidan. They offer excellent cover. We could locate an appropriate area and lure them in."

Angela shook her head. "Dirk Radick will not stumble into another ambush. We saw that at the Rapidan. He would never chase us up into the mountains. Nor would I in his place. He knows that the terrain would favor us too greatly."

"There are the Falmouth Plains," Star Commander Tseng said after a moment or two.

"What about them?" Breedfelt asked. "They are covered with tall reeds and cane at this time of year. What good is that except to obscure our movement?"

Tseng smiled slightly. "You speak as if you have reviewed the tactical data the way the Wolves have."

Angela realized where he was going. She smiled too as her mind played over the thought. *It might just work . . .* "Doctor Drogan, what is the condition of the plains at this time of the year?"

The doctor was caught off guard by her calling on him and even stammered a bit as he began to speak. "I, well, uh, usually the plains are pretty dry. Our farmers have pulled in their crops and in a week or two they usually burn off the cane fields. It helps promote growth next season. If they don't burn them off in controlled fires, accidental or natural circumstances start uncontrolled burns."

"Are the plains dry this year?"

Drogan nodded slowly. "As a bone, Star Captain."

"And the prevailing winds?"

Tseng pulled out his datapad and punched away furiously. "To the northeast during this season. From what our meteorological datafeeds in orbit are telling us, it looks like there will be steady breezes for the next week."

Gregori also smiled broadly as he grasped the idea. "We lure the Wolves to the Falmouth Plains and burn them off."

"Aye," Angela said confidently. "At present, it is our best option. We will need a way to ignite a large area of the plains, though, and set it off all at once if possible." She cast a glance past her inner ring of warriors to where Chief Luray stood. "Chief Technician, do you have a way of setting a fire, a fire of incredible size?"

He, like Drogan before, was caught off guard, mostly by lack of sleep to the point of exhaustion. "We have about forty barrels of pentaglycerine that we buried about fifty kilometers from here when we abandoned Fort DelVillar. It is a very deadly explosive liquid, but when sprayed, it is more flammable than napalm. Since it does not evaporate, we could use that all over the area you are talking about. One spark or even some remote-controlled devices and you could burn almost anything."

Angela nodded. "We have seen the plains during our training exercises when we first arrived on Toffen. With the reeds and canestalks so tall and thick, I think a fire in there will be too hot for even the best OmniMech to fight or survive.

"The fires would have to be set in such a manner as to prevent retreat by the Wolves. Also, it would have to be in an area where the growth was so thick that the flames would generate a sustained heat, enough to keep them unable to move or fire."

The doctor spoke up. "Star Commander, I have lived on this planet my entire life. The heat from the cane fires that the farmers set is so intense that often times there are three or four days of clouds from the smoke that is kicked up—not just here but all across Toffen. Most people say they can't be within fifty meters of a cane-fire without passing out. It'll be more than hot enough for you."

"You cannot do this Star Captain," said Breedfelt. "The use of a controlled blaze lacks honor. Our people suffered a loss on Tukayyid when the Com Guards used just this kind of tactic." His voice was bitter, as if he still tasted the ashes of the fire in the Holth Forest of Tukayyid.

Angela's eyes narrowed. "I understand your concern. I was on Tukayyid, too. I was in the fires in the Holth Forest and only barely survived."

"Then you agree we cannot employ this tactic."

"Neg," she replied. "For several reasons. One, the circumstances are different. I included this terrain in my bid, and Star Colonel Radick has the same information at his disposal. Two, there is no loss of honor is using the terrain to win a victory. Three, it will work. I know. I survived the use of such a fire used against my unit. We are Ghost Bears. We are known to be set in our ways, but in this case we must adapt."

Neta spoke up as well. "The Wolves remember Tukayyid as well as we do. They know that our whole

Clan was scarred by what happened in Holth Forest. We must employ this tactic if only because they would never expect us to do so."

Breedfelt was still not totally convinced. "Are you speaking as a Nova Cat or a Ghost Bear, Neta?"

"As a Ghost Bear that desires victory as much as you," she said, then turned to Angela. "And as a warrior who believes this tactic will work." From that point on, the debate was closed. The matter was settled.

"There is another matter that bothers me," Tseng said. "Radick is not bringing this Binary down for another twenty-five hours. Why wait? They could drop in a matter of an hour with no difficulty."

Angela shrugged. "We may never know for sure. Based on Stone's after-action report, chances are it was the defeat of Radick's Aggressor Star that forced this hand. His forces still on planet are badly beaten up. He must be doing what he can to repair what he has and is using that time to do it."

"If he drops that Binary and its supplies at Fort DelVillar and refits, the odds will be even worse against us," Tseng said.

"Aye," Angela replied. "So we must force his hand in such a way that he commits to battle before he is fully ready."

"Star Captain." The voice came from the massive figure of Dolf. "Your words raise another question. It is not in my place to ask, but where is the rest of our Clan? Reinforcements should have arrived in system by now."

Angela glanced at Tseng, then back to Dolf. How could she answer his question when she herself did not understand why some relief had still not arrived? "I have yet to receive word from our commanders. I assume that our kin are sending additional units to relieve us, but they have not signaled us yet."

Neta began to speak, her voice taking on a strange, otherworldly monotone, like an oracle or seer of centuries long past. "It has been more than forty days, Star Captain. If reinforcements were coming, they should be in system by now."

The silence was uncomfortable as Angela struggled with her own doubts. But it was only a moment before she rekindled her courage through sheer force of will. "We have not heard from our Clan, that is true. Even if they were in-system, the Wolves are in orbit and would get here first. We have fought this entire Trial without any outside help, and I say we can continue on to win it in the same way—with our own blood." Looking at the faces around her, she saw that they had been lifted beyond their fears.

She again caught the eyes of each one of her surviving warriors and support staff. "The only question you must each ask is this, can we defeat these Wolves? Can we bloody them enough to drive them from Toffen in defeat? Can we crush them one more time in battle, a final battle?"

In unison the Stalking Bears roared a resounding, "Yes!"

Angela beamed. "Excellent. There are many details that we must work through. Chief Luray, get a team under Star Commander Tseng's direction to lay a pattern of pentaglycerine around the Falmouth Plains. We also need every available warrior who can pilot a Battle-Mech or suit up in Elemental armor ready to fight."

"And what are your plans for my Sweep Star?" Stone asked.

Angela smiled. "You have suffered some damage already. I have plans for you and your people, Stone.

Done correctly, we should be able to let you deliver a special surprise for Dirk Radick." Stone cocked an eyebrow in surprise, and Constant Tseng looked at her with an inquisitive tilt of the head.

"Star Captain, you have hit on the key issue from where I sit," Chief Luray said. "The lack of warriors. We were able to somewhat repair the *Summoner* we recovered from the Wolves, but we have no warrior to pilot it."

Angela looked over at Doctor Drogan. "No matter what drugs I use, neither Bethany nor any of the others in my care will be ready for battle in time," he said, his tone leaving little room for debate.

Tseng came toward her in one long stride. "Star Captain, I may be able to solve this issue," he said, then glanced back toward the small gathering. "Barthelow, come forward."

The Inner Sphere bondsman stepped up to his master and held out his hand. Constant Tseng reached down and grabbed the small band of fur on the man's wrist. He tugged it away from the flesh and slashed it with the blade of his knife, freeing the man's wrist. "Barthelow, on this day, in the eyes and minds of the Ghost Bears around you, I release you from your bonds. You are no longer Barthelow the bondsman of Constant Tseng. From this day forward, Barthelow, you are a warrior of our Clan."

The other Ghost Bears, Angela included, lowered their heads for a moment. "Seyla," they chanted in unison, a single word that sealed the ceremony for all time. As she lifted her head, Angela saw Barthelow, still somewhat stunned, rubbing his wrist where the bondcord had once been. "Welcome to our ranks, Barthelow."

"Thank you, Star Captain," he said, looking dazed.

Gregori raised his fist in a victory salute. "At last,

another freebirth in the unit. I cannot wait until Bethany recovers."

"That solves one problem," Tseng said, "but does not answer the question, Star Captain. Exactly how do you intend to get the Wolves to the plains to fight?"

"By giving Radick something he desires. Something he cannot resist. Something he has wanted since the moment he arrived." Angela activated her wristcom and held the microphone up close to her face so that her words would not be lost.

"Star Colonel Dirk Radick of the Wolves, this is Star Captain Angela Bekker. I grant safcon to your Binary grounding at the eastern edge of the Falmouth Plains in the time frame you indicated. At that time, I will be on the plains. Once your troops have landed, I will transmit to you my Trinary's position."

"Your *entire* Trinary?" came back the disembodied voice of Radick.

"All of us that will be engaging you on the plains. This is what you wanted, Dirk Radick, a final climactic battle of our two Clans. I must warn you, though. You must be ready to move against us or I will never agree to such a stand-up fight again.

"The winner will own Toffen. The loser will either be dead or wish he was."

25

Falmouth Plains
Toffen
Ghost Bear Dominion
21 April 3062

"It is a trap, you know that, quiaff?" Star Captain Jergan said as she maneuvered her 'Mech around a huge tree, trying to keep up with Star Colonel Radick. Nearly a hundred meters behind her lumbered the massive *Dire Wolf* piloted by Patton Ward, also trying to keep up. Radick's *Executioner* moved through Richart Forest as if the trees were not even there. This was not the first time Jergan had seen him like this, in the grip of a compulsion no one in the Blood Drinkers could control. He was driven, totally obsessed with the Bears, oblivious to anything else—including reason.

Radick's voice crackled back in her neurohelmet. "Aye, of course I know that this Bekker is up to something. I am not some ignorant freebirth. You have checked out these Falmouth Plains. What do you think she is doing?" It was the kind of verbal trap Jergan had come to dread with her commander, but she had no choice but to respond.

Much had been done in the last two days, most of it in a rush. Vaul and his *Mist Lynx* were all they had left behind with the DropShip at Fort DelVillar, mostly because Vaul's 'Mech had been stripped for parts to keep the rest of the command operational. That, and the fact that Dirk Radick was still angry at Vaul for the last ambush by the Ghost Bears. Leaving him behind was a message, the price of failure. Off to her flank, Drew in his *Ice Ferret* skirted the trees and undergrowth to keep pace with them. This was her command, or all that remained of it.

They had been racing through the forest, heading west to where the forest gave way to the vast and rolling plains. She had reviewed every byte of data on the Falmouth Plains three times over, each time sensing that she was missing something. The terrain was good for concealing visible movement, the reeds and unharvested cane stalks tall enough to hide most 'Mechs. Combat could only effectively happen in those areas where the reeds were thinned out or low enough to see the enemy 'Mechs. But that did not make sense. Their sensors would be more than adequate to track the Ghost Bears even if they could not see them. Jergan had learned enough about Angela Bekker to know that she would not have chosen these plains if it did not it some way suit her plans.

"From what I can tell, she will use the plains to obscure her movement. The canestalks will offer only limited fields of fire. Bekker has proven herself quite adept at turning the terrain against us. I would advise caution."

She lost sight of Radick's *Executioner* as it dropped down the other side of a hill that loomed in front of her, but his voice stung at her. "Caution has gotten us into this predicament. She is worn down and knows it. Our

Angela Bekker is getting desperate. We outnumber and outgun her. If this place offered such a vast tactical advantage, why did she not use it earlier?"

Jergan felt her *Warhawk* strain slightly as it moved up the hill. "You have forced her to play your game, Star Colonel. I am only suggesting that she is adapting, and rapidly."

As she reached the top of the hill, she saw the dominating oval shape of a *Union-C* DropShip sitting at the very edge of the forest. Beyond the last saplings was the start of the Falmouth Plains. The brown grasses and reeds swayed in the breeze, like waves on a lake. The 'Mechs gathered at the bottom of the hill near the recently arrived DropShip were the Binary of troops under Star Captain Lark Radick—her peer and her rival.

"Nice of you to join us," Lark Radick taunted from the cockpit of his *Timber Wolf*, his tone so arrogant Jergan was beginning to think it was a genetic trait of the Radick bloodline. "I suggest you park for a moment and let my technicians reload you properly."

She came to a stop next to Dirk Radick's *Executioner* and climbed down the battered rungs to join her CO. Lark was already there, standing with arms crossed and a sly grin on his face. Jergan tried not to let it annoy her. She knew he really had no idea what they had already been through on Toffen or what they were likely to face in this final battle.

"Jergan, good to see you again. It appears that this Ghost Bear ristar has given you quite a bloody nose," he gloated, tipping forward on his toes slightly, then rocking back, savoring the moment.

"Before you say too much, Lark, I might remind you that this operation is under the direction of our commanding officer." She glanced at Dirk Radick, who appeared far from amused by the younger Radick's tone.

"If there is something you think I have overlooked, Lark, perhaps you should tell me now." Dirk Radick's eyes narrowed angrily, and Jergan saw that Lark had better choose his next words more carefully or he would find himself in a Circle of Equals with his commander—an undesirable position, at best.

"Neg, Star Colonel, I have nothing to add," he said, his tone subdued. "I have reviewed the data on your encounters thus far. The Ghost Bears are indeed a foe worthy of the Wolf."

"Enough of this chatter," Dirk Radick said as the technicians began to load missiles into what remained of his *Executioner*. "You are about to learn how crafty Angela Bekker can be."

"Aye, Star Colonel. I have reviewed her position. The area is open, but firing will be difficult because of the heavy growth covering the area."

"Did you scan these plains on your approach to see if she was here?" Radick asked.

"I did permit scans, but only enough to make sure we had the right location, nothing that would violate the honor of this Trial or place this DropShip as a potential combatant," Lark said. His use of the sensors was stretching the terms of the Trial slightly, but not enough that it would ever be verified. "After our ship touched down, I honored the intent and spirit of the bid."

Lark beamed over his ploy of contorting the bidding process and his seeming lack of honor at scanning the Ghost Bears. "I did inadvertently detect a force of BattleMechs on a hilltop nearly eighty kilometers from here, spread out nearly a kilometer in a line formation. If memory serves"—he let his eyes roll upward slightly as though trying to remember—"I seem to recall there being eight such 'Mechs in total."

Dirk Radick nodded in admiration. "Eight 'Mechs. In

all of this fighting, she has managed to keep over half of her Trinary intact." He threw a sharp glance at Lark. "Do not let your little games go to your head, Star Captain. I have faced this Ghost Bear in battle. She is cunning."

Jergan had no argument with that. She, too, had come to respect Angela Bekker, not as a Ghost Bear but as a compeer—an equal in an ages-old art, the art of warfare.

"What is your plan, Star Colonel?" Lark asked.

"Trying to repair the 'Mechs of Jergan's Trinary would be a waste of time. Bekker is waiting for us, so we will go and find her. We will not rush in blindly, but watch her carefully. When we do engage her, I want our forces to spread wide. Get on the flanks and hammer this Ghost Bear until she and her command succumb."

Lark beamed confidently. "We will defeat her. By nightfall, this planet will be but another dot on the map of the holdings of Clan Wolf."

"Status, Chief Luray," Star Captain Angela Bekker said calmly from her position on the small hilltop. From here, the sea of dried brown grasses and reeds seemed to go on forever, gently waving in the breeze. Her *Executioner* stood tall, the wind at her back. From her cockpit, it was hard to believe that these fields of cane and reed would, in a matter of minutes, become a battlefield where the fate of this world would be decided.

"Everything is in place," came back a voice in her earpiece. "I have spread every drop of pentaglycerine we had in a wide circle. Charges are rigged on the command channel that you specified."

"Good work," she said. "Star Commander Tseng, are you and your Star in place?" It was information she could obtain in an instant by checking her secondary tactical display, but there was something about getting a personal report from one of her officers. Something more reassuring.

"Striker Star is ready when the Wolves are," came the voice of Constant Tseng. He, along with Gregori, Barthelow, and Angela, would form the center of the formation. Out on the right flank were Neta and Sprange; Breedfelt, Kate, and Scarry were holding the far left.

"Good. Everyone keep sharp," she said. They had all seen the Wolf DropShip sweep over the plains and knew that the battle was only minutes away. Seeing the ship, Angela felt her heart swell for an instant, hoping somehow that the vessel might bear the markings of the Ghost Bears, her own Clan. But it did not. Where were they? Had she and her people been forgotten here on Toffen?

The flyover had been over an hour ago. All that remained was the combat. Somewhere, in the fog of the battle, victory would be decided. Angela was proud of what they had accomplished thus far. Soon, very soon, it would be all over.

She reached over to the comm panel and switched frequencies. "Star Commander Stone," she said.

"This is Sweep Star," Stone answered. Kate and Scarry were members of his Star, but for the time being they would serve under Constant Tseng. She had sent Stone, along with Dolf and Raul—the last of the Elementals who could still fight—off on a special mission. One that was aimed at providing the crippling blow to Dirk Radick, hopefully at the right moment.

"Are you in position?"

"Aye, Star Captain," Stone said. "We await your signal."

"Good. I wish you luck, Star Commander."

There was a pause. "Would you not prefer that the battle be won on skill, Star Captain?"

"Aye," she said, "but at this point, I think we had better take whatever we can get—even if it is luck." A light flashing on her comm panel told her that someone was signaling on another channel. She switched over rapidly. "This is Command One," she said briskly.

The voice on the other end was familiar, but sounded weak and drained. Bethany?

"Star Captain, our stravag doctor disapproves of this, but I wanted to speak to you." In Angela's mind, she could almost hear the argument that must have taken place between Drogan and Bethany. She smiled slightly at the thought.

"Go ahead," she said.

"Give the word, Star Captain, and I will join you and the others."

Gone was the bitterness of Bethany's past outbursts. Gone was the hatred. All that remained was the loyalty Angela had sought from the start. She wanted to tell Bethany to mount up, to race over to the plains from the supply cache where she was recovering. But that was wrong, and it was too late now anyway. "You are here," she said.

"Aye," came the breathless voice, weary and worn, followed by a drawn-out sigh. "Then all that remains is for me to wish you success in battle. Pulverize these Blood Drinkers. Make them pay for their arrogance."

Angela's smile grew. "We will. All of us." She was about to tell Bethany how proud she was of her as a warrior, how she had grown beyond her petty self-interest. But the emergency comm channel automatically kicked in, cutting off their dialogue.

"This is Sweep Four," came the crisp voice of Kate on the far end of the flank. "Contacts. Multiple. Repeat, I have 'Mechs and Elementals on the outer marker. Confirmed on long-range sensors. They are moving due west and closing on our position."

Angela dumped the long-range tactical data feed from Kate's *Mist Lynx* over a kilometer away. The Wolves were coming straight at her and Scarry. She checked the datafeeds on the BattleMechs Kate's battle computer was tagging as Wolves. She gritted her teeth. Heading this way were Lark Radick's Binary along with what was left of Dirk Radick's battered Bloodied Wolves Trinary. They were there, all together.

"Stalking Bears, remember the fire zone and stay clear of it if possible. Scarry, Breedfelt, and Kate, hold your positions and engage at maximum range. Star Commander Tseng, take your center force and sweep, using Breedfelt's position as your pivot point. Hit the Wolves and fall back to reform the line in its original position. That should pull them toward the center. Be careful with your shots. We do not want the fires to light up too soon."

From her position on the hilltop, she saw Tseng, Gregori, and Barthelow move off to the left, cutting a swath through the tall reeds as they went. In the distance came a rumble of fire, missiles and autocannons. Her heart pounded in her ears as it always did at such moments, a roar of excitement and energy.

Star Commander Jergan's *Warhawk* waded into the seemingly endless wall of cane reed, the stalks whipping at her viewscreen with a sound like a thundering rainstorm. Reaching a small area where the reeds were low enough for sight, she saw Lark Radick's *Timber Wolf* break into the opening as well, and just beyond that, the battle-scarred *Executioner* of Star Colonel Dirk Radick. The smaller forms of the Elemental warriors moved through the dead brown grasses like snakes slithering through a marsh.

From across the shadow grass area, a barrage of missiles seemed to come from out of nowhere, slamming furiously into Dirk Radick's *Executioner,* mangling the scant few replacement plates of armor in the center torso. The Point of five Elementals ignited their jump jets and rose into the air, lifting up and forward as the rest of the Wolves began to move into firing positions.

The flames from their jets left a smoking black wake as the armored warriors rose in the air, their short-range missiles streaking toward an unseen enemy in the distance. Out of the corner of one eye, Jergan saw something else, something that instantly set off an alarm bell in her mind. The cane reeds where they had stood sparked and burst into flame, then the flames quickly spread to become a wave of fire that seemed to take on a life of its own.

She turned her attention forward just in time to see a Ghost Bear *Mist Lynx* wither under a barrage of fire from Lark Radick's *Timber Wolf.* Suddenly she understood why Angela Bekker had chosen this location for her contest. The flames lapped up at her 'Mech, and Jergan side-stepped her *Warhawk* to avoid them.

Before she could speak, the voice of Dirk Radick cut in over the Wolf command channel. "We have multiple contacts to the southwest. All units sweep in that direction. Hit them fast and hit them hard."

As she turned her body slightly in the command couch to better access the communications systems to send a message of warning, her *Warhawk* rocked under the impact of an autocannon barrage that tossed her hard to one side and banged her neurohelmet hard into the cockpit controls in front of her. A warm trickle of blood tasted oddly metallic on her lips as she stared at the spider web cracks in her cockpit glass, dazed, confused, and her ears ringing from the impact. Just inside her field of vision was the shimmer of light from the growing firestorm.

26

Fort DelVillar
Toffen
Ghost Bear Dominion
21 April 3062

Star Commander Stone stopped his 'Mech in a small cluster of young trees that marked the edge of the cleared forest surrounding Fort DelVillar. Using the enhanced scanning capabilities of his aged *Viper*, he swept the fort. The 'Mech had been held in reserve, and with good reason. It had fought in the initial invasion of the Inner Sphere, and been damaged and refitted so many times that it was, in the words of Chief Tech Luray, "technologically unsound." By that he meant that damage to the internal structure was such that many of the repairs were cobbled together by a variety of technicians. Yes, it could fight and was a potent weapon, but it had quirks in its operation. Now and then the long-range sensors failed, if only for a few seconds. And the targeting system drifted to the low right.

But it felt good to be in a cockpit again.

Dolf and one of his Elementals were almost a kilometer away, also skirting the edge of the fort. His sensors did not tell him much. The thick granite walls of the centuries-old structure not only provided protection but shielded the interior from most sensor sweeps. He did pick up a reading of a 'Mech reactor running in the interior—just one. The class and type of 'Mech were unknown. Also unknown was whether there were any other surprises such as the Elementals from Lark Radick's Mauler Trinary. But, if Stone and Star Captain Bekker were right, the Wolves had sent almost everything they had to Falmouth Plains. That left Fort DelVillar almost empty.

"Dolf, are you and Raul in position?" Stone asked.

"Aye, Star Commander," came back the static-filled transmission from Dolf.

The gate to the fort was closed. Stone knew that what they had to do would not be easy, but it was possible. Few victories ever came any other way. "You will wait until I have cleared the wall, then move in on your objective." They had planned this as much as possible, given the time and resources. Surprise was their chief advantage. A surprise big enough to shake Dirk Radick's soul—if he had one.

Throttling the old *Viper*'s reactor, Stone felt it quake under him rather than begin to throb the way most 'Mechs did. *One more battle is all you owe the Ghost Bears,* he silently told the *Viper*. Then he broke out of the woods in a dead run, heading for the gated wall of Fort DelVillar. The ground blurred past on either side of his viewport as the fort seemed to loom before him like a mountain. A scant forty meters from the granite wall, he triggered the *Viper*'s jump jets. The quaking he had felt now became a violent shaking, and Stone strained to keep control of the BattleMech.

The *Viper* rose into the air, slowly at first, then, almost begrudgingly, it began to soar. The massive wall of the fort seemed to rush forward at him, and Stone feared, if only for a moment, that he might not clear it. Then he saw the battlement at the top. It was a wide stone platform carved into the granite. He landed on it, his cockpit temperature spiking so high that his thin shirt was soaked in sweat.

He saw the figure of the *Mist Lynx* as soon as he landed. Something was wrong with it. It was almost skeletal. There was no armor left to speak of, little more than an occasional plate on each limb, more near the cockpit. One of its weapons pods was gone, removed or blown off in an earlier battle. Almost to his shock, it moved forward, closing the distance between them, seeming to drag its right leg like a wounded animal.

Stone did not linger over thoughts of what they had done to bring the Wolves to this point. He swung his weapons around, charging them as he did. The five extended-range medium lasers' full power lights lit one after another, though the last one seemed to flicker on and off until he slammed his fist against the cockpit control panel. He heard the audible metallic grind as the short-range missiles loaded.

The *Mist Lynx* stopped its seemingly tortured gait ninety meters away and tipped back at the torso, raising toward him. It fired, but instead of the deadly volley he had anticipated, all that came was machine gun fire, pattering up the *Viper*'s legs to the cockpit, crumbling only a single plate of armor in the process. Stone realized that the machine guns were all the *Mist Lynx* had left. He could destroy the Wolf 'Mech with a single

volley if he wished. But that would be wasteful. There
was no honor in a fight against nothing.

Stone linked only his short-range missiles on the primary target interlock and triggered the joystick control,
aiming low into the legs of the *Lynx*. The missiles spiraled and snaked in the air, slamming into the legs of
the Wolf 'Mech. There were a series of explosions, then,
unceremoniously, the *Mist Lynx* fell forward, its right
kneecap belching black smoke. It crashed onto the ferrocrete roadway, creating a spider web of cracks from
its impact. Stone activated his jump jets one more time
and fluttered downward to the ground in front of it.

Stone saw, out of the corner of his eye, through the
side cockpit window, the forms of Dolf and Raul drop
down and start moving. Raul broke and ran for the
command bunker. Dolf, to the DropShip sitting on the
parade field at the far side of the fort. He activated his
communications system and called to the fallen Wolf.
"Wolf warrior, I am Star Commander Stone of the
Stalking Bears Trinary. You are defeated. Shut down
your reactor."

An angry voice came back. "I am Vaul of the Blood
Drinkers, the Bloodied Wolves Trinary. Kill me now,
Ghost Bear. I have no desire to face Star Colonel Radick
as the reason this base fell."

Stone looked down at the shattered remains of the
Mist Lynx. "I am a warrior, not a murderer. If you seek
release, find it elsewhere. For now, know that you have
lost here. And on the plains, my Star Captain is handing
your Clan another defeat that pales this one. The
Wolves have lost this Trial of Possession. Signal those of
your Clan in this facility that you surrender it in the
name of the Ghost Bears."

It took a full minute for Vaul to comply.

* * *

The *Union-C* DropShip *Houndstooth* stood oddly quiet in the middle of the parade field as Dolf stepped out into plain view and began to walk toward the loading ramp to the DropShip's massive cargo bays. He moved openly, not trying to hide. The turrets on the outer hull of the ship, domed humps of death and destruction, were also oddly quiet. He knew that the Wolves inside must surely see him. The Ghost Bear insignia painted on the armored plate over his heart was as brilliant as any banner he might carry.

Suddenly a voice boomed in his headset inside the Elemental armor. "I am Star Captain Kevin of the Clan Wolf DropShip *Houndstooth*. Stop there, Elemental, or you will be destroyed."

Dolf halted and stood facing the ship, hopelessly outmassed and outgunned. It was time to play their honor like a musical instrument. "Star Captain Kevin, I am Dolf of the Sweep Star of the Stalking Bears, who have been waging this Trial of Possession. I come bearing a message from Star Captain Angela Bekker, my commander and the defender of Toffen."

"Speak this message," the voice said.

"She sent me to say that if I reached you, it means that Fort DelVillar has fallen. As such she claims your ship and crew as isorla." His use of that word, Clan short-speak for the spoils of battle, was not an idle threat.

"You are a mere Elemental. You are alone. We can blast you out of existence and there is nothing you or anyone else could do about it," Kevin taunted.

"Aye, you could. But heed this. Your ship was never bid in the battle for this planet. Fire one shot at me and you violate the bidding for this Trial. Whatever shred of honor your Star Colonel claims will be lost, and the Ghost Bears will contest this Trial before all of the Clans in the Grand Council. The honor of your Clan and your Khan will be called into question. We will tell the others how you have obviously been tainted by the ways of the Inner Sphere warriors. For this single action, your genes and those of your commanders will be lost for the rest of time, dumped into a latrine. There will be no future for a commander who led his warriors to such disgrace. No lines in The Remembrance for your actions. If anything, others will see you as a symbol of what to avoid rather than to follow."

Dolf grinned broadly. "So, Star Captain Kevin of the *Houndstooth*, do you violate centuries of our traditions and ritual, or do you submit with honor?"

27

Falmouth Plains
Toffen
Ghost Bear Dominion
21 April 3062

Angela braced herself as her *Executioner* took a blast from a spread of long-range missiles. Many of them missed, plowing into the grass in front of her, sending sod, then flames into the air. The rest hit her torso and leg armor shotgun style, leaving an erratic pattern of destruction. The *Timber Wolf* that had unleashed the attack was nearly three hundred meters away in a clearing where the reeds and dried grasses were less than cockpit-high.

The signs of battle were masked by towers of flame and smoke that rose and drifted in long trails to the east of the plains. Using her targeting joystick, she brought the targeting reticle squarely over the lower torso and legs of the *Timber Wolf,* switching her gauss rifle and large lasers to the same trigger. She fired, but in her mind it was as if her eyes alone guided the shots. There was no sign of the gauss slug in flight, but its impact on the left leg of the Wolf 'Mech was evident as the entire 'Mech rocked back and down under the impact. The lasers then swept the small, relatively clear knoll. One went wide, leaving only smoking embers near the feet of the BattleMech. The other laced up diagonally across its left torso. She sidestepped her *Executioner* and moved quickly off to the southeast, knowing that her opponent would pursue.

She checked her tactical display to see that her 'Mechs ran in a short line north and south, and a longer line to the east and west, a lop-sided "L" shape into the plains. The Wolf forces were in the middle of it, attempting to backtrack to the east, apparently in fear that she was moving beyond their flank. The green dots of light, hers included, moved to the south and east, and the Wolves, identified by glowing red dots, seemed to follow. *Almost in position . . .*

"Sweep Four!" came an agonized voice over the commline. Angela opened her mouth to respond, but Kate beat her to it. "Punching out!" Static was all that remained as somewhere, beyond her field of vision, Kate ejected from her 'Mech, the last resort for any MechWarrior.

The cane reeds around her *Executioner* rippled as if a scythe were cutting them as forty long-range missiles from the *Timber Wolf* attempted to hit her in a dense growth. Ten did, striking her left torso and arm hard enough to rock the 'Mech slightly as she moved. Most disappeared into the never-ending sea of dead grass.

Constant Tseng's voice came over the command frequency. "Sweep Four is down. Sweep Three is down as well." She knew that Scarry's battle-weary *Viper* had been at the far northern edge of her line and that he had followed her orders well, as had Kate. They had held their ground long enough for the rest of the Stalking Bears to lure the Wolves to the south. A part of her felt remorse. She had ordered them to hold, and in doing so, they might well have died by her word. But years of training pushed such thoughts back, deep into her mind and soul. Such things were not for now, in the middle of battle. They were for later.

"Star Captain Bekker. They are in the ring. It is now or never," Tseng said. From the static that interrupted his message, she knew that he too was under a heavy fire.

She switched to the channel that Luray had pre-set for the explosive charges and triggered it. Before her and off to the north, the sea of reeds suddenly became a crimson and orange wall of death, roaring upward as the pentaglycerine burst into flames. Even from this distance, she could feel the heat. It reached into her cockpit and sent tingles of sweat all down her face and body. "Ghost Bears, pull back a few meters. Pick your targets and continue to engage."

She checked her sensors and saw that all but one of the Wolf 'Mechs was now encircled by a five-kilometer ring of fire. With the winds carrying the flames to the east, the Wolves would be roasting and constantly forced to fall back, only to find their exit cut off. A BattleMech could survive a raging fire, but it was a risky undertaking and no 'Mech could engage in combat at the same time. The spikes in temperature would be so intense that it could cause a 'Mech's fusion reactor to shut down, ammunition to explode before it was fired, or roast the Mech-Warrior alive.

She knew. She had survived such a battle once.

On Tukayyid Angela had been fighting in the Holth Forest when the Com Guards set fire to it. Her 'Mech had barley escaped, and when she did emerge and

tried to fire, it shut down. That had been one of a handful of times she had come close to death as a warrior. It
was the only time when she had felt that all was utterly
lost, and was prepared to embrace death. Somehow she
survived instead.

Now Dirk Radick and his Wolves were enduring the
same kind of firestorm.

Memories dissolved as she made out the form of the
Timber Wolf outlined in the flames. He was on the other
side of the wall of fire, the side that was hottest and
where the air was choked with smoke and searing heat.
Angela did not hesitate, nor did he. He fired at her with
his lasers, followed by the *Timber Wolf's* impressive
wall of missiles.

The lasers carved into her center torso, savaging her
armor plates and melting the ferro-fibrous armor. Her
own large lasers swept the arm and chest of the *Timber
Wolf,* splaying armor but not seeming to do much damage. A moment later the Wolf's missiles struck her right
and left torso and arms with such force that she tipped
back, falling into a heap as her own blasted armor plate
rained down on her *Executioner's* limp form. Her shoulders ached from the restraining straps that cut into her
upper arms but kept her in her seat.

The fall had done some damage, mostly to her rear
armor. Rocking the throttle and punching the leg controls, she managed to get her 'Mech onto its knees. She
knew she was a ripe target like this, but no shots came
as she worked the arm and leg controls furiously, finally getting her *Executioner* to a standing position. She
spun around and saw the form of the *Timber Wolf* almost exactly where she had left it, but now the wall of
flames had overtaken it.

She scanned it rather than just firing wildly and saw
that its reactor was shut down. Firing all of its weapons

so close to the fire, it had overheated. Now it stood still, engulfed in flames, turning a charred black. Angela wanted to fire, to finish the 'Mech off, but did not get a chance. The remaining rounds of long-range missile ammunition suddenly went off inside the 'Mech. The compartmentalized storage system designed to vent internal explosions outward popped its doors open and tried to channel the explosion from within. It only seemed to add a stark yellow rage to the bright red fire all around the Wolf 'Mech. The *Timber Wolf* vibrated under the explosions of its own ammo, and its boxy right long-range missile rack exploded into hundreds of pieces. Then, unceremoniously, it tipped sideways, consumed in fire.

To her left she saw Neta's *Kingfisher* cut loose with a barrage from its particle projection cannon at a Wolf 'Mech that was attempting to charge through the wall of fire to break out against the Ghost Bears. The Wolf, a *Linebacker*, reached the edge of the burning area just in time to get hit by Neta's PPC fire, which ripped into its right weapons pod. It turned slowly but did not bring its weapons on line.

Watching, Angela understood all too well, knowing what it was to fight in fiery conditions. If the Wolf warrior attempted to fire, he or she would drive the 'Mech's temperature even higher. The Wolf warrior was trying to wait and cool off some, hoping to weather the attack long enough to take out Neta.

Neta had other plans. Her LB autocannon swept into action along with her short-range missiles. The autocannon hit the already damaged torso of the *Linebacker*, adding to damage she had inflicted before Angela had begun to watch. The missiles raked the center torso and cockpit of the Wolf 'Mech, almost crushing the cockpit under the assault. The *Linebacker* warrior decided to take the risk of firing, seeing Neta planning yet another barrage. He triggered both his long- and short-range missiles in a combined strike that mangled much of the legs of Neta's Kingfisher, leaving long, black, comet-shaped scars on the unpainted replacement armor plates. He was still holding back his heavy-hitting PPC, knowing that the heat from that weapon would be too much to bear.

But not Neta. She fired her PPC as soon as it re-charged, again mauling the already damaged weapons pod on the *Linebacker*. Angela might have savored the victory, but checking her tactical display she real-ized the battle was far from over. Breedfelt's *Kodiak* was showing as downed, apparently having suffered under the long-range weapons of Dirk Radick's *Executioner*. The Wolves were falling back, but they were still pump-ing out considerable damage, despite the losses her dis-play told her they were taking.

A beeping of her command channel told her of an incoming message from Sweep Star. "Command One," she barked. "Status, Stone."

"Mission accomplished," came back the emotionless voice. "No losses. We hold the fort, Star Captain."

"And what of Dolf?"

"He was successful, as anticipated," Stone said with just a hint of pride. The two of them had planned his role at the fort.

The burning of the cane had suddenly left vast, open, charred black fields of vision, hazy with wind-blown smoke, the smoldering fires still burning in spots. She watched as Constant Tseng's *Timber Wolf* suffered a barrage from an unseen Wolf 'Mech concealed behind the wall of fire that still raged to the east. As she had earlier, Tseng tipped back under the assault, falling on his back with a thud that she felt under the feet of her own BattleMech.

Catching sight of the wave of missiles streaking at his fallen form, she instinctively moved toward him, even knowing she could never reach him in time. Then a blur swept like a ghost in front of her field of vision, a running BattleMech in full sprint. It stopped just as the missiles would have reached their mark, taking the blast for the fallen Tseng rather than let him die lying on the ground. The 'Mech withered under the barrage, plates from its already damaged armor dropping in every direction. Angela was glad to see one of her Stalking Bears attempting to save another, and even more so that the 'Mech was Gregori's *Grizzly*. Behind him, Tseng slowly and painfully brought his *Timber Wolf* to a standing position, his left missile-carriage box all but smashed to an ugly blob of worthless metallic scrap.

"Gregori, are you all right?" she said.

He did not answer immediately, but instead fired at his unseen opponent in the flames, cutting loose with his long-range missiles and gauss rifle before responding. "I am operational, Star Captain. Just don't tell anyone I saved the life of a trueborn. I do have a reputation to uphold. But the Wolves have started to engage multiple targets. The rules of engagement are canceled."

"Aye," she responded. "Everyone maintain your distance and concentrate your efforts with long-range weapons only. Let the fires do their work." In the background of her view of the field she saw the fallen form of a *Dire Wolf* lying on the charred black ground as the flames fanned in tighter and tighter on the Wolves. In the orange hell of the fires, she saw Sprange's foe, a Wolf *Pouncer*, eject its pilot into the air as the damaged 'Mech fell into its own funeral pyre.

Checking her tactical display once more, she saw that the circle of fire was turning into a mere pocket. She advanced her *Executioner* to keep pace with the rest of the Stalking Bears as they moved in forcibly on the retreating Wolves. She considered her options. Her force had been badly injured, but so had the enemy. Star Colonel Radick was a rabid Crusader as well as a skilled warrior. He would be looking for any and all means to end this bit of hell erupting on Toffen.

Perhaps it is up to me to provide him with a way out. She set her comm channel to a broadband transmission, so that the Wolves as well as her own people could hear her. "Star Colonel Radick, this is Star Captain Bekker. You have lost, Star Colonel. Capitulate now and save your lives."

"Neg," came back a bitter and angry voice. "We will walk through this fire trap of yours and still outnumber you."

"Perhaps," Angela said. "But for what? Check your command channels and attempt to raise Fort DelVillar, Star Colonel. You will find that it is under Ghost Bear control. Even if you beat me here, you will have to lay siege to that fort, and you do not have the forces to do that successfully. Also, I have claimed your DropShip *Houndstooth* as isorla. Contact them as well if you do not believe me."

The pause was long enough for her to spy another *Dire Wolf* moving amidst the flames. She squeezed off a snap shot with her lasers and gauss rifle. One laser missed, but the rest of her shots seemed to find their marks. The hundred-ton BattleMech stopped in its tracks and attempted to return fire, only to lose sight and target lock on her in the raging flames that rose between the two of them. Neta moved up on Angela's right flank and matched her pace forward.

Then she heard Radick's voice again. "You are a worthy foe, Angela Bekker. But I cannot surrender to you. To do so would violate what honor I have left. And though you believe me beaten, I will fight and die for what little honor I still possess."

Angela considered her words carefully. "There is another way." She knew that Radick would understand. *Hegira.* The rite by which one Clan commander granted an enemy permission to withdraw from battle without loss of honor. If granted hegira, Radick and his Blood Drinkers would be allowed safe passage out of the Toffen system, but they would have to concede this Trial of Possession.

"I do not take your meaning," he said, but Angela knew that was a lie.

"Then my warriors will finish you and your warriors off. Hear this, Dirk Radick. Death in defeat brings no honor."

Much damage had been done. Angela and her Stalking Bears had humiliated the Wolves in defeat after defeat through long, drawn-out weeks of fighting. Radick had arrogantly believed his seasoned warriors could easily best an untried unit and steal the world they were bound to defend, had even brought down additional forces against her when his losses became too grave. Yet the Stalking Bears had proven themselves true warriors, true Ghost Bears. They had prevailed through patience as well as courage and strength.

"Star Colonel Dirk Radick of the Wolves, what has happened here will be remembered by my people as well as yours. You can still save what honor remains to you. I, Star Captain Angela Bekker, commander of the Stalking Bears Trinary, defenders of Toffen, grant you hegira."

The silence lasted only seconds, but is seemed like an

eternity. For several long heartbeats, only the hiss of the open commline answered her. Finally a weary voice came over the line. "In the name of the Wolf Clan, I accept the offer of hegira," Dirk Radick said, almost inaudibly.

"Well bargained and done, Star Colonel Radick," Angela said, more for the sake of tradition than true respect.

"Well bargained and done, Star Captain Becker."

Angela raised the arm of her *Executioner* in a victory salute. "Stalking Bears," she said. "Our foes acknowledge our victory in this Trial. Stand down and allow them to exit the fire."

28

Falmouth Plains
Toffen
Ghost Bear Dominion
21 April 3062

The forces of the Ghost Bears and the Wolves lined up face to face on the charred grounds of Falmouth Plains. Smoke still hung in the air as the two rows of Battle-Mechs stood a mere thirty meters apart. Angela's ranks were small and showed signs of a vicious battle. Next to her was Constant Tseng, his *Timber Wolf* covered with soot and severely damaged from the fight. Neta's *Kingfisher*, missing an arm from the final moments of the fighting, came next. Sprange stood without his 'Mech in the line, still garbed in his coolant vest and shorts, now covered with gray and black soot. His 'Mech was on a hillside nearly a kilometer away, having fallen taking out a *Warhawk*—whose pilot Sprange had claimed as his bondsman. The next place in line was a *Summoner* piloted by the newest Stalking Bear,

Barthelow, its legs blackened by the charred cane. Last in line was Kate, with Doctor Drogan trying to tend her injuries as she tried to ignore him and savor this moment. Her 'Mech was gone, as were some members of the Stalking Bears Trinary. No one had yet found the remains of Scarry or Breedfelt.

The Wolves had more numbers, but looked worse off. The seven 'Mechs that had survived the inferno were black from top to bottom, and most had lost significant pieces of their armor protection. Some, such as Dirk Radick's *Executioner*, were missing limbs. In his case, the left arm was severed at the shoulder. What was left of a Point of Elementals were three blackened warriors who seemed to sag in place as they stood.

Angela sat in her cockpit and stared at the *Executioner*. In a fight the odds would have been even. But how many more of her people would have been injured or killed? She kept her own *Executioner* in place, facing the enemy warriors she and her people had defeated.

"We will depart now," Star Colonel Radick said coolly. "I had hoped to make you my bondsman, Angela Bekker. You would have made an outstanding Wolf."

She spoke into her neurohelmet's microphone. "I doubt that, Star Colonel. You would find that I am more Warden than Crusader in my beliefs. As you have seen with our Clan, it is easy to become the defender of mankind. It is much harder to mold a defender into a Crusader."

"Perhaps," Radick replied. "You fought well. But now we face essentially the same problems."

"Which are?"

"Our upper commands."

Angela was confused. Problems? She had triumphed. Her Stalking Bears had won the Trial of Possession. They had fulfilled their mission. Toffen was still a part of the Ghost Bear Dominion. "I do not understand, Star Colonel."

"I must atone for attempting to take Toffen without authorization from my superiors—and failing. I have suffered losses that will take much time to recover. My commanders and my Khan will be furious with me, of that much I am confident. I have met Khan Ward many times and his rage is not something to be invited.

"And you, Star Captain Bekker," he said, "why was your Trinary left here alone to defend Toffen? Where were the rest of the Ghost Bears as you faced us? Every day I expected to detect the arrival of Ghost Bear Drop-Ships, but none ever came. And what about the massive stockpiles of supplies brought here? I am sure that by now you see your real reason for being on Toffen in the first place.

"And so," he continued, "that is why I say we both have problems to be dealt with."

As if by some unspoken cue, the Wolf BattleMechs turned and began to walk away into the smoke and haze. It would take them hours to reach their DropShip and then depart from Toffen, but they were now bound by honor to do so. Angela watched as the last Wolf 'Mech, a burned, flat black *Naga*, passed through the wisps of smoke and then disappeared from sight.

The Wolves had lost, but it was Dirk Radick who had fired the last shot of the Trial. His words had found their mark. She too had so often looked up into the night sky hoping to see signs of Ghost Bear ships arriving to relieve her, but all she ever saw were the cold stars.

Angela shifted in her seat as if suddenly chilled at what Radick had implied. And while what was left of her Trinary rejoiced in their victory, Angela Bekker contemplated the unthinkable and the undeniable.

Epilogue

Field of Honor
Alshain
Ghost Bear Dominion
25 June 3062

Angela stood at attention along with the rest of Stalking Bears Trinary, Eighth Bear Cuirassiers, Delta Galaxy. Gone were the stained and tattered uniforms of the campaign, replaced for the occasion by new gray dress uniforms. Gone also was the weariness on the faces of her warriors who had survived the fight. Some still sported casts on their limbs or bandages on their burns, but their faces showed spirit and a sense of purpose. Even Bethany, with her arm still in a sling and with bionic replacements carefully rigged in place on her hand. That alone helped take the edge off the confused mixture of anger, frustration, and embarrassment that Angela felt.

They stood on an elevated platform of stone, the bright Alshain sun beating down on them. The shimmering grass of the parade field before them was filled with the rank and file of every available Ghost Bear warrior on Alshain. Behind them were also gathered members of the lower castes. Ghost Bears all, they had come here by order of the Khan. They stood at full attention, line after line of eyes staring up at the platform where Angela stood, looking back.

These last months had seemed almost anticlimactic after their victory on Toffen. Replacement troops, an entire Cluster, had come to relieve her Trinary nearly two weeks after the final battle with Dirk Radick and the Wolves. The Stalking Bears had been loaded onto fresh ships that brought them back to Alshain, apparently at the behest of Khan Bjorn Jorgensson. Angela had asked several times to speak with her superiors, but her requests had been ignored. Now, today, on this platform, she saw them. Star Colonel Dana Vishio stood alongside Galaxy Commander Roberto Snuka, and both gave Angela nods of encouragement. SaKhan Aletha Kabrinski stood with them, silent and stern. Khan Jorgensson moved to a small, pillar-like podium at the center of the platform. He wore the traditional garb of his office, a fur cape and hood cut from the hide of a ghost bear over a dark black body suit. Around his neck was a necklace of teeth from the ghost bears he had slain during his Clawing ritual years ago. The Khan did not look at Angela or her Trinary members, but instead faced the legion of his Clan, removing his fur hood so that all might see his face.

"As Khan of the Ghost Bears there is no greater honor than a day like this one. Some months back I authorized the formation of a new Trinary in the Eighth Bear Cuirassiers. Star Captain Angela Bekker was given command. It was a new unit, green, untested in battle. As their first assignment, they went to the planet

Toffen, where they alone assumed garrison duties. Both bloodnamed and Clawed, Angela Bekker represents the best of what makes us Ghost Bears, and her assignment to that world was intended to honor her and those in her command.

"Our former Clankin, the Wolf Clan, came stalking at our borders. They came to Toffen to wrest the world from our Dominion. Facing the Blood Drinkers, one of the best units the Wolves have to offer, Star Captain Bekker and her green unit engaged them in a Trial of Possession for the planet. The battle was fought not in an hour, but for some forty-six days. Angela Bekker and her Stalking Bears Trinary defeated not only a Trinary of Wolves, but also an additional Binary of Wolf Clan forces. Despite her losses, her command remained intact and I am ordering it refitted with new equipment.

"And while the Wolves were making their vain attempt to take Toffen from us and these brave warriors were holding them at bay, we Ghost Bears launched our own offensive against the Wolves. Victory was sweet, for we won from them the worlds of Nox, Satalice, and also Altenmarkt, the planet the Blood Drinkers called their home. Star Captain Bekker helped make this possible and it lends even greater honor to the sacrifices made by her unit."

His words made Angela's face hot with rage. The reason her Clan had not come to relieve her was that she was tying down an entire Cluster of forces on Toffen, in order to permit the rest of the Ghost Bears to wage their own separate war against the Wolves. She could not help but think of the words Dirk Radick had spoken on the day of his defeat. Why, he had asked, were the Stalking Bears left alone to protect Toffen? Now she had her answer. They had been set up as bait to lure the Wolves in.

Khan Jorgensson continued. "And in recognition of her selfless dedication to our Clan, we come here today to award our most prestigious honor, the Shield of Tseng, to Star Captain Angela Bekker. To Star Commander Constant Tseng, Star Commander Stone, and to the rest of the Stalking Bears, I offer you my highest commendations for your courage and dedication to the ideals of the Ghost Bears."

SaKhan Kabrinski then rose and came to stand in front of Angela, still mute and stone-faced. She held the Shield of Tseng, which she pinned to Angela's uniform, pressing so hard Angela could feel the cold pin on her flesh.

Bjorn Jorgensson turned back to the assembled warriors when she was done. "Behold the strength of our Clan against those who deem themselves worthy enough to be our foes. Join me in honoring these warriors!" He began to clap his hands and the gathering of Ghost Bears joined in until the applause became an immense roar all around them.

Angela entered the office of Galaxy Commander Snuka and stood at attention. The room was much smaller and darker than she remembered it. Star Colonel Dana Vishio was also present.

"As you were, Star Captain, and congratulations." Roberto Snuka motioned for her to sit, but Angela remained standing.

Snuka rested his elbows on his desk and steepled his fingers at his chin while looking at her for a few moments. "Khan Jorgensson has told me how much he appreciates your great service, Star Captain. So much so that he is planning to form a new Cluster that will, of course, need a commanding officer. He will nominate you personally for the Trial of Position, and he assures me that no others will challenge you."

Angela controlled her temper, but just barely. "That is not necessary, Galaxy Commander," she said, staring straight ahead, but not at him.

"Is there a problem, Star Captain Bekker?" Dana Vishio asked.

"Aye," Angela said bitterly. "Medals do not bring back the dead, nor do new commands. You sent me and my unit to Toffen and left us there alone, all the while knowing that the Wolves would come for us, quiaff?" She snapped her head around and glared into the eyes of her commanding officer.

There was a pause as Vishio cast a quick look at Roberto Snuka, then back at Angela. "Aff. Information was leaked to the Wolf Clan Watch regarding your posting. We transported an inordinate amount of supplies and spare parts to Toffen weeks before your arrival, to make our enemies believe the world was more important than it really was. It was all necessary to lure them into the Khan's trap."

"We were bait," Angela said, almost spitting out the words. "No relief was ever planned for us."

Galaxy Commander Snuka spoke up. "It was a strategy, Star Captain. A necessary strategy. Your work on Toffen handed us several Wolf Clan worlds."

"And you knew of this?" Angela said, still looking at Dana Vishio.

"Aye," Vishio replied. "The execution of strategy is the duty of a Star Colonel. Surely by now you realize that."

"Tell me, Galaxy Commander, Star Colonel, were my Stalking Bears and I expendable?"

Roberto Snuka locked his eyes with Angela's. "We all have our duties, Star Captain. And in that respect, all are expendable when necessary to preserve our Clan and our way of life. What happened on Toffen was you and your Stalking Bears serving in a strategic capacity—performing your duty. Nothing more. Nothing less."

Angela nodded. "I am a tactician. I win battles. That is my duty, to the Clan and to my command. If developing and implementing strategies like that of Toffen is the kind of service you would expect of me as a Star Colonel, I want nothing to do with it. My honor would never permit it."

"What are you saying, Angela Bekker?" Snuka demanded, rising to his feet. "You would turn down promotion and remain a Star Captain, quiaff?"

"Aff, Galaxy Commander. Especially if the price is my conscience or my honor. And after what I have been through, both would be tainted if I ever had to do what was done to us.

"I want only to remain a Star Captain, leading the best Trinary in the Ghost Bear Touman."

Angela did not wait to be dismissed, but executed a perfect about-face and left the office.

"How did it go?" Constant Tseng asked as he and Stone jogged to catch up to Angela outside the command center.

"As well as expected. They offered me a chance to be a Star Colonel—uncontested. A chance to form a new Cluster."

"Did you accept?"

"Neg," she said. "I told them I have no wish to ever do to others what they did to us."

"I am sure that did not go over well. Hopefully you are still in command of us," Stone said.

"Apparently so. I received new orders a few minutes

ago. Refit the Trinary and join the rest of the Eighth Bear Cuirassiers on Toffen within the month. Apparently they do not plan to punish my insubordination."

"It would not serve the Clan to punish their newest hero," Stone said.

"I do not feel like a hero." Angela could not help the weariness in her voice.

"I doubt that any hero does," Tseng said. "Welcome back to the Stalking Bears, Star Captain."

Angela chuckled. "Thank you, Constant. It is good to be home."

"There is one more thing," Tseng said. The trio stopped walking as he reached inside a large leather bag he had been carrying. Out came a velvet cloth bag, capped with ivory and rosewood drones and ringed with pieces of silver. "This is from the unit to you. A new set of bagpipes, made by the finest craftsman we could find on this world. We were told that it took him several months to turn the drones."

Angela held them up and looked at the chanter. Near the top was a small silver plate. On it she saw the insignia of the Ghost Bears and the individually carved names of each member of her Trinary, in letters so small she could just barely read them.

She held the pipes with reverence. "Thank you, both of you, for this. But it is time for us to go home, quiaff?"

"To Toffen," Stone said.

"Neg," Angela returned. "To the Stalking Bears. And that is the only home I will ever need."

About the Author

Blaine Pardoe has been writing for BattleTech® for over thirteen years. He has contributed to over forty books, including the BattleTech® novels *Highlander Gambit, Impetus of War,* and *Exodus Road.*

He is also senior manager, in charge of Technology Education Services, at the firm of Ernst & Young LLP in his day job. He is a recognized industry expert and his articles on technology education often appear in trade journals. He earned his B.A. and an M.A. from Central Michigan University.

His book on office politics, *Cubicle Warfare,* was a bestseller and earned him international media recognition as an authority on the workplace. He has authored numerous books on computer games under the Brady imprint. He is also a fan of the American Civil War and has written several articles on the subject as well as having an interesting collection of artifacts.

Blaine lives with his family in Amissville, Virginia, near the mountains in a new house dubbed Desperation Overlook. On those evenings when he is not writing, researching, or playing computer games, you can hear the mournful skirl of his bagpipes in the breeze—much to the chagrin of his neighbors.

For those that wish to reach him personally, he is available at Bpardoe870@aol.com.

**Don't miss the next
action-packed
MechWarrior,**

By Blood Betrayed

available soon from Roc!

Birdsong Ridge
Caldarium, Rim Collection
The Periphery
15 January 3059

"**O**wlflight One, this is Lantern One," said Lieutenant Livia Hawke as she checked her BattleMech's primary and secondary sensor displays again. Her *Quickdraw*'s sensors picked up no enemy movement in the area, but two other 'Mechs of her company showed up clearly on the head's up display. Ditto for the infrared scans and the magnetic resonance checks that usually picked up the fusion reactor signatures of nearby BattleMechs.

Owlflight One was a *Jenner* Class 'Mech. Like the enemy 'Mechs, it wasn't showing up on her long- or short-range sensors, but Hawke knew it hadn't simply disappeared. The *Jenner* was a scout machine with enough onboard ordnance and speed that it wouldn't go down without so much as a puff of smoke. Battle-Mechs had dominated the battlefields of war for the last three centuries. Powered with fusion reactors and armed with enough firepower to level a city block, the three-story machines were fearsome, even the lighter ones like the *Jenner.*

She'd ordered radio silence as soon as the unit had moved into the hill country from the DropShip. Only the *Jenner* had gone up into the ridgeline towering overhead, to scout for any sign of the pirates. Owlflight was supposed to signal via a burst-transmission blip, just a friendly knock to let her know he was still ambulatory. But nothing came.

The long wait ate at her nerves like ants crawling on her skin. She glanced up from the secondary display and stared into the night through her cockpit's polycarbonate viewport. A feeling of unease settled over. She and the rest of her company moved forward slowly, hoping Owlflight One would stumble on any real trouble before they did.

The terrain was deadly to 'Mechs, filled with plunging cliffs and rugged hills covered with tall trees and dense undergrowth. A 'Mech could climb well enough, but it took a lot of skill to keep one upright under these conditions. The pale moonlight rendered the landscape almost in 2-D to the unaided eye. Even the *Quickdraw*'s IR scanners struggled to keep up with the changing geoforms. Some of that was the terrain, some of it was that her 'Mech was an older model lacking some of the newer technology. Such was the lot in life of a Periphery MechWarrior. Out here, among the far-flung planets at the edge of colonized space, they did not have the advantages of newer tech enjoyed by those living in the Inner Sphere.

Hawke knew from the mission profile given her by Major Able before she'd left the mercenary unit's command post on Gillfillan's Gold that this area had once been a vast mining area. Tunnels had been blasted through the hard rock, snaking deep into the earth, and the ore dug out. It had been shipped by rail down the mountains and into processing plants in the foothills. Factories had turned the ore into metals, and the metals had been pressed and shaped into components to be shipped off-world. When the ore petered out, the factories and combines had left too.

That had been a hundred years ago. Now Porth, one of the cities on Caldarium's southern hemisphere, lived in the ruins of the great refineries, its people scavenging what they could to construct what they needed. Here and there through the underbrush, Hawke spotted timbers that had once been railroad ties, laid in straight rows like the graying spinal column of some great beast that had died there. When the combines left, they'd smelted the tracks and the ore cars, leaving almost nothing behind. Now the people living in Porth were mostly an agrarian society, trading grain to the Federated Commonwealth in exchange for the goods they needed.

Six weeks ago, Porth had been attacked. It wasn't the first attack. Pirate raids were all too commonplace in the Periphery. Three to five 'Mechs, the militia and local news reports had said. The stories conflicted, changing from witness to witness. It was something Hawke was used to. Her unit, Able's Aces, had taken on the job of protecting the emerging Rim Collection planets from raiders twelve years ago. Livia herself was a Rim native, born and bred there in one of the few industrial cities on Otisberg. And she knew from experience that Major Able always took his responsibilities seriously. Able had invested in the Rim Collection even before the Council of Planets was financially able to pay his people, covering the expenses himself because he believed in the future they were trying to create. Able's Aces were the only real protection for the locals living in the Rim Collection, the last bastion between some semblance of order and civilization and the chaos of pirate rule.

In the Rim Collection, the Aces kept all 'Mech replacement parts scavenged from recovered and disabled miner 'Mechs left behind by the combines that were discovered or unearthed as the planetary populations grew and spread out. All 'Mech supply was handled through the Aces, and Major Able kept a stockpile of component parts as part of his contract with the Council of Planets.

The Major himself had been set to head up the hunting expedition for the raiders until Morgan's Extractors had hit a munitions plant on Waypoint. The Extractors were only one of the pirate groups in the area that preyed on the Rim Collection, but they were the most flagrant. "King" Hopper Morgan, the Extractors' pirate leader, held two planets in nearby space. He'd christened them Pain and The Rack, and had dug in so fiercely that no one could blast him out.

When the Clans had ripped through the Inner Sphere in their drive toward Terra, the Aces hoped the invaders' path would take them through Morgan's territory. That didn't happen. As it turned out the invasion weakened the Lyran Commonwealth and made it easier for Morgan to raid the Commonwealth's border planets. But with the Truce of Tukayyid in 3052, Morgan's attentions had returned to the Rim Collection.

The Aces had taken advantage of the reprieve, using it to add another 'Mech battalion to Major Able's original two. The three battalions, along with their support personnel, made the Aces regimental in size, but spread out over the six worlds that made up the Collection.

Morgan's raiders had identified themselves when

they'd hit the munitions depot, destroying two 'Mechs and killing sixteen personnel. It was an attack designed to sow doubt among the Council of Planets about the Aces' ability to protect the Rim Collection. The raid was as much political as it was military. Each time they struck, they drove more of a wedge between Major Able and the Council leadership.

There'd been some talk over the last few years of adding another mercenary company to the Collection's defenses, but Major Able had managed to get that idea shelved. So far. Having two different mercenary groups might look good on-screen to a frightened civilian population, but it played hell with chain of command over the area. And it would have cut the Aces' profits in half, making it difficult to keep filling their ranks with the kind of loyal personnel they'd always attracted.

Thoughts of the enemy finally brought her patience to an end. Hawke keyed the com channel open. "Lantern Two, this is One."

"Go, One," Benjamin Rassor said in his calm voice.

Despite the tension of the moment, Hawke smiled as she scanned the night. Benjamin always came across as the professional soldier. Two years with the Aces and he'd promoted quickly because he was trainable and aggressive. Perhaps a little too aggressive in what he wanted. He was always ready for another promotion, another chance to get into a bigger and better 'Mech. Benjamin was obsessed with technology, and even broke more than a few of the rules to lay his hands on the latest and greatest in battlefield technology—battletech.

His ambition and drive were some of the reasons she'd taken him as a sometime lover. He could be passionate all through the night and never blur the lines of the chain of command that separated them.

"Stand ready, Two," Hawke said, grabbing the control joysticks. "We're going to recce the area and try to find out what happened to Owlflight. If things turn bad, we're going to need the back door."

"Affirmative, One," Benjamin replied. "We're standing hard here. Good hunting."

Hawke rocked against the cockpit's restraint straps as the *Quickdraw*'s leg and hip actuators pushed the sixty tons of 'Mech into a walk. Cruising speed for the *Quickdraw* was fifty-four kph, too fast for the terrain under the existing conditions.

"Raptor One, this is Lantern One," she called.

"Acknowledged, Lantern One, you have Raptor One," Jamison, the air lance leader, replied. The aerofighter lance consisted of two SPR-H5 *Sparrowhawk*s equipped with medium and small lasers. The speed of which the *Sparrowhawk* was capable made it a choice first-response attack craft.

"I want a fly-by, Raptor One," Hawke instructed. "A full sensor array over a five-klick spread from my mark. Do not engage unless fired upon and you can identify the target. We've got a unit down somewhere out there."

"Not to worry, Lantern One," Lieutenant Jamison said. He was a careful, capable pilot, and as brave as they came. "Raptor One is the angel on your shoulder."

She swept the terrain again with her sensors, growing more uneasy. With the onboard programming and vids on the 'Mech, a full 360-degree view outside the *Quickdraw* was compressed into a 120-degree arc on the HUD. Learning to manage her movement by the compressed full-scan had been one of the hardest things in her training.

She scanned her target interlock circuits and did a fast weapons check. The *Quickdraw* carried two medium Omicron 4000 lasers at the end of its arms and two more on its back. A Delta Dart long-range missile 10-rack was mounted on its left torso, and a Hovertec short-range missile quad occupied the 'Mech's chest cavity. She knew the *Quickdraw* and its weapons like the back of her hand and felt much better as she saw the pre-heat and load lights on her tactical display show that she was armed and ready. The *Quickdraw* was painted black and white, the colors of the Aces, and an Ace of Spades was painted on its massive left shoulder.

Hawke sat in the cockpit seat dressed only in a cut-off black military tank top under her cooling vest and camouflage shorts hacked off well above the knees. In combat or when pressed to run or jump, a 'Mech could generate tremendous heat, more than its heat sinks could vent. When that happened, the coolant vest would help protect her or at least buy her some time in a firefight. It would not save her if her ammunition cooked off or if the heat corrupted her reactor's magnetic core, though—the worse fears of a MechWarrior.

She was twenty-four years old, and her body was hard and lean from a daily regimen of calisthenics and martial arts. She wore her dark red hair pulled back, shaved near the temples for better contact with the neurohelmet. Her skin was bronzed by the sun, but freckles still lingered, including a spattering across her cheeks and the bridge of her nose. The only incongruency was the pink splash of burn scar tissue on her left elbow. It was ten centimeters long and four centimeters across at its widest point. She'd picked that up in a skirmish with pirates four months ago, and the skin grafts hadn't quite taken enough to return the original color.

She opened the com channel. "Crosby."

"Here, Lieutenant," Crosby replied.

"We're moving in. I've got point and Amos is walking slack. That leaves you the middle."

"Affirmative, Lieutenant. Waiting around like this was about to drive me out of my gourd. Kicking butt's what I signed on for."

Hawke watched Crosby's *Dervish* step out from the copse of trees he'd used for cover. Crosby had an irrepressible nature and a quick temper. If not for the fact that he was a damn good MechWarrior and knew how to deliver fire-support in the heat of battle, by now Major Able would have busted him down through the ranks and put him out on the street. As it was, Crosby usually ended up pulling extra duty as punishment for infractions, or fined. Or both.

Behind him, Derrick Amos moved his *Orion* into position behind Crosby. "Ready," he said in that whispery, soft voice of his. Around the Acers' barracks, Amos was something of an enigma. He had no real personality, no past, was as functional as any 'Mech replacement subsystem, and as easy to talk to. He was also completely dependable.

"Move out," Hawke commanded. She worked the joystick and foot pedal controls, pushing the *Quickdraw* into cruising speed. All the while she had a sinking feeling in the pit of her stomach that they could well be walking into the jaws of a trap. She glanced up and saw Raptor Lance's two *Sparrowhawk*s sweep in on her right flank. Then there was a brilliant double flash in the air. To a civilian, it would have appeared like a bright blue bolt of lightning. To Hawke, it was something more, something sinister. Particle projection cannon fire . . . PPCs. More than one. Not a good sign.

She reached for the communications controls but was too late. Swarms of missiles arced up at the already damaged aerospace fighters as they reeled from the

PPC attacks. There was a hiss in her earpiece just as Jamison screamed, cutting off his death wail. The missiles laced across his fighter and enveloped it in a ball of fire. The other *Sparrowhawk*, attempted to bank, trying to evade the attack. Bright amber laser lights lanced upward, slicing into its wing at the apex of its arc, tossing the small fighter about like a child's toy plane caught in a tornado. Neither of the aeropilots had time to eject. Neither could have survived. Her company of twelve 'Mechs and fighters had suddenly lost one-sixth of its firepower in a matter of seconds.

"This is Lantern One to all personnel. They knew we were coming. Fall back to your perimeter markers immediately!"

Hawke's voice boomed into her neurohelmet's microphone, but all she heard was the irritating hiss of static. Jamming. The enemy had let them wander into the rocky crags of Birdsong Ridge, then had cut them off from the rest of the universe.

"It's a trap!" she barked.

Grizzly

Timber Wolf

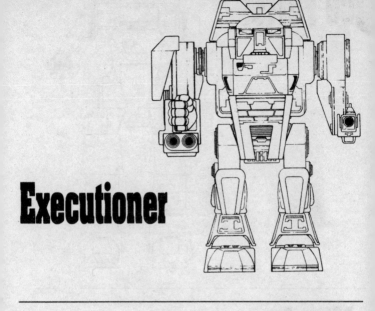

Executioner

Nova

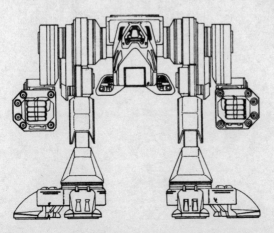

Ice Ferret

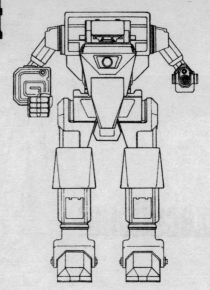

Mist Lynx

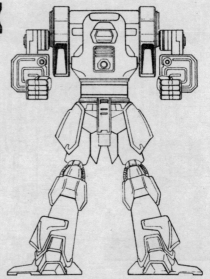

Union-C Class DropShip

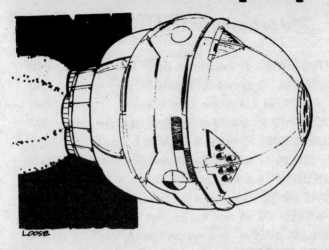

Merchant Class JumpShip

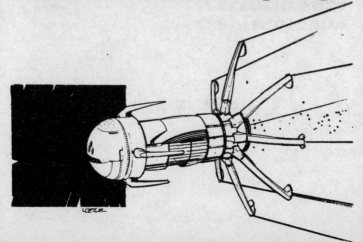

■ *Don't miss out on any of the deep-space adventure*
of the Bestselling **BATTLETECH**® *Series.*

To order call: 1-800-788-6262